Ed Crutchley was born in Cambridge, England and has also lived in France and the USA. He is married with one son and now lives in Kent, England. *Bad Days in Broadacre* is his second novel. He has also written *The Black Carriage*, *Hummingbird*, *A Most Unfortunate Affair*, *Procession*

www.edcrutchley.c

Praise for *Bad Days in L...*

"A family deals with a sleepy Northern town's secrets in this enjoyably energetic romp…. An engaging and thoughtfully conceived plot."—*Kirkus Reviews*.

Bad Days in Broadacre

Edward B Crutchley

Copyright © 2016 by Edward B Crutchley
All rights reserved

Summary

A struggling screenwriter is invited to 1990s USA to prepare a television drama series in New York. For peace and tranquility, he installs his family in a small and enchanting town in New England, but life at home soon finds itself competing with his script for entertainment.

Dedication

To Eugenie and James

Author's Note

This story is entirely fictional. Any similarities between the characters portrayed and people living or dead are unintended.

BAD DAYS IN BROADACRE

1

They had arrived at last, but the suspended wooden floor had barely finished reverberating from their falling suitcases than there was a knock at the door. It had been closed less than ten seconds before.

"I'll get it!"

Bill regained his sagging composure with the help of a handrail on the wall left by the previous owner, a cripple or ballet dancer or both, and opened up. At the top of the short pathway, their limousine had been replaced by a fortyish blond in dark glasses, her hair bunched behind her head to make her look intelligent. She was ostentatiously revving the open shiny black Saab in which she sat.

Her face was long and determined, at a stretch attractive, and she was beaming in his direction. She had no doubt drawn up her unscathed object of pride on the wrong side of the road so that Bill could better admire it, and her as well. Indeed, he thought, the late afternoon July sun blessed them, as well as the magnificent ginkgo biloba on the side of the road.

"I'm Mary Lou. I'm a lawyer!"

It figured.

"Pleasure!" he called back, trying to work out how she had knocked on the door from her car, ten yards away.

He shouted his name.

"That's Debra, my daughter," she shouted back, pointing towards his legs.

He had missed tiny Debra standing right in front of him, next to a strange cat. He looked down and smiled, relieved that he hadn't kneed her by accident. It wouldn't have been a good start.

"I'm your neighbor," called Mary Lou, as Debra, her duty fulfilled, proudly hopped and skipped with a telltale hint of a swagger back down the path to the car.

"Which side?"

"Honey, you get in this side," she said, seemingly not listening.

She had opened her door without bothering to get out as Bill watched.

"Never go on the road! Remember what I told you!"

Little, blond-haired and chubby Debra climbed over her slender mother and flopped out of sight on the back seat.

"The gray clapboard behind you, Bill! Hey, come over to our party in an hour. You must meet Tom, my husband."

"Tom?"

"He's a builder," she said, suggestively angling her hidden eyes upward towards the roof just above Bill's head.

"Look forward to it!"

Bill wondered how to take the hint.

"Hey, what about the cat?"

"That's Oswald. He'll get home on his own."

He closed the door, slowly for politeness, but she had already screeched off and negotiated the sharp corner into the driveway that skirted the left side of their modest property. As far as he could tell, theirs was much smaller than Mary Lou's, or any of the other neighbors for that matter. He hurried over to the back window to watch her park, and to observe how she looked once out of her car.

Catherine wasn't noticing.

"Who was that, Dad?" quizzed Daniel, disappointed that his father had blocked his view.

"Your new girlfriend, Daniel. Hey Catherine, we're invited next door in an hour's time."

"*Oh great!*" moaned Catherine, remaining prostrate on the rest of the couch, the back of which was helping to mask the invading sunlight from her forearm-covered eyes.

"I thought we had come here for peace and quiet."

"*She's* a lawyer. *He's* a builder," Bill pointed out excitedly. "And it looks as though they have a sizeable garden, maybe a pool."

"*A pool?*"

Daniel sprang up, full of energy.

Despite Bill's outwardly glamorous profession, he was a screenwriter, pools and enormous gardens only belonged to the luckier ones.

"Aren't we supposed to be zoned?" said Catherine, finally getting up to stare beside her husband and son into their back garden.

The realtor lady had appallingly called it a yard despite the grass.

She scratched her short brown hair. Mary Lou had already disappeared.

"I thought all the plots here were supposed to be the same."

"We're grandfathered," Bill sad.

His comment only drew a blank.

Catherine's ephemeral interlude gave way to thoughts of buying curtains. She asked that they scout the main town, ten miles away, first thing.

Bill could have insisted that she not rush, that she should purchase cheap blinds to give her time to rework their old curtains. Instead, he welcomed her idea. Their successful seven-year *Pax Romana* was based on what those squabbling kings of the animated world, Tex Avery and Fred Quimby, would have called 'yes only' discussions, to move forward and keep the peace. But an instinctive urge meant that he would annoyingly remind her of her request as soon as they woke up.

Such was marriage.

They were strangers to this side of the world. They had been living in France, yet another challenge to their Britannic ways. The entry signs to their newly adopted New England town had announced its eighteenth-century incorporation. It had seemed odd to be so reminded of history in America of all places, and at first sight, the place seemed charming. The countryside around was littered with old stone walls that followed the undulations and inclines that smacked of Scotland, were it not for the occasional turkey vulture. Many of the walls were still fully maintained, and there was even a disused windmill a mile away, although the limo driver had said that it had relatively recently been built by an eccentric. Only the buildings in the town center were in brick or stone. The rest, in timber, breathed oxygen, humidity and radon, just as they needed to in order to preserve a thriving economic Catherine wheel of ant and termite exterminators, builders, painters, carpenters, timber merchants, roofers, and hardware stores. These were aided and abetted by a notoriously hegemonic Historical Commission that set the pace for appearance.

The local people Bill had met before the arrival of Catherine and Daniel seemed remarkably pleasant and civilized. The only downside he saw was the absence of the early morning whiff of French croissants that they had gotten used to in recent years, but he knew it would soon change as the world warmed up to international trade.

Bill had chosen the town as a suitable retreat for his writing. It was convenient for occasional sorties along the Silk Road southwards into New York, but far enough away to remain out of the minds of his collaborators there, so he hoped. He might have risked a larger house, and even a pool, as debt seemed a status symbol there, but he didn't want to be invaded by colleagues from the metropolis. They had already proved to be too noisy, egotistical, and riotous for his weekend preferences.

Bill had been lucky to find work in America. He had been hired by no less than Samuel T. Rosenbaum, a producer at the top of his profession for two decades. Sam had long turned his back on the West Coast to live over an hour away near the shoreline. His Manhattan enterprise had long been regarded as second to none in its ability to innovate and minimize production costs and to call off dud projects in time. Backers turned up in droves as a result. He reputedly forced such a hard bargain with his distributors that he was, in effect, in part, financed by his competitors.

Despite this rapid change, Bill felt ready to compete in the great seesaw, attention-deficit and novelty-obsessed nation that this country was reputed to be. His job was for a new series that would start filming within a year. After being lodged for his first two months in a hotel near the office, he had fallen for the post-war timber house in the leafy town they now called home. It stood in a backstreet about half a mile from the center of the community, itself lost in a wooded and hilly region that was much sought after by New Yorkers who could afford to commute so far.

The house had gone cheaply. The previous owner had used it for a recording studio and had not bothered to seal up the dozens of cable passages between the rooms, or paint over the dreadful tobacco smells embedded into the plasterboard walls. After a lone ant timely chose to gatecrash Bill's showing of the white kitchen, he had it made.

He had instantly taken to the bouncy wooden floor, the handrails, and the long corridor to the bedrooms that looked outside on one side and had emulsion-painted bookshelves on the other. He had also praised the quaint oxblood potting shed in the garden and the huge ceps growing next to the large yew tree in the front. The French would have killed for those.

As soon as the house had been given a cleaner bill of health than Bill's bargaining had suggested, he had put his money down, hired an electrician to install the all-important 240-volt plug for an English kettle, and called for Catherine, Daniel and all their belongings from France. The hotel in New York was sorry to see one of their rare long timers leave, but Bill looked forward to the prospect of at last sleeping properly and no longer being so invalided by noise. It had been wearing him down. He had only survived on overdoses of caffeine to keep himself upright in the morning. Too many times at breakfast he had caught himself putting sugar in the orange juice instead of the coffee, helping himself to one of the decorative plastic bananas that adorned the counter, and mistakenly trying to get back into the room he had been moved from the week before.

Bill and Catherine's new home stood between large trees on a plot much less illustrious than those either side of it. It benefitted, however, from the absence of walls or fences between properties. The neighbors were a mixture of local artisans and professionals, lawyers, doctors, schoolteachers, writers, and industrialists, some of them retired, a few of them commuting south during the week. New York was a couple of hours away by car, except for one of the wealthier denizens just outside town who reportedly commuted in his helicopter kept in a field next to his home. Neighbors said it sounded like a tractor when it started up in the early morning dark, early enough not to be caught. The realtor lady had said that the town was overtly ruled by a First Selectman, covertly guided by powerful influences so well established that their names appeared on street signs, each vying to leave their fingerprint on their community. Helicopters were banned.

The town was littered with plush gardens. It had been the first thing Bill had noticed. The quaintness of many of the properties was apparently helped by two gardeners, called Jesus and Maria.

"With a hard 'J'," the fiftyish and impeccably tweeded realtor lady had pointed out.

They were a Mexican couple who had already been working for the previous owner for years. The presence of Latinos there was a little unusual, and the realtor lady had been quick to assure Bill about them. Maria, for example, was as considerate to animals and flowers as to her waspish customers. She once famously stumbled upon two frogs copulating on the pavement and boldly held up traffic until they had finished, and Jesus had scooped up the satiated amphibians to carry them to the nearby pond. The word had soon got round. The couple became instant heroes and had for ever since been considered family. That had been a decade ago.

Their story contrasted with where Bill, Catherine and Daniel had just hailed from, a first stop after his struggling start in England. They had lived at the opposite end of France to that which had been gassed during the First World War. For as long as anyone could remember, the village frogs fatally chose the same full-mooned early summer night to migrate *en masse* from the village pond. Each year, their adventure was anticipated by the entire village, salivating and armed with flashlights, hurricane lamps and recycled plastic bags, and unashamedly reeking of the garlic sauce impatiently prepared days in advance.

The massacre that ensued had been typical of life there in the country. Other practices, such as the communal killing and dissecting of a pig for every edible part down to and including its trotters, or the force-feeding of geese, to the more discreet dining on onetime pet rabbits, would no doubt resonate with Jesus and Maria, but not their customers. As the realtor lady assured, apart from the use of carbines or crossbows to hunt deer, or the occasional fatal accident to their human hunters, the worst the New Englanders ever did was to clip the ears of their dogs.

But all this was no surprise at all to Bill and Catherine, and they were glad for the change from one weird environment to another. Living in *La France profonde* had become stifling for them, even if they were to forsake such ubiquitous and gentle maladies such as *crises de foie* for dreaded American diseases such as strep throat and Lyme disease.

During their after-hour boozing sessions, Bill had recounted the improbable stories to his New York colleagues. His friend and landlord, the village mayor, in the true French tradition of making one's point in the street, used to ride to work on a horse several times his size. His briefcase was always securely strapped to the saddle, and a fresh baguette to make his lunch carried in a purpose-made bag swinging from his shoulder. His dramatic and noisy early morning canter down the tarmacadam street oozed authority and tradition, intent on influencing his *commune* into line.

Keeping the conversation alive, Bill had described how everything about France had seemed to involve the State. It ruled graciously, at least for its own, and the mayor's family also profited from its employment handouts. His brother, a retired gendarme, was tasked with investigating all types of accident that occurred in the commune. He had stories to tell at parties. There had been the case of a falling bomb. One of those familiar ornaments that decorated the village memorial had crushed a council worker's foot. After losing count of the number of men and women with missing fingers Bill encountered during his endless daily ritual of shaking hands, he knew the mayor's brother was kept well occupied. Behind each withered grip, he couldn't help visualizing the traumatic event that had caused it and the mayor's family somehow making money out of it.

"France was the world capital of the Enlightenment," Bill had said.

He described their village neighbors who had a small dairy farm. They had suffered constant problems with cows that braved the electric fences to escape into the village and create havoc. The wife had the habit of smacking her head each time she made a mistake or forgot something, and that gave her husband an idea. He equipped their entire herd with antennae made from coat hangers. The metallic prostheses touched the electric fence well before their wearers and forced them to have second thoughts in time.

He described life behind closed doors. The mayor, just like his subjects, would eat garlic for breakfast and drink wine-chased coffee out of a bowl. He would only set out for work after a swig of blinding alcohol made from apples, potatoes, or grapes. His first action of the day at the office would be to listen to the ritual swearing over the hated Parisian visitors, the seventy-fivers, as they were called after their license plates, speeding through the village at weekends and buying out properties at extortionate prices. America had to be better.

On hearing Bill's story about his mayor, the realtor lady compared it with the youngish First Selectman who also ran the local bookstore. He would limit himself to a light breakfast, arrive jogging at the town hall no later than his ego, and meet with the attorney first thing to make sure there were no new liability crises to anticipate or take care of. His only overt stab at displaying authority would follow a couple of late-night bourbons at home, after which he would menacingly call his closest rival to remind him that most of the electors who would ever vote for him had not even been born yet. As for New Yorkers, they were disliked almost as much as the seventy-fivers, but at least they paid the rates and parking fines, and kept the local stores solvent.

Finally, along had come their opportunity for change. Bill and Catherine's stay in France, where Daniel had been born, had lasted several years, until Sam Rosenbaum had unexpectedly knocked on their pastoral front door on a Christmas Eve and made an offer that couldn't be refused. Bill was to script an American version of the series he was already working on. The salary would be nearly double, and Sam would fast-track the immigration business so that Bill could be in place within weeks.

And so it came to be. The purchase of the new house was only marred two weeks later by an unpleasant letter from a neighbor who had just discovered, so he wrote, that the delightful oxblood garden shed, that gave the property so much of its character, jutted onto his land by all of two feet, as it had done for forty years.

It was his first taste of the New World order. Bill called the realtor lady straight away, and she said he should speak to the surveyor before getting legal over it. An early storm was rising.

Welcome to America!

2

Two hours later, after rummaging through the packing cases lining the living room wall, Catherine had completed her habitual shouting match with the talking scales and a subsequent self-inflicted battle over what to wear.

She, Bill and Daniel walked to the edge of their property and onto Mary Lou's seamlessly adjoined and vaster front lawn that boasted a tiny fishpond beside the driveway. There were cars already there. Daniel pointed out that the first of them had bumper stickers that read *SUPPORT YOUR LOCAL POLICE,* and *THIS COP HAS NOT SHOT ANYONE - YET*, and another that read *HONK IF YOU'RE SCOTTISH*, and while Catherine had said to him that 'car park' and 'parking lot' were the same, Bill was wondering who on earth they were about to encounter.

Bill told Daniel to remove his hands from his pockets.

"These people will be sensitive to our presence. Especially today," he warned. "We mustn't turn up looking as though we own the place."

"But we do, Dad!"

Bill gave Daniel a hard look, and he complied without really understanding why.

They knew why the occasion. They had heard about it from the limousine driver on the way in. It was a July 4th party, one of many around that had been heralded by the earlier traditional firing of a canon and an A10 Warthog fly-past along North Street. Catherine and Daniel had missed all that when standing in the airport immigration line while Bill had waited for them outside.

A tall, broad-shouldered man walked out towards them. He had a slim, sun-tanned face with an unsightly upper white line towards the top of his forehead, short black crewcut hair, sweatshirt, and pinkish pants that stopped just below his broad knees. With a beer can in one hand, he waved the three of them over with the other.

"You must be Tom," Bill said.

"Nope. I'm Harry. Local state trooper. Tom's inside."

"Anything wrong?"

"The barbecue's doing just fine. Come on through!"

They all shook hands as if to celebrate the news.

"You sound foreign. Are you from California or something?"

"We're aliens from England!" Daniel announced, citing what he had heard earlier on at the airport.

"*Old* England," Bill said.

"I knew it!"

Harry looked over to their back yard.

"Hey, I mow lawns in my spare time. Let me know if you are looking for someone. Leaves and snow as well."

"Great!" Bill said, mentally knocking those tasks off his accumulating to-do list, but wondering if policemen of all people could really moonlight in that way.

Daniel was looking up at Harry.

"Where's your gun?"

At that moment, Mary Lou, looking taller, walked out of the French windows that gave Tom and herself a panoramic view of the rear of the house. She was wearing a light, inconspicuous dress that covered up to her neck and went below the knees. She stepped down onto the lawn to reach her actual size, physically below Bill's shoulders.

She sided up to Harry and remembered Bill's name. Bill reminded himself how important this was. In his mind, he scraped for his mnemonic tools that would support his struggling memory.

"Well, Bill, has he been selling you yard work yet? It sure would help the view from here."

She had a point, although she didn't have to make it that way so soon. The modest lawn had missed more than a few weeks' attention, as Jesus and Maria did not cover that. Catherine nudged her husband to show her disapproval of the newly discovered brashness.

"Are policemen allowed to do that kind of thing?"

Harry and Mary Lou did not reply and looked around instead.

"Tell me it's not all like this," Catherine whispered into Bill's ear on her toes, still aggravated over the intrusion into the state of the garden.

Bill pretended not to listen, although he secretly admired her perspicacity. It brought him down to earth.

"Mary Lou, this is my wife, Catherine."

"A pleasure to meet you, Catherine."

Mary Lou's telling squint seemed to betray her intent to challenge her about what she had evidently overheard.

"Come on through and meet Tom, but promise first you won't take him from me."

"I doubt it," snarled Catherine under her breath.

She transformed her earlier nudge into a telling glance back in Bill's direction as the two of them walked off together.

"But you haven't seen him yet!"

Mary Lou led the way.

Tom duly appeared on cue at the French windows. He looked remarkably fit, almost consigning the short-sleeved running vest he wore to a virtual oblivion. In this land and life of more, Tom looked as though his fortyish yet impressive torso was putting up and succeeding in a noble resistance. Bill's Britannic bias saw a man desperately striving to live permanently in his comfort zone. Catherine seemed distracted. Bill, alarmed, caught up just in time and they all shook hands as Daniel looked up from below.

"Hey!" Tom said, taking Catherine's arm so gently that she couldn't refuse or pull away. "Let me introduce you around."

Mary Lou smiled as they disappeared into the house, and Daniel ran off to look for Debra and her brother. She turned towards Bill, who was now alone.

"There he goes! Hey, Bill, you're English, aren't you? I thought I recognized the accent. Come on through to the back. We've got quite a few people here, but I want you to meet someone who just *loves* your country. She's such a devoted anglophile and refuses to believe you really are a bunch of inverted snobs."

Bill tried to forget what she had just said. They walked the entire length of her long back garden, past the pool and its raised deck, where Bill, still at the lower level, was struck by a sea of roofs of wagging mouths, past groups of people increasingly fueled by alcohol and trying to shout each other into submission, past a bevy of men on their own walking in circles on the grass as they spoke into their cellphones, to find, some way off, a Spartan-looking fiftyish woman sitting on her own and smoking, far away from the noisy but balmy crowd. She was in walking boots with short socks. He detected the familiar whiff of *Gitanes* as he approached. This woman had evidently found her label.

As he approached, the world about them seemed to slow down. The various conversations going on in the distance appeared to follow a pattern, alternately growing louder and then subsiding, rather like cicadas. It was at least a relief to discover that the local anglophile had an English sense of calm.

"So, you're an anglophile?"

Mary Lou had all too blatantly escaped.

"Well, not exactly. I once went to England, back in the seventies."

"I'm Bill."

They shook hands. She appeared obsessively frugal.

"I'm Barbara. I paint."

Bill showed his interest.

"My wife used to be a court artist, of all things. What do you paint?"

"Homes, mostly."

Gracefully flashing through his mind returned the long grass and the worn-out sidings of the house, the bowing roof and attic that needed converting, and the beautiful small, red garden shed that the real estate agent had said had been there for over forty years, but that two feet of it had just been discovered to be sitting on land belonging to the property on the other side. In one sweep, on their very first day, Bill had met people itching to solve every one of the problems he thought he had. What a delightful convenience! What a neighborhood!

Then he shuddered when he remembered that the realtor lady had already offered the services of her husband for any building work. He had to avoid antagonizing the locals by overstretching his promises so soon.

Barbara interrupted his thoughts by confessing that she was actually a writer. So, there was a Bohemian strain in Broadacre, thought Bill. Something to resist pecuniary obsession.

"But I paint to bring in money."

Bill couldn't hold back.

"I'm a writer too!"

"You look like a huckster to me. Brits always make good hucksters."

After he said what he did, she seemed to have lost interest. She watched little television anyway, she mumbled. Then she said that her age allowed her to forget what she had already seen and make it just as enjoyable the second time around. So, her appetite was moderate.

"Mary Lou said she was a lawyer. Does she practice?"

"*No way!* She's at home with the kids. As far as I know, she hasn't seen a customer in years."

Bill was already learning about the precariousness of first impressions in his newly adopted country. He had already been warned about this by Sam. Barbara went on.

"She enjoys giving advice, though. She could eat two men like Tom *before* breakfast. If you need an opinion, think of her. She needs the attention before she gets destructive."

Bill obligingly made a note of it, gesturing with his finger to show that it had been properly registered.

"I see you smoke French cigarettes. They bring back memories."

"Is that your wife over there? The English-looking one?"

He looked over to spot Tom in the distance. He was cornering Catherine against a tree.

"She *looks* like an illustrator."

"I'd better go."

"Oh, don't worry about Tom. There's nothing lascivious about him at all. He's all talk. But he's fun."

"Thanks."

"Now, when are you planning to paint your house?"

But Bill needed to reclaim his wife, not to mention an intermission from all the blatant solicitation. His mind had blackened. Had they landed in a country of thieves and beggars? Would they discover that an honest friendship without underlying motivation was an alien concept here? How safe was Catherine in all that?

And he had thought that the French were a challenge!

He made a solid excuse to Barbara and went searching for Catherine, who had by now moved on from the tree and disappeared altogether. After a tense minute he found her pinned against a wall instead, once again Tom's burly arm blocking her only escape.

She caught Bill's eye with a telepathic cry for help, and he was relieved to be of service.

Tom caught on and turned around.

"Your beautiful wife is telling me you're Catholics, Bill."

"Well not quite..."

He wondered what on earth Catherine might have been driven to say.

"We're having a clambake at the Church on Saturday at eleven," Tom said. "We'll pick you up on the way over."

The veil of religion had fallen earlier than Bill had expected, and he prayed it had not been Catherine's fault. For compensation, he guessed that the local padre would be someone worth knowing. He could advise on schools and local culture, if not plenty else. If his only vested interest was God, it might even bring relief from all these others.

Tom asked Bill what he did for a living.

"I'm a screenwriter. We moved from France."

Tom became angry.

"*The French*! Strange and unpatriotic people. I don't understand them at all."

"Unpatriotic?"

"To *us*!"

"They supported your revolution, Tom. Rochambeau, Lafayette, Statue of Liberty."

"Well, it doesn't seem like it anymore. They're against us on everything, ever since De Gaulle. My uncle got thrown out of France back in the sixties. He worked for NATO near Paris."

"Their only real problem is that they're always at each other's throats," Bill assured him. "But for a foreigner that makes things easier."

Tom laughed.

"I bet you Brits must love that!"

He seemed to be about to ask Bill more about his job when a young boy, a little older that Daniel, ran into the room, across towards them, and tried to bring Tom down with a head-on tackle.

"This is my son, Jack."

It sounded like an admission. Tom regained his balance and composure and, struggling to free himself, Bill noticed he appeared to be hurting where it might have counted had he planned for more children.

"He's three years older than his sister."

Tom fought to gain the upper hand. Jack gave up trying to emasculate his father and ran off to attack Mary Lou instead.

"Leave your mother alone!"

But he had not been heard. A loud crash and a scream came from the kitchen.

"Do you English have hyperactive kids?"

Tom was still recovering and bending over a little, trying to ignore the aftermath in the kitchen.

"More garrulous than like that," admitted Catherine, relieved at having been freed.

Bill guessed she was about to blame again all those hormones Americans left in their meat, over-indulgent potty training, or even the quality of the local water. She had equivalent theories for the French. Tom luckily cut her off.

"Hey, let's go out to the barbeque before Mary Lou tells me I'm not doing my duty."

"How come Mary Lou has her say on that?"

"Bill, you're dead right!" said Tom, determinedly striding off towards the kitchen. "Hey, Mary Lou, give me back the skewers."

"All those hormones!" whispered Catherine.

Harry the trooper walked in. He was sweating profusely. They had just finished a bout of flag football that he had noisily initiated on the lower lawn. Daniel, who had never played before, had apparently scored twice, no doubt because he was so small, and no-one wanted to hurt the new arrival. Harry was followed by an older man with short graying hair with Daniel on his tail, and Daniel seemed to lecture him from behind.

"This kid! He doesn't stop. Does he belong to anyone?"

"Me," Catherine said, turning to be heard.

He was evidently embarrassed and swung back apologetically to face her. He said that she should be proud of such a precocious youngster. Daniel, meanwhile, ran off to play with some of the other kids at the end of the room.

"I'm Josh Villeneuve."

He offered an arm of peace.

"Your son showed me an earthworm out there in the garden, but I really don't know if they go backward. He needs to understand that."

Catherine laughed at his plight. She had instantly found him beguiling, but now noticed that he had become distracted by Bill's nose. She wondered why.

Josh was clearly still embarrassed by his *faux pas* and resolved to make up for it.

"Hey, kids!"

They came running over.

"Who wants to see me imitate a lighthouse?"

Before they could ask what he had meant, he went into the corner of the room and rotated on his feet, gradually opening and closing his mouth when his face came into view. The kids watched mesmerized, but only the grown-ups laughed, and the kids ran out to the pool.

Josh moved on. Harry started talking about the small town they were in, how he had landed his treasured job after leaving the army, and how Bill and Catherine would soon discover that the United States was the very best country in the world. He had an Irish surname. Bill asked him if he had ever been to Europe.

"Not yet. Didn't even do Nam."

To make up for this self-perceived shortcoming, he blithely talked about hunting instead. He had just made his annual trek over to the Catskills and had amazingly found seashells there, way up. He talked about all the game he had caught in the past, and how his wife, who was presently away in Michigan looking after her ageing father, introduced him to an Argentinian meat restaurant on Long Island where he had to guess what he was eating. It had been a sort of revenge on her behalf, as he always boorishly called her out of the blue from the wilds straight after bagging an animal, any animal, and asking her to guess what it was.

Bill asked after Harry's father-in-law.

"In his nineties. She had to go. She was on the phone to him every day and having to shout louder and louder. I would fall asleep and wake up much later and she was still on the phone trying to get the same message across."

"And everything's fine now?" asked Catherine.

"Well, he's now in a home, and who knows what they are putting into his system behind her back. He's constantly complaining about monkeys in the trees outside."

Catherine asked how Harry survived without his wife. He said it had become easier once he had learned to tell himself off at least ten times a day. Only Bill laughed.

Harry talked about the local community, about the exclusive golf club which had a waiting list of over twenty years, of mysterious town elders who ruled like despots from behind closed doors and, finally, of the crime he had to deal with as the resident state trooper. They were in a quiet and affluent area with only the occasional drunken gunshot, he said, but more regularly subjected to sprees by seedy characters passing through between New York and Boston when avoiding the turnpike, stories which the elders did their best to suppress in the local media.

"So, I guess then it's mostly rape and incest they talk about," Bill said.

"Sodomy and buggery as well, Bill."

Harry hadn't had a moment of hesitation. He vainly tried to suppress a grin.

"You English must know about that."

"Nothing else?"

"Once stopped a guy for speeding while towing a whale."

He hurriedly said that the man was a professor rushing back from the coast in order to put his cargo under refrigeration, and he had to let him off because of the smell. Later in the conversation, they talked about burglaries, although guns kept at home managed to keep them down. Harry joked about how often people returned home embarrassed at discovering themselves burgled after not having made their beds.

"A bit like going out in dirty underpants. You never know."

Bill made a mental note. It would make a good story. They had been burgled twice in France and had learned the hard way. Photographs of their untidy home probably still lingered in the local gendarmerie's files. Catherine had taken it as an invasion worse than the burglaries themselves.

There were constant reminders of the darker sides of life in this idyllic setting all the same, Harry went on. Right in the middle of town stood a small state prison that had been there since long before the Civil War.

"Hey, they even kept Brit sailors there!"

He warned Bill and Catherine that two or three times a year the siren would go off to announce an escaped convict, and he imitated the sequence to listen out for. Catherine asked if they were in for anything serious.

"Not *that* many murderers."

Catherine showed some degree of relief.

"But anyway, this State does not pursue the death penalty, Catherine. Your lights will never flicker, at least not for that reason."

He talked about tourists, the more innocent type. They came up from the southern shoreline, often from New York as well, and a select few kept second homes in and around town. Most summer weekends yielded a sufficient trickle of parking fees and fines to pay for himself and a part-time traffic warden who chalked the parked cars' tires to catch their owners out. In the fall, straight after Labor Day, everyone would at least stroll along the long boardwalk in the local wildlife sanctuary or drive or fly over the Hills to swoon at the color. For most people, the shift in the climate meant that lazy summer strolls around town metamorphosed into frenzied bursts of weekend energy in and around the forests that were turning to all shades of orange and red.

"We're a nation always on the move."

The half dozen conversations with Harry and others, an invitation to lunch that came from the Villeneuves, not to mention the plentiful illegal fireworks that Tom had smuggled across the state line with an apparent customary blind eye from Harry, all buzzed in their minds as they trekked the thirty yards uphill back home. The cars with the stickers had gone, so neither of them had been Harry's.

They had abandoned Mary Lou and Tom to a dwindling, but ever louder, group of friends. Harry would no doubt advise them to retrieve their cars the following day.

"Bill, did you notice all their Biedermeier furniture in the living room? That was the last thing I expected."

Before they reached the front door, Catherine and Daniel had each come out with things they should do right away. Catherine had the curtains, and Daniel, the neighbors' pool, followed by an ice-cream on the way. Alcohol and a friendly crowd had spoiled Bill and Catherine, and Daniel, who had become chlorinated by the pool, was equally euphoric.

By all measures, they had landed well, each of them thought. They had just been successfully welded to the best friends on offer in the best region of the best country in the world, and Bill's meeting with Barbara at the extreme end of the garden had given him one of several ideas for the script. He had benefitted even more from overhearing so many conversations throughout the evening, most of them far more revealing than what anyone had intended him to hear.

Bill was full of thoughts. He would call Sam about them in the morning.

3

The disturbingly laconic Fritz Gargano was never likeable, even when he doted on his only daughter, presently absent on her 21st birthday. His tiny blue eyes danced sideways in his wide and mean-looking puffy face. They warned of feral intention. His curly and thinning gray hair brushed backward, and his broad jaw lined with so-called designer stubble, each helped to project meanness and cruelty. Every hidden thought that he harbored, each fastidious gesture that hinted of his current mood, made even the firmest minds around him rush, seeded panic in those who did not know him, and sowed revulsion amongst those who watched from afar. Even his name gave away the nefarious mongrel that he was.

His capricious mind was tough to anticipate. His temper and misogyny were legendary and had long driven two wives and three sons away forever. Refuge from his unpredictable emotions, which randomly bounced from hot to cold and back again, was reserved for his daughter Tanya, who was as beautiful as he was ugly. She alone had any sort of freedom of his vast home and fortune. She had the brains and education to be certain to succeed him. And despite his foibles and the short leash he accorded her, she treated him with respect and a smattering of love.

He had little sense of humor. It had always been so. Any attempt to tease him at school had been instantly met with a flying fist aimed straight at the nose, or just under the eye. Sometimes he had used brass knuckles, always at the ready in his back pocket. Other times, it had been a switchblade. Occasionally, his vicious reaction would go further still. After one of his closest friends had once jokingly forged a set of Viet Nam call-up papers, he had shot him in the head in the street in full daylight, without even a silencer.

Fritz's upbringing had always been violent. Son of an obese, frequently out-of-work Italian stevedore and slender German seamstress, who from time to time 'defended herself', as one writer used to describe it, just off Times Square, or in Central Park if she could get away with it, he had barely completed junior high. The family lived in one of the cruelest projects of the fifties Bronx, where brute force and violence ruled over an economy of influence peddling, prostitution, alcohol, and drugs. With his parents on such precarious incomes, as a teenager, he had to help provide for his three younger siblings, still supposedly at school. Fritz developed an ability to take ruthless enterprise several steps beyond what was ever asked of him. It earned him a valued lieutenancy under a local warlord. It landed him in the even harsher environments of state and federal penitentiaries.

Fritz owed his brain to his mother who, intelligent and of impeccable memory, had always refrained from tobacco, alcohol and drugs. He exploited his long years locked away from society by reading and learning. In recent years, to the frustration of federal agents who still patiently kept an eye on him while he was outside, Fritz had learned to divert most of his ill-gotten gains towards safer enterprises.

Tanya, Fritz's precocious and equally temperamental daughter, had graduated from business and law schools. She was presently headed for the arms of a young and only son of a modest Albany widow. He had been a fellow student, destined for heights of his own, but despite this turn of events, Fritz knew his daughter would never stray far. Their business of cheating the world, legally or otherwise, was certain to survive and flourish.

Fritz put down his Marshall McLuhan and seemed relieved. Carmine, his long-time lieutenant, had already been standing there for several minutes.

"I need to speak to you, Boss."

Fritz trusted Carmine almost as much as his daughter, but likewise, it did not go far. The trouble was that Carmine *always* needed to speak to him and Fritz *always* had to make the decisions. It was the problem of being so strong. He could never rely on anybody. His entire entourage presented a permanent challenge. Everyone he dealt with, even his daughter, continually tested his patience. They forced him to have to remember everything in order to stay one step ahead. He had to keep them in check and on their toes.

And they tried to cope with him in return. Their manner of keeping any sort of handle on their situation was through planting deliberate mistakes. These channeled his wrath away from areas they each sought to protect. It had turned into a game. Like Siamese cats, they constantly watched him with at least one eye.

But Fritz's advancing age was coming into play. At least, that's how he perceived it. It made him afraid of mellowing. His home-grown paranoia grew. His memory was no longer what it used to be. Often it looked as though everyone around him was doing their best to wipe it clean, one surreptitious stroke at a time. He saw it as a battle of mind games. It conformed with his second nature. He compensated by structuring his life as much as possible. He ordered his meals always at the same time. He worked to checklists, just like in prison, to keep their attempts at disorientation and subterfuge in check. And above all he never stopped trying to anticipate their next moves.

"You know, Carmine," he sneered, briefly glancing back at his book, "everything you say I can see, and everything you f***ing don't say I can f***ing feel!"

Carmine had long become used to such bouts of oppressive philosophy. He too had read extensively in and out of prison, and his even temperament that had kept him in his job had also kept him above the emotional waterline.

"Is that called *synesthesia*, Boss?"

He meant it seriously.

"Carmine, don't make me f***ing…" Fritz growled.

He hated others trying to be clever with him. Very few got away with it. And he always had something to return.

"Hey, did you cut down that f***ing tree already?"

The small apple tree in the middle of his stunningly beautiful lawn that looked out onto the Sound had been the object of his wrath the day before. It had been the eve of Tanya's birthday. At the very last minute he had hired a film crew to record a time lapse setting of the sun. He intended to project it in the background right there on the lawn on the day. But the sun had descended less vertically than expected, and at the last minute had disappeared behind the tree. And then she had called to say that she wouldn't be there.

The film crew had left unpaid. They had discussed another try for another occasion, the wedding, for example.

"What about just before she loses her…," had jokingly whispered one of Fritz's men before never being seen again.

"What did I f***ing tell you?" Fritz shouted.

Carmine was about to stutter an excuse. It could jeopardize the rest of his day. He remembered in time that what he had to say was even more important than the tree.

"Tell me about it," Fritz invited, half rolling his eyes, half looking sideways at his subaltern.

"Yeah," said Carmine with relief.

"I said *tell me about it!*"

The lieutenant apologized.

"Well, Boss. Lenny the Limp didn't have a condo on Martha's Vineyard as we'd thought. That's why we never found it."

"*What!*"

This was out of the blue and unexpected. Fritz stood up in shock at the news of ten years of misconception.

"Turns out he had a property in Connecticut with land around it," said Carmine, talking even faster, "and he dressed as a woman and ran a recording studio."

"Well f*** me!"

Fritz walked towards the middle of the room while stroking his cactus chin.

"How the f*** did we find him?"

"He kept that painting you gave him. The boys spotted it for sale in one of those magazines."

Fritz had always tried to improve the worldliness of his entourage of bodyguards. It angered him he had not spotted the article himself. Perhaps he had been distracted by all that world news that would never change his life. Perhaps it had been when Tanya had momentarily gone off the wall.

Whatever.

But why had Lenny sold a prized possession?

"He didn't," said Carmine. "He died a year ago, and it was being sold off by his estate."

Fritz briefly panicked. He hated not having the initiative.

"The house! How much is it going for?"

"Well, that's the problem, Boss. It's already been sold."

Fritz realized that this was far too important to get upset about. Lenny the Limp had been evading him ever since the Melville heist. The bullion was worth millions. If he had disguised himself and purchased a home, he must have buried the loot somewhere there.

He thought of the opportunity it presented. The gold could be easily laundered, no problem. He needed to get his hands on the house and grounds. It was too bad if they had already been sold.

He turned his back to gaze outside to the front. A team of four Haitian gardeners were sweeping the driveway and mowing the lawn either side of it. But the outsized fountain in the background had been turned off, and it distracted him. He needed freedom of thought. He swung back, skirted past his lieutenant, and walked towards the back. Then he saw the apple tree standing there in the middle of his view.

"And now this!"

It could be down in minutes. Why hadn't it been?

"Find out who conveyed it and get it f***ing un-conveyed or something. I want that house. Whatever it takes!"

Carmine had enough to act on and headed for the door. He would take the Cadillac and drive up north after he had cut down the tree.

"Where did you say?" asked Fritz.

"A town called Broadacre. Two-and-a-bit hours away."

"Isn't that where…?"

Carmine's face lit up. He hadn't thought of that. He promptly walked back to the doorway to face his boss.

"Hey, you're right, Boss. Should I speak to him first?"

"No. Leave that to me," said Fritz. "Take Gin Bottle and get up there and scout around. Bring back photos."

Carmine left the room and swooped up the keys and camera from the side table right next to where the sallow Gin Bottle was sitting. Once he reached the outside sun, he smiled to himself. He enjoyed driving north. It reminded him of all those missions to Boston. Best of all there were two McDonalds a few miles from each other on I95, just enough to finish one burger before collecting the next.

He beckoned Gin Bottle to accompany him, took command of the Cadillac, and sped off having forgotten to down the tree.

"Dressed as a f***ing woman, heh," thought Fritz, finally on his own and looking out towards the miniscule waves lapping his shoreline.

He wondered what the bastard had called himself. He looked forward to hearing what Carmine found out and examining the photos. He walked through the conservatory and onto the soft smooth lawn and headed past the tree to stand on the water's edge. Finding Lenny the Limp had been an obsession for so long. It had been secretly wearing him down.

He thought about those hallowed times, of Lenny's music activities and weird friends. The pressure from the feds had been worsening. Just after the Dapper Don had been sent down to Illinois, Fritz had reoriented his affairs towards more legitimate ways of satisfying his avarice.

It had taken time. He had thought of everything. He had dreamed of making money from Broadway until he fell asleep during Cats. He planned to invest where there were guaranteed needs. He read books about innovation. He had crazy ideas of his own. They came thick and fast. From his strolls along his shoreline, he thought about glasses that magnified feet when rummaging. Carmine's overeating made him imagine a calorie tally linked to the supermarket food bill. After the cook screwed up yet again, he planned a voice-commanded smoke detector. After he found himself arguing in the car with Tanya, he thought of a GPS device that politely asked first if directions given were agreed with by all parties. And then there were the bedroom windows that automatically closed at an approaching aircraft. That one was brilliant, and he almost fitted some in.

After Tanya came to the rescue, he had lowered his sights. He read that most fortunes in history had been made by copying other people's ideas. The printing press had come from squashing olives. The French had copied the guillotine from the British. Americans had copied the British Comet jet.

Fritz had searched for stranded ideas still awaiting rescue. He read about relieving drought by towing icebergs, or water transported in barges made of flexible membranes. There were dozens of others.

"You need ideas that have already gone further," had advised Tanya.

Along came Eli Mendelsohn, a stroke of luck. Everything was luck in the end. Tanya had briefly interned at the Manhattan company where Mendelsohn worked. He was recognized for his assiduousness. He had talked to her about new opportunities in what he called 'intellectual property'.

Intellectual property. When she repeated the words to Fritz that evening, his bushy eyebrows almost hit the ceiling of his Long Room. The very expression made him quiver with excitement. Tanya had stumbled on an opportunity for 'abstract' loot - no need for secret warehouses, or concealed pits in the back yard or under the house. The feds would have nothing to train their binoculars on. It was brilliant.

He had asked her for more information. Mendelsohn, she said the next day, was involved in litigation over patents. They formed the embodiment of intellectual property. She then showed her father an article Mendelsohn had written that talked about making money out of other people's ideas without even having to invent or make anything. It just got better. The more Fritz heard, the more he adored his daughter for her find.

Out of the blue, Fritz had turned up at Tanya's place of work and demanded an interview, saying he was an investor and hiding the fact that he was her father. He had read the article, he said. While a flattered Eli gave his rather frightening visitor a two-hour lecture on how existing intellectual property could be manipulated to make streams of money, Fritz Gargano realized he had finally met his dream.

Eli painted the full grimy picture, the savage war over patents and invention that no-one outside saw. He talked of reputable companies, and even countries, discreetly seeking illegal monopolies by taking out patents in targeted industries. He showed how the Second World War losers had found their way back to the top. He talked of covert operations by corporations and governments. He described a world awash with patents, several thousand new ones every day. Many of these were never exploited by their owners. Some, though, were illegally copied by others. There was an opportunity, Mendelsohn said, to buy the rights to such patents and to prosecute the copiers. He described how the high costs and vagaries around litigation forced most defendants to pay up without asking questions.

Fritz's eyes had stopped dancing and moistened, just as they had at the birth of his daughter. As his brain salivated out of control, he had continued to listen and absorb. His mouth salivated too, Pavlovian style. He had to put the back of his fist to it. He had read that Pavlov had made a fortune selling saliva at a liter per dog to treat dyspepsia. Fritz would make his own by becoming a patent troll.

He went to work right away. He put Tanya onto scouting for candidate patents going for a song. They recruited a team of young business graduates and lawyers, as well as chemists and physicists who would master the subject. They began to prosecute. The newly created Gargano Associates rapidly became a universally detested multimillion-dollar enterprise that yielded huge profits for everyone involved.

But Eli Mendelsohn was never on board. He fell out of the picture almost straight away. In fact, he had bailed out. Yet after he came to realize what he had spawned, he kept himself aware from a distance about what Fritz Gargano was up to. It might one day make another book.

Fritz picked up one of the flat pebbles that Carmine and Gin Bottle always discreetly planted and threw it towards the water. It bounced three times. What if it was no coincidence that Eli Mendelsohn and Lenny the Limp had lived in the same town? There was no reason possible. He dismissed it straight away. Then he thought about his resolution to only stay with things legit from now on. Well, this was going to be one last time, and anyway the bullion was his.

He glanced at a golf ball lying a few feet away on the lawn. It was new. He never played golf, but he had seen them there before.

"F***ing seagulls!"

Had there been visitors, he would have explained his theory about seagulls stealing from the course a few miles away. In fact, it was Tanya. She'd been playing the trick on him for years, just to watch him from afar pointing into the air to his captivated friends. Each time she laughed so much that she wanted to pee.

He returned to the house to continue his book, then changed his mind. The news of Lenny had resurrected his old instincts. He went over to the bookshelves, that covered the entire Long Room wall from front to back and reached for Salvador Dali's memoirs. The idea of a primeval man examining his daily rhinoceros horns fitted his new mood perfectly, more than an unreadable saga of hot and cold media. The real Fritz had returned. He sighed. Life was about to go basic again, from its cerebral interlude back to the animal. It was a reawakening, a return to the Hades he had always loved. And yet the first thing he did was to remember a poem as he sank into his chair.

"*Lightly flows the mind, that leaves the load of yesterday behind.*"

4

It was getting dark by the time they turned up the highway that headed northwards from the shoreline. Carmine had been satiated. He had finished his second burger several minutes before and was now concentrating on getting there faster. Gin Bottle was already asleep, ever since they had said to head for a hotel certain to have space. Carmine took a final swig of soda from the container that looked disgracefully like a baby's bottle, knowing that his colleague was too far gone to notice.

He thought about what he had just achieved. He was delighted and proud. His news about Lenny had resurrected the old Fritz that the guys had missed. Staying legal had taken every bit of zest out of their existence. He, Gin Bottle and the boys would once again live for a reason, and hopefully there would be action just like the old times.

He was now doing seventy. He suddenly realized how he was driving. His mind had wandered as much as the Cadillac swayed from side to side. He tried to figure out what would happen if they crashed. Would their souls continue moving at the same speed?

He rapidly closed in on a run-down truck. It was rattling. Its back doors were rubbing and sliding against each other in their twisting and shaking frame. Somewhere from its underbelly it was slowly leaking liquid onto the roadway. He knew what it was up to. He recalled Fritz's short-lived hazardous waste venture and the money they had saved doing the same along the Expressway.

A car came up and overtook on the inside lane. He instinctively reached for the glove box but hesitated. Fritz would kill them if they got distracted. He accelerated and tailgated, and it deliberately slowed down. He reached for the glove box again. Gin Bottle stirred and Carmine came back to his senses. It wasn't worth it.

They turned off the highway and onto a secondary road. A car came up from behind. Carmine instinctively gaged its front tires in the rear-view mirror. Unmarked cruisers always had thicker wheels. When he saw they were normal, he pulled over to let it pass. It stayed behind with its headlights now on beam. He reached for the rear-view mirror to teach a lesson, give it a dose of its own medicine. He had gotten distracted. The Cadillac careened off the road and up the side bank before regaining the road. The car behind soon pulled back and dimmed its lights.

Gin Bottle woke up. Something was on his mind.

"Lenny always had it for graveyards, Carmine."

Carmine recognized the truth in what his colleague had just said. Lenny always used to hide his loot in graveyards. His share of the jewelry from the Hamptons heist had even been hidden next to his mother's coffin.

"Let's check out if this place has a graveyard."

They arrived just before eleven and sure enough there were plenty of spare rooms. Carmine called Fritz from reception to announce that they would scout around first thing and include any graveyard. Fritz gave him Eli Mendelsohn's address.

"Only take photos. And remember, not a word of this to Tanya."

After a dinner of buffalo wings and beer, Carmine placed the tray outside his room and fell asleep fully dressed. Gin Bottle's snoring next door vibrated the separating wall.

They were greeted outside by a beautiful early morning sun, but for the first time the Cadillac wouldn't start. Carmine swore. The day had already started badly when Gin Bottle drank his orange juice at the breakfast counter. Carmine hated that. He lifted the hood but saw nothing untoward. Leaving Gin Bottle with the bags, he walked back to reception to ask for help.

The veteran's badge that he, like Gin Bottle, supported on his vest did no good at all. The young man at reception passed him a telephone directory. The rescue truck arrived over an hour later. The Cadillac was back in action within fifteen minutes.

Carmine was at the wheel again, still swearing, as they emerged onto the main road to Broadacre.

Gin Bottle was reading a magazine as they drove along.

"*You've got to be kidding!*"

He had stumbled on a double page spread for the same hotel chain. He read out the story of a customer who had been helped by staff after his car would not start. Carmine was tempted to turn around to speak his mind, from the glove box if necessary.

It was still quiet when they arrived. Broadacre appeared small and tidy, and they negotiated each of the principal streets and then the narrower streets behind them. In its splendid isolation the town appeared a prime example of autarky, independent from everywhere around. They passed several churches in stone and two in timber, a few stores and bookshop, a large well-cut green, and a donut shop and hardware store further out. The white, cream, red and gray cladding on the buildings and houses, the wide tree-lined streets, the short lawns in front of the houses and paved driveways either to the fronts of the houses, or directly to garages of more modest properties, spelled a typical New England environment.

"Hey, Carmine, a restaurant called Equus! Maybe it's Italian."

They passed a state prison building. It had red-painted brick walls and a white portico. It made them instinctively shiver and look away.

"I swear I saw someone mooning from that window," Carmine said.

Not far from there they found Eli Mendelsohn's, and Gin Bottle took two photos on the fly. A little further down the same street they photographed the house that had belonged to Lenny. A SOLD sign was still posted in front, and the realtors were local.

There was a delightful pond nearby, and they got out to sit for a while by the water. Then they returned to the center to case the town on foot. They purchased a map and ice cream from the corner store and headed for the cemetery.

"Would you like to retire here, Carmine?"

They were well out of sight of the prison and had spotted the first graves and cypresses in the distance. Carmine said that the place seemed better, more civilized, than Long Island, even if dead.

"Yeah Carmine, it seems a bit closed."

They eventually found themselves searching among the graves. Several of the headstones went back at least a hundred and fifty years. There were large ones, some whole, others chipped, split or leaning, and many that had half lost their markings, either through weather or a covering of moss. Graves on one side of the cemetery were quite new and had flowers deposited in small glass or metal vessels. Carmine took several photographs in various directions before they headed back towards the center.

On the way, they spotted the office of the attorney who had handled the conveyance of Lenny's property. It was set back from the roadway and was being opened up for the day. The cheerful secretary greeted them, and they announced they came from Gargano Associates.

She glanced at their identical badges and declared that she was always ready to help veterans. She confirmed that Attorney Hughes, the senior partner of two, had handled the affair. The seller's name had been Leonora Long, and the purchasers were an English couple.

"*Leonara Long!*" they chuckled.

Carmine asked who had ordered the sale of the property. She said it had been written into the deceased owner's will which had also been handled by Attorney Hughes. The proceeds were to be dedicated to charities.

"Which ones?"

She would not say. Carmine then asked if she knew anything about the English couple. She said they had just arrived, and that he worked for a film producer in New York. Their eyebrows rose. She obligingly dug into her files and gave the names of the couple and film company.

They decided they had discovered enough for the time being and took their leave. As they walked back towards the center, the secretary briefly peered through the front window blind. There had been something troubling about the men and their interest. Before she forgot all about it, she jotted down a quick note to tip Hughes off.

Carmine and Gin Bottle decided to return to Long Island and discuss the next move with Fritz, but before leaving they picked up a couple of coffees and a box of donuts and parked close to Lenny's house in order to sneak a snapshot of its new owners. No-one showed during the two hours they waited.

As they prepared to take off, Gin Bottle asked that they first call in at the local hardware store.

"I need some twelve-inch nails. You never know."

Fritz was itching to hear what they had found. They lovingly described the small town that had so impressed and produced the map and Polaroids.

"A prison, eh?"

They examined the photos from the cemetery.

"What the f*** is that?" Fritz asked.

Carmine and Gin Bottle quizzically looked. Fritz pointed to a small structure behind some graves in one of their shots. It appeared to be fronting the road. It might be a mausoleum or something, but it seemed to be the only one around.

The three of them looked at each other and said that it needed to be checked out next time they were up there, no doubt when they returned for a gentle chat with this Hughes.

Gin Bottle left the room. Fritz pondered for a while.

"No, I've got a better idea. Leave it with me."

Carmine headed for the door. Fritz had yet another thought. One day they might need a local contact whom they could trust.

"Find out if we have a friend in Broadacre. Just in case."

5

Mary Dunne, known behind her back as 'The Countess' because of all the unlikely people she said she knew, inched her Lincoln Continental out of her driveway and into the near lane of the grandest street in town, exquisitely lined with tall maples. Once her car had effortlessly slipped through its gears and was coasting in a southerly direction, she adjusted her GPS to its first pre-set, her closest friend's house not so far away. Then she peered through the rear-view mirror to assure herself of the graceful automatic closing of one of her three garage doors, as well as the double wrought-iron gate in front.

All was well. Her take-off routine satisfactorily completed, she gave a quick second glance in the mirror for herself. Her bushy white hair, well past worth dying, in fact quite grand, looked in place, her Roman nose stood impeccably in the center of her broad face, thanks to fine tuning by Dr. Villeneuve a decade ago, and her contrasting eyelashes, exquisitely thickened through a combination of her steady hand and Lancôme, meant that all was well with her as well.

It was ten to twelve, and she was aiming for Anne Kaplan's, another spiky radiolarian and her alter-ego. Her doughty and equally punctilious but querulous Jewish friend had called in earnest, and Mary had rushed her departure in consequence.

Halfway to the crossroads, she made her customary sign of the cross as she drove past the cemetery, and then glanced down to the leather seat next to her to ensure that she had remembered her *New Yorker*.

Oh dear! She had forgotten it.

The magazine was too important to forget. The articles and cartoons were accessories to her real enjoyment, the treasured restaurant reviews, that made one's mouth water, and reminded them both of headier days when they each lived even grander lives in the metropolis suburbs.

That's what happens when you rush things, she murmured to herself in the mirror with a slight frown. She should have known better.

She was still cursing under her breath as she power-swung the limousine without stopping, only just making the width of the road, let alone missing cars coming in the opposite direction. After dutifully making a second sign of the cross as she passed the cemetery again, with her left hand on the steering wheel, and somewhat clumsily clasping the control stick at the same time, she pressed the button that would reopen her gates just in time for her arrival.

She mentally slapped herself as she prepared to cross the road into her drive. She ruminated that these instances of carelessness were becoming more frequent. Her once formidable mental bolt of steel had developed a habit of jumping its threads by surprise. She had begun to lose faith in her long-held motto that a person's weakness was their strength, and she searched for reasons. Perhaps it was due to what they were presently calling the 'bright tax', imposed on clever people once they got older. It wasn't her memory that had showed signs of weakening, *Oh no*, she argued, it was her finely honed system of checks and balances that for so many decades had pre-warned her of any pending oversight. The compulsiveness, that had taken over the void that had usually been satisfied by finding new projects, was debilitating her. Her control system had come into question. But her memory was intact.

She parked next to the front door and, leaving the motor running, boldly swung the car door open to its maximum, stepped out, and regained her composure with the gentle sound of bling-bling in the background. She walked gracefully towards the front door, and once on the step, opened the bag hanging from her folded arm and deliberately took out the key. Her eyes purposefully glanced into the bag while she spread it open. Her brain had always made her do one thing at a time. Her late husband, of Italian descent through his mother and practical, used to badger her about taking out the key while she was walking over, but after ten years of his being buried, such annoyances had been all but forgotten. She had always done things one thing at a time, and her life had been a darn slight neater for it.

She opened up and turned off the alarm. Her entry into the hallway was greeted by a sudden flutter of wings as Horatio fled towards the coffered ceiling of the back conservatory. Her one-track mind meant that she ignored her mynah bird completely as she spotted and scooped up the magazine just where she had left it, next to the rococo filigree on the side table by the door, so as not to forget.

A couple of minutes later, the periphery alarm reset, car re-departed, and gates re-closed, Mary was once again making her third sign of the cross in front of the passing cemetery where her husband lay.

Her mind turned to Anne Kaplan, her permanently carping friend to whom she had to remain close to in order to maintain control. 'Best' friend, as others sometimes labeled her, was a manner of speaking. Their relationship, born out of the need for two aging fossils to continue to impose themselves on their surroundings, and especially each other, and from time to time console one another in case of setback, was in reality nothing less than akin to the Hitler-Stalin pact, with a gender-adjusted smidgeon of the tragic seams that underlay such relationships as those of Cain and Abel, Romulus and Remus, Henry II and his Archbishop of Canterbury, and Kennedy and Johnson. But then again, she knew, that's what old friends were built for.

And this time it sounded as though Anne needed consolation yet again. In fact, it was nearly always down to her. She had called an hour before, wanting to see Mary as soon as possible. She did not explain why, but Mary had easily guessed. Anne's life comprised consecutive long-running themes. Her best friend had had only one thing on her mind for months, and at present it was the gerrymandering of their immutable environment through a powerful body called the Historical Commission, revived after decades of being prorogued by the town council. Yes, thought Mary, it had to be something to do with the group of half a dozen regressive citizens that to most of the town prevented anything novel, controversial or imaginative ever happening to it. Mary was sure of it. Anne would breathe the name of that august and ensconced body once they were within hearing distance of each other, regrettably just a little closer than when they were younger.

And now she thought about it, she knew precisely why her friend had called: Mary had good hold over the leader of the Commission, the town's First Selectman, the undoubted *bête noir* of Anne's *ennui du jour*, as her Canadian friends might say.

It was true that Mary had a good hold over the First Selectman, and by implication the Town Clerk and every other churlish character and parsimonious bureaucrat who had a hand in herding their community. Her attitude towards these effete beings, as towards any official at all with whom she had to deal, was that *de facto* they had reached their level of incompetence, constantly squabbled between themselves, and never learned properly to manage shortcuts in order to get things done. They had climbed the full heights of their individual trees, well beneath her own, largely because of their potted and over diversified personal histories. It was a case, she firmly believed, of too many broths spoiling the cook. Eclecticism is dangerous, she believed. It makes people want constantly to move on. It makes them understand things too easily where blissful ignorance better helps to drive the bravest and most difficult decisions. So much for an America on the move!

But Mary's belief went further than conquering the contretemps presented by lowly venal bureaucrats of one sort or another. It was an attitude she held against everyone who presented her with obstacles of any sort, any form of chutzpah, social or otherwise, the cantankerous Anne counting among them.

Not that Anne Kaplan was a write-off, however. Her friend remained as shrewd as ever in her business dealings. Anne knew people got too easily confused by kerfuffle placed before them. She knew how to get them to focus on what she wanted and provide a yardstick by which she and they could judge their progress. Her approach, with which she had been imbibed by her own parents, had been also nurtured by her husband. She and Mary shared this in common. That's why they had always got on so well, at a certain level.

Mary cursed again as she remembered it was her own birthday, on Independence Day no less. She had been born to the sound of fireworks, and it had always nurtured in her a desire for surprise. She had grown to love to forget her anniversaries until the evening, and then suddenly remember. She would ceremoniously cook herself a five-course meal in celebration. It was very special to her, and it was why, for all those years, she had kept the date secret from the likes of Anne. Since her friend was manipulative, and certain to destroy such enjoyment, Mary kept out of touch for days ahead. But this time her ploy had failed when she had fatally picked up the telephone before waiting for the voice.

Mary cursed when she remembered she was about to be asked to bring people to heel yet again. She had once thought that she had successfully trained those who discreetly did her bidding to keep such annoyances at a distance, and only provide what she wanted to hear. If Anne did indeed have it in for the First Selectman, Mary would strategically pull a direct punch by aiming instead at his full-time assistant, the Town Clerk, who usually got saddled with the hard stuff, and anyway always looked the convenient patsy.

"He's not doing his job again!" she would complain, her alcoholic breath disguised by vodka instead of gin in order to maintain her credibility. "Find out what he is doing instead and tell him to stop it!"

The First Selectman would dutifully listen and comply. After all, she had paid several times over for his election, and so far, no-one else knew about it.

And today indeed was no exception, but as usual, the smooth glide of her Continental through town gave away nothing of her weakness for a tipple. In any case, her discreet and sometimes dubious philanthropic activities ensured her place on a list of untouchables, provided to Harry the resident trooper, among others.

In fact, Harry knew of her particular habit firsthand. A couple of years ago, he had been alerted by his New York colleagues who had arrested her trying to stuff a dollar bill into the coin machine on a parkway toll and staying there while insisting. They had carried her to the state line to where Harry had been dutifully summoned, and her car was recuperated a day later by the Broadacre limousine driver aided by his wife.

Harry always remembered the alcoholic fumes coming from the old lady snoring away on the back seat as he drove her back. His standing instructions never stopped him suspecting that he could smell gin each time he spotted her car.

Mary turned left at the central crossroads that presented her with an imaginary demarcation line, rather like the bridge in Ottawa next to their onetime hotel that had divided the so-different worlds of Anglo-Saxons and French.

Once again, she sensed the immediate change of the world she was entering, in this case Anne's world. The people she saw changed. They looked different, their faces more ruffled, their stature often shorter, no doubt because several in the area raced horses for a living. They behaved differently too, and sometimes it was hard to get used to.

Half a mile later, the GPS android softly announced that she had arrived. Mary sneeringly nicknamed it the 3H Ranch, for horticulture, horses and hunting. She crossed the road into Anne's gate-drawn driveway, and her friend came out in person to greet her with her usual equally alcoholic scowl.

She eyed the woman who was shorter than herself and had a more pointed face. Wait for it! Wait for the words 'Historical Commission' certain to be mouthed even before she had unwound the window.

Their 'amicable' feud was nothing new. Their relationship had always been tense and competitive, spiced with envy. Mary was once made jealous by rumors that Anne's husband had imported a rickshaw and forced her to pull him around their large garden, both stark naked. Their adventure always climaxed at the water's edge, underneath, and in part courtesy of, an age-old weeping willow. He had eventually been diagnosed with bipolar disease, only a decade after the term had been invented. He gave up his business, and they moved to Broadacre, and a nasty road accident mysteriously locked his bipolarity into permanent positive mode. He became impossible to handle and eventually killed himself on his treasured vintage motorbike. By the time Mary had arrived at the scene, all that was left was his blood-stained helmet and a dirty initialed handkerchief that had fallen out of his pocket, the sight of both of which had stuck in her mind ever since. It was a strange way of remembering him. The helmet and handkerchief reappeared more often than his face.

Mary flinched a little as soon as her nemesis and friend came out with those so hotly anticipated words. At least she was out there in front of her and not going through the pathetic motion of deliberately talking to her phone messages as soon as she spotted her through the corner of her eye or insisting instead on continuing to traipse around her house with one or another unknown acolyte while Mary was forced to wait.

Mary liked to believe that Anne had always admired her. It may have been partially true. But Anne also treasured any one-upmanship she could gain over her friend, like the time she surprised Mary's husband improbably vacuuming the house, or Mary herself just after she had popped a hot potato into her mouth while she thought she had been alone in the kitchen. Their rather unique wavering bond had been resealed after they had gone out together for a walk in the local wildlife sanctuary and, thanks to beavers, an electricity pole had crashed in front of them, surrounding them with so many live cables that they had to be rescued.

Enough of these thoughts! Mary braced herself and got out, and they nonchalantly ghost-kissed each other on both cheeks with a *moi-moi*.

Mary studied her friend's painted face, enshrouded as usual by her dark brown wig to cover her receding hairline and withering body of hair. Her friend now looked like an American geisha, she thought. In certain lights she even looked as though she had been embalmed. Time had changed her. It had placed a toll on her looks that even all her dollar bills could never rescue.

Anne Kaplan ended up playing it cool. She did not want to appear that she was in a rush, so she decided they play Scrabble. They sat down in the living room that opened onto the garden and commenced in their usual aggressive style.

The mood changed. Within minutes they started scowling at each other's moves. Had it not been a national holiday, they would have called the New York Public Library multiple times in order to validate the words they argued over. Anne was brash with her moves. It conformed to her belief that any decision, even made rapidly, was infinitely better than dithering or no decision at all.

After a couple of hours, Anne got down to business, and her friend was almost relieved. She led Mary outside to her glorious Technicolor expanse that was tended by the gardeners Jesus and Maria, and they sat down on wire chairs on the vast patio. Then Anne got out her pipe, as much an annoyance to Mary as her friend's permanent reminder of gin was to her.

Anne reported that someone just outside the zone controlled by the Historical Commission was planning to build a windmill in his garden. The egregious idea of putting up zany structures around town was in danger of catching on, and contrary to the secret plan she had been hatching with the First Selectman. It would be a death knoll to the town's tradition and future as she saw it. The restricted zone needed to be expanded before it was too late, but the First Selectman was dragging his feet on a proposal that had been under discussion for nearly a year already. Hence her desperate call.

"So, what do you intend to do?" asked Mary, deliberately distorting her voice to pretend she was trying not to cough, while avoiding any suggestion at all that she would provide help.

But in fact, Mary agreed with the problem more than she wanted to be agreeable to her friend. As they continued to pour down their drinks, they brainstormed every solution they could think of. The culprit was the vulgar Tom the builder. Jesus and Maria worked for him as well. Mary wildly proposed using them unknowingly to introduce termites into the building, or even to cause a chemical leak that would necessitate digging up the land and pulling down the windmill. Then again, the English couple who had just bought the house in front might be persuaded to launch a complaint.

And so it went on, as one of the town's *eminences grises* repeatedly helped herself to the other's gin, while her opposite regularly puffed away at her stinking and ungainly pipe, and they both wasted their time skirting around the true mutually acceptable solution of expanding the zone covered by the Commission.

Deep in alternating thought and conversation, and clouded by the smoke and alcoholic fumes, they heard the low-flying Warthog and the concurrent boom of the cannon from the town center.

"Thank God that wasn't a crash," exclaimed Mary, just as she did every year, always hoping that something would fall on the mutually detested new library building near the center of town.

They continued to divert from their original conversation. Anne complained of her loss of sense of smell in the last few days. Mary disguised her schadenfreude as she knew it was considered a first sign of impending death.

Then they returned to the subject of the day, this time unified in agreement. Both of them had long dreamed of a town bathed in tradition, of rigorous planning rules imposed by a powerful and repressive Commission, of an exceptional town becoming famous and visited by several times more tourists than ever before, of the rise in property values, of the riches provided by a new local museum, of actors prowling the streets in seventeenth century costumes, of cars being banned from the center for the sake of horse carriages and carts, of a bubble of yesteryear that would in a weird way even make them feel younger and revitalized.

And then there was Anne's secret project. She had land that abutted the town that she wanted, with the help of investment money from the town, to convert into a model working village. It would bring tourists by their tens of thousands. There would even be old-style hotels.

Their mutual smoothing and soothing session was to last for a couple of hours more, through a two-course watercress and smoked salmon sandwich lunch, followed by their favorite lemon meringue pie, all prepared and chilled by Anne's cook Rosa the day before, before they each went their separate ways in order to somewhat noisily sleep the rest of the afternoon off.

6

It was light outside. Bill had been dreaming of his Golden Globe. Trophy in hand, he had been eying the enthusiastic audience of his applauding peers. They were thumping their feet in unison. He woke up and for a second still believed it.

Thump, thump, thump.

He had expected to be disturbed much later by Daniel or Catherine champing at the bit, or by his own urge to update Sam in New York. Catherine was still fast asleep and quiet. Daniel was never up so early, even for his new school.

Thump, thump, thump.

He had long believed in ninety-minute sleep patterns, but the sky was already too light to wait this one out. He got out of bed, little better than a newborn foal, but managed to tip-toe alongside the rail down the wooden corridor to the living room to peek at what was going on. Just as he entered, he sensed the full onslaught of lucidity. Doing something other than lighting up the computer would make the whole day go better. It was the way he started the day that always counted for the rest. He looked outside.

It was Tom the builder.

Tom had started the grand windmill that he had boasted about during the party but delayed until afterwards. He had wanted to free himself from the dictatorship of the power company that had sent them one exorbitant bill too many, to become green and independent, and to complete it before the Historical Commission finally carried out the threat to extend its boundary. The edifice would stand behind Bill and Catherine's house in such a way that they would only see the top part and its canvas sails, but Tom's meagre description had been enough to make them picture a rather awful challenge to any standard of architectural decency. This was the land of the free after all.

The incessant noise soon aroused the others. Each sleepily joined Bill at the window, Catherine in her slippers that she dragged against the wooden floor, and Daniel in bare feet that seemed to stick to it. Without saying a word, the three of them peered into the misty abyss to follow a super-caffeinated Tom darting around from task to task at the top of a ladder, unrecognizable inside his safety hat and goggles, thick rubber pads on his knees, and no doubt wearing the same steel-tipped safety shoes that had set off every alarm at La Guardia.

"Lucky if he doesn't fall."

Catherine hadn't noticed that Tom had even harnessed himself to the ladder.

Bill pulled the window open, and they heard Tom's singing, quite out of tune with the display he was putting on.

"The change in the weather has brought us together…"

Catherine swiveled her eyes and pulled away, appalled at the inhuman display of energy outside.

"I'll make coffee."

Bill closed the window.

"Forget the work in the garden today, darling."

He'd better order earmuffs, gloves, glasses and safety hat first, so as not to invite any comments from his neighbor.

From the kitchen, Catherine agreed. She recalled Tom had donned the next thing to a bomb disposal outfit for the fireworks.

Daniel was otherwise inspired. He went to search the packing boxes for his hammer set. From the kitchen window Catherine spotted Mary Lou and Barbara outside on the road, both spandexed in unimaginably awful colors, power walking their bodies along with weights in their hands.

"What does it take to slow these Americans down?"

Bill called Sam Rosenbaum at ten.

"Good to hear you, my dear friend."

Sam spoke in his usual smooth manner. Bill wondered for how long such euphoria would endure. It was surely a case of happiness being provoked by forgetting the past and not thinking of the future, a dangerous path by any standard.

Bill described to Sam the arrival of a mysterious down-and-out hobo in a small and rough Long Island community. This man would become the leading protagonist in a picaresque story about a violent gang - French, Jewish, Italian, Fascist, Communist, he didn't know yet - intent on wrenching control of their small town. Bill described the sorry man's meeting with a lonely nervous woman smoking foreign cigarettes who was the only person prepared to listen to him. She was the one, he had decided, who had the ominous bumper sticker on her car.

Sam was delighted and chose not to challenge Bill.

"The grit's in the oyster, Bill! but do me a favor, leave out the Jews."

At precisely eleven thirty, Tom and Mary Lou and their two offspring drew up in front and honked for the short drive to the clambake, to which they could have easily and more enjoyably all walked together. However, the journey took long enough to show that Tom was none the worse for his earlier exertion or any residual caffeine. In fact, he was in better form than ever. As if bonhomie was always rationed, it made Catherine feel even worse.

Father Arnold, the avuncular organizer, appeared to be more cosmopolitan and altruistic than anyone Bill and Catherine had come across so far. It was a good sign. How strange it had been, had thought Bill, to so rapidly sense the insular perspective of neighbors whose origins were from such widely differing far-off lands and cultures. Then he had second thoughts. These first impressions must surely be wrong. He should wait for better proof.

Nevertheless, Father Arnold, who had a huge and imposing frame, talked about himself. His parents had been teachers in remote Newfoundland, and in a tortuous conversation this led to a discussion about making one's mark in life. At one point, he cited the morning's news about a spate of Arab suicide bombers, and Catherine carelessly joked that he could never be a candidate because of his vows.

Father Arnold smiled.

"You mean the seventy-two virgins? I'm going to invite them to my funeral instead!"

He had taken it well, and they all laughed in relief. The priest was well over seventy. Bill was tempted to challenge him about how far he had already got in his endeavor. Father Arnold's tone changed instead.

"You wouldn't believe how many parishioners die without anyone left. I'm often the only living one there."

"Even Karl Marx only had eleven at his funeral," said Bill.

That tone lasted for a while. Catherine glumly recalled that, had it not been for her sister and herself, their father would have been in the same predicament.

"He caught on once he saw that his time was getting close. He read about Polybius who never went to the forum without making a friend. He started going out for walks just to make friends. He learned to look at dogs before their owners, as it nearly always facilitated a greeting that might turn into something more. But in the end, we were the only ones at his funeral."

Father Arnold had at one time taught at a school, in New York.

"I came to realize that in reality I was preparing my pupils for death."

Bill tried to divert the moroseness, but only made things worse. He talked about his last experience in church, in his early twenties. He had gotten high on weed and decided that it would be fun to go to confession to enjoy the memories. He admitted he had more or less already given up back in the sixties after they had dropped Latin. The half-understood language had always seemed more powerful and spiritual than the mundane vernacular by comparison and trying to learn its structure by chance also helped with math. Then they demoted Saint Christopher. The fatal blow came when the local bishop had turned up at church with a vast accolade of hangers-on, all willing females. Bill spotted a mafia. It became the last straw, and he gave up forever.

Catherine tried to steer the subject her way.

"Confessions must twist your view of life, Father."

The priest, still recovering from what Bill had just said, accepted that confessions brought him in line with the authorities who had to deal with troubled and troublesome people.

"They know, I know. It binds us together, even though we cannot talk about it. Whatever the limitations of our professions, we are all trying to put things right."

He recalled one or two fellow seminarians who admitted how much they found pleasure in listening to confessions. Sometimes it seemed as if it were their only ambition, and he often wondered whether they had ever been tempted to sell indulgences just as in the Middle Ages. Catherine thought that scary. A shocked Bill was meanwhile coming to terms with the wild imagination of an America ruled by religious police and an exploitive clergy. Father Arnold tried to push Bill's thoughts to the edge.

"We need people to monitor us. Godparents, auditors, trustees, confessors, best-men, and inspectors…and us priests as much as any."

Bill had images of his Dominican boarding school. It had developed into a hotbed of teenage agnosticism, despite all the liturgical practices and paraphernalia that provided a comforting familiarity across the seasons. Alongside his comrades, he had competed like a jackal to bring down even the best of their teachers. After his alarmed parents had transferred him to a local day college instead, he had difficulty acclimatizing to people who were so pleasant and civilized to each other all the time. There were no more trivia like waking up in the dormitory in the morning with boots around his head, punishments that included kneeling on a stone floor for hours on end or being condemned to walking a thousand times up and down an outside path in the rain or snow, or niceties such as being ostracized for suggesting that *Citizen Kane* might have been a good film after all.

He stopped his daydreaming. He was not sure if there had been a pause in the conversation and he looked around. Everyone was talking peacefully, so unlike at Tom's and Mary Lou's party or the violent beginning of the day. It reminded him of the eerie quiet of parties given by friends who practiced transcendental meditation back in England. Their center had been one floor up from the Samaritans, and Bill had always suspected some kind of collusion between them. Here it was different. In front of Father Arnold's church, it had to be the influence of a looming Catholic purgatory. The congregation no doubt became more civilized at the thought of impending death. Bill then recalled a few riotous Irish funeral boozes and promptly shook off the thought.

Father Arnold reverted to his own world once again. He talked about his parishioners and the challenge he faced with army veterans, mostly from Vietnam. Many felt compelled to talk endlessly about their horrific experiences, and he admitted he wished that he had been like his First World War colleagues who had famously been the only ones of their kind to have stayed at the front.

"The more you think you know about those poor guys, and what they went through, the less you actually do. Sometimes it's best to stay ignorant and accept what they say."

One of his parishioners had written a book about his experience which Father Arnold had read. He described the disturbing contrast between the author's beautiful prose and the killing and destruction it was describing.

Bill recalled when he had first started work in the south-east of England. Some of his oldest colleagues had been prisoners of war after the taking of Singapore. Nearly a quarter of a century later they were still showing symptoms of their punishment and deprivation. They commanded deep respect from the earthly northern warlords, many from Yorkshire, who ran different parts of the company, and many were still going for yearly check-ups for malaria. The difference, recounted Bill in comparing with what he had just heard, was that none of them ever talked about their experience. One just saw it in their bodies and faces.

Catherine asked Father Arnold if he enjoyed his pulpit. Did it give him a feeling of power?

"Well, yes. Now that you mention it, Catherine, I look forward to it all week. But whether my sermon registers with anyone is another matter."

Before they left, Father Arnold offered to show them his church. While Daniel played outside with Jack and Debra, they entered from the bright sunlight and squinted to adapt to the dark. They walked side by side toward the altar and at that very minute the organ lit up. They glanced at each other, wondering if it had somehow been fortuitous.

"He's practicing," Father Arnold said.

As they were emerging, he said he had something for Daniel. He disappeared and returned with a small lion carved out of ivory. Bill called Daniel over to receive the gift.

"A lure to go to church, or a sign of guilt about keeping something illegal?" whispered Catherine.

They walked back home to see that Jesus and Maria had turned up with a pretty Puerto Rican girl whose clothes seemed barely to hang on her as she forced her trowel into the ground.

"We have an assistant, you see," Jesus said to Bill. "Yolanda's a friend."

She seemed to be every now and again picking flowers and pressing them into a canvas-covered book she kept at her side. Bill wondered if that was theft.

The telephone had rung as soon as they got inside. It was Sam. He had been trying for an hour. He wanted Bill in New York right away for a meeting with his backers. A hired two-pilot twin-engine was headed to the local airport about half an hour away. The plan was to fly into Republic where a limo would be waiting to take them into Manhattan.

"Bring Catherine. We have a party tonight."

7

Daniel was dispatched for a sleepover next door, and Bill and Catherine headed for the isolated airfield that Bill had already used before. As they approached, half an hour later, they were confronted with an unexpected scene. The small country road leading to the terminal was lined with identical shiny black four-by-fours with multiple antennae protruding from their roofs. Their undersides were being sniffed by excited Alsatians directed by crewcut men alternately pointing for the dogs and talking into their cuffs.

Bill caught on that the Secret Service had descended upon a normally silent neighborhood and, for want of better distraction, it had turned to bizarrely checking itself.

They parked easily in front of the small terminal and went inside, eager to find out what was going on. There was far more than the usual number of individuals loitering inside. Bill picked out their two pilots standing on their own opposite a large plate window that fronted the staging area and runway beyond. One of them announced the skies had been closed for an impromptu arrival of no less than Marine One.

It made no sense. Bill asked why the President would come there of all places, a run-down airport belonging to the featureless industrial city ten miles away, an entire apartheid away from where they lived.

One pilot knew the answer. He had overheard mention of a local billionaire fundraiser who was the President's friend and who lived on a large estate nearby. This man had reportedly made his fortune developing a high-speed winch for army special forces and was rich enough to possess his own private airfield that for some reason the Secret Service chose to avoid.

The distraction started to be fun, despite the inconvenience. A small military helicopter dropped out of the sky right in front of where they stood, its blades almost stripping the roof off the terminal they were in.

Minutes later, two clean-shaven pilots in dark glasses and fatigues climbed down from their respective sides with notepads in their hands. They entered through the only glass door and looked around before walking over to the control room to the right which doubled as the airport reception desk and snack bar.

One of Sam's pilots went over to ask if there was any chance of flying out any time soon.

"Not for the next hour or so, Sir," Bill overheard.

He marveled at how polite and civilized everyone remained in the face of such perturbation. The gathering in the small lobby remained almost quiet. A tall marine in full ceremonial uniform, and chained to an attaché case, walked in from nowhere and stood in front of them, blocking their view to the runway.

Perhaps the arrival was imminent. The first pilot, unmoved by it all, made a proposal.

"I suggest we have breakfast."

Bill would have liked to have waited and watched but did not want to admit it. Catherine was already fed up. There was no proper restauration on site, so the four of them had to drive a couple of miles to the main road. They settled on a fast-food outlet selling miniature lukewarm greasy hamburgers, which were all they could get in the short time available.

Just after they passed the fleet of black cars again, the once empty country road beyond was by now bursting both sides with a flag-waving rent-a-crowd, enough to make any dictator feel at home, let alone the President of the United States. Bill was busily taking note, trying to figure out how to incorporate such an event into an upcoming script.

The burgers were truly dreadful, as promised, a far cry from their once favorite Hard Rocks, as Catherine would call it, and they all regretted the diversion. On the way back, each of them privately wondered if they could ever fly after that. By the end, the short ride had thankfully seemed to have downed the sickly burgers for good.

All had changed at the terminal. The crowd, crew-cuts, dogs and armored vehicles had gone. They parked where they had before.

In no time at all they were taxying past a parked Marine One with its crew at the ready, listening to their radio while surrounded on the ground by rifle-toting men in dark suits. As the stationary presidential helicopter disappeared in ripples at the edges of the portholes behind them, they reached the end of the only runway.

The engines revved to shaking point. Both pilots in front of them braced as they took off and narrowly dodged the multiple pylons that reportedly made landing there such fun, especially in poor weather.

"Wow!" exclaimed Bill.

Over the nonsensical noise coming over the radio, as if the air traffic controller had just attacked one of his donuts, the lead pilot announced he had changed the flight plans to make it directly into Kennedy. The small plane lifted upward fast enough to make them all feel twice their weight, and then on, having flattened out, from time to time both pilots checked a penciled plan clipped to the dashboard between them. If they were arguing about their route, thought Bill, they were doing a good job at disguising it.

The short flight south was smooth, but Catherine felt queasy over the Sound. She had already read how many aircraft disappeared there, and after Bill tried to reassure her, she only got worse. It made him start to feel the same. The crossing went on forever. The short stretch of water never seemed to give way to land. Bill swore he detected Catherine praying.

After an eternity, once they were at long last beyond the opposite shoreline, their tiny plane found itself miraculously sandwiched between two 747s as they lined up to land in Kennedy. The landing fees and the general aviation facilities there would be horrifically expensive, thought Bill, but Sam was paying, and so he told a recuperating Catherine to enjoy the rare experience. Everything would be smooth, and a limousine was promised to be waiting for them.

"On the tarmac?"

The second pilot twisted his head as much as he could.

"Hold on! It gets shaky between these giants."

They glanced at each other, and Catherine reached for a rather creased paper bag just in case. They rode the wake of the jumbo in front as if on a mechanical steer. Even the pilots seemed on edge as they helplessly bounced on their seats in orderly synchronization. The temporary respite accorded Bill and Catherine just beforehand had become entirely voided, and the affair had developed into an experience that both intended to forget forever.

Then, finally, there was the relief of a smooth touch-down. Bill's cell rang to announce that they would have to make their own way into town after all.

Catherine became angry.

There were no cabs in front of the terminal, and so Bill darted for the rental counter while it was still vacant. The only vehicle left was a silver Mercedes S-Class at an astronomical rate, but it was the same model that Bill had seen George Clooney crash during his flight from France. Avoiding mentioning the Clooney link to Catherine on the way in, Bill decided it would be wise to hide the rental once they got there, so that Sam's backers would not see how their money was being spent.

They found the right building and a parking lot around the corner, far enough away from the squeegee men mounting guard at the traffic lights nearby. After a quick exchange on the intercom in the empty hallway, Catherine waited for Sam Rosenbaum's wife while Bill headed for the elevator and pressed for the eighth floor, only seven floors up.

As the elevator made its way upward, Bill glanced at the list of occupants posted next to the panel. He was in a mind to joke to Sam about Schindler's lift until he realized the pun would be lost in American, let alone be distasteful to his employer.

He walked into a meeting that had only just started. He had lost the opportunity to plan anything ahead with Sam, so he would have to be extra careful about what he said.

There was no time for niceties. Sam introduced his three visitors by their first names only. One was American and the two others had just flown in from Europe. Sam said he had called Bill in at the last minute in case they needed to talk about the script.

The American took the lead. He asked Sam about the schedule which he insisted was running about three weeks behind. Sam at first underplayed this and mentioned reasons for the delay, including Bill's later than planned arrival in the country, but he did not seem to get through.

"How did we get here?" asked the American again.

Bill had the answer.

"One day at a time. We'll make it up the same way. You'll see."

The man refused to accept and was becoming tiresome. Bill started to dislike him. The man boasted that his daughter had read Jean-Paul Sartre at high school.

"You know, that man published twenty pages a day throughout his entire working lifetime."

Sam glanced at Bill, almost giving away his own annoyance. Only the money was keeping him silent. The man went on.

"And anyway, you know very well that if something doesn't get done in twenty-four hours, it won't in twenty-four days."

Bill was now angry and ready to show it. Who did this creep think he was? Even a telling glance from Sam could not stop him now.

"I'm sorry, Mr., er, Mr...."

"Gargano's the name. Fritz Gargano."

Bill was happy with the Europeans on the other hand. It made him feel less isolated. One of them, named Sadini, had arranged to ship in some very special camera equipment from Rome. It would enable spectacular shots, Bill learned. The problem was that his Italian office may have loaded the wrong equipment. It would be a permanent admission into the country, and the duties would amount to tens of thousands of dollars. They had at all costs to check out the shipment, before it went through customs, and turn back anything unneeded.

Sam called a friend and was told it was impossible.

"But this is America, for heaven's sake!" he shouted in frustration.

Fritz Gargano kept quiet. He was not about to expose his links to men who could have seen things righted. The Italian office told them they had contacts in New Jersey where the equipment was in bondage. They said they would call back right away.

They decided on a working lunch while waiting. Catherine and Sam's wife returned from Manhattan and joined them. Bill chatted to Sam about Harry the trooper's Long Island Argentinian experience, and Sam, eying Sadini, said he would take them next time to an Italian restaurant where they discreetly served horse and donkey. It proved to be a gigantic *faux pas*. To Sam's horror, the second Italian was a horse breeder and had even written a book that had sold well both sides of the Atlantic. He predictably took exception to Sam's gesture.

"Why they do that, I'll never understand. Half a million horses gave their lives in the First World War, and God knows how many donkeys."

For the heck of it, Bill mentioned his uncle had explored the Australian Outback with camels in the 1930s and once or twice had to eat one in order to survive. Fritz Gargano reacted.

"I had camel down in Florida once. It came with alligator."

The Italian duly silenced, Fritz Gargano then asked Bill how he got his ideas for the script. Catherine joked how easy it all was because of all they had already experienced in their new home. Despite his permanently sour look, Gargano's eyes lit up with interest.

"What sort of things?"

Bill had no way of knowing to whom he was talking. He could never be blamed for all that he now said. As he described the problems he had with the neighbor's land, the weird windmill that was going up that was bound to cause an eruption at the Historical Commission, as he talked about the local cop who seemed to spend all his time mowing other people's lawns, and the old lady who had sold them the house and had left holes in her walls, Fritz Gargano lapped up the free lowdown he was being handed while pretending to appear as indifferent as he could. His ugly face adopted the allure of a Cheshire Cat. He asked for more, and Bill too readily obliged. Gargano even asked if the old lady had done any alterations to the foundations or the garden.

Rome called back, and the deal was on. The wives decided to continue their tour in town and, much to Bill's chagrin, Sam decided they drive to New Jersey in the carefully concealed Mercedes.

As they stood on the curb, Fritz Gargano announced he would take his leave. When he came over to shake hands with Bill and Catherine, he said how delighted he had been and that he might come over and visit them soon.

"To see how the script is going, Bill."

As soon as Fritz was out of hearing, Catherine whispered what she thought of him. She had never been so reviled in her life. Bill pulled a face that made his own feelings equally clear.

"And the way he kept leering at me."

She took off with Sam's wife. Fritz Gargano, meanwhile, pulled out of the parking lot and headed for the highway that would take him to Long Island.

The traffic across the Verrazano and along the turnpike was relatively light. They eventually turned off, drove a few miles, and finally parked in front of a diner across from the dock gates. Inside the diner, a short, insignificant-looking man in his forties, sitting at a far table, appeared to recognize them and stood up. He made a sign for them to approach. As they walked over and sat down, he said he was from the local forwarding agent and introduced them to a younger man at his side who had worked in the customs opposite until just recently. Sam was delighted.

"Quick work!"

The young man said that he had been let go only the day before, but he knew how to get people inside and open up a container held in the bonded area.

"I did it many times."

He gave them instructions on what to do and how to behave, and passed a badge to the agent, saying he would wait for them right there at the diner.

As they walked over to the dock entrance, the agent repeatedly assured them he had all the right contacts if needed. He saw to the security passes according to the young man's instructions and led them the long walk to where the container was already being isolated. It had been surrounded by other containers to keep everything out of sight. Sam couldn't believe his eyes.

"This is America!"

Bill was equally taken aback.

The container was opened up before them. Leaning against containers all around them were men in dark suits and sunglasses, together with two armed officers who had evidently been brought in on the operation. Sadini and Sam went inside and opened up the crate as Bill and the others remained exposed to the glorious sun.

There was a stir from just outside the area they were in. The two customs officers stood to attention. A balding stubby man in his fifties with metal-rimmed glasses, closely trailed by a young dark-haired female assistant, stormed into the area and pushed past Bill. He strode right up to the container, saw that people were inside, and demanded to know what was happening. The men in dark glasses behind him glanced at each other shiftily but said nothing. The officers remained rigidly to attention. It became clear to Bill that this man was in charge, and that he did not approve of what was going down.

The agent kept his cool and moved in to intervene without flashing the badge he had been lent. There followed a tense ten minutes of subdued discussion, after which the intruder walked away in a huff with his assistant still trailing behind. The agent told them they could carry on, provided it was quick.

The goods turned out to be just what they needed. Sadini appeared relieved. The agent said he too was relieved because their surprise visitor had made the prospect of turning anything back very difficult indeed. Everything was closed up and sealed as before and they walked back to the gates, handed in their passes, and went over to the diner. The young man, who had not moved, was on a fresh coffee.

"How did it go?"

Handing over the badge as he sat down, the agent said it had been perfect, and then he slid him a small envelope. While Bill was trying to come to terms with the contrast between what was now being said and what had actually happened, he a saw look of terror on the faces in front of him. He turned around and saw the stubby man and his assistant walking in through the door, presumably for a late lunch.

They spotted the young man whom they evidently knew. The standoff became tense. They continued to stare at him severely. Then, ignoring everyone else, they walked up to him and asked what the hell he was up to. The young man turned to his previous company.

"You'd better go."

He was obviously in deep trouble, but there was nothing they could do. The five of them escaped outside, and the agent revealed his relief that they had gotten away. Then he said goodbye to everyone as they stood by the Mercedes.

"And don't forget, if you ever…"

Bill accelerated towards the turnpike. No-one spoke the entire route back. At the office, they finished up business and the two Italians left, not showing any signs of wear from their experience on the dock, but no doubt keen to rid themselves of their jetlag.

They were alone at last. Bill asked Sam what had been so special about the Italian camera equipment that warranted so much attention.

"We'll be able to take pictures from the air for nothing. What they had in that container was a flying robot. Developed by the Italians. It's way ahead of its time."

Bill asked why the customs cost for such a useful and expensive piece of equipment was something to worry about. Sam had the answer.

"It was a lie. Sadini told me. They were afraid that they had accidentally sent a version modified for their military. It would have caused a scandal if the authorities had caught on."

The wives returned from Manhattan with their arms full.

"For heaven's sake, Bill," whispered Sam as they all headed for the elevator to head for the party. "What got into your head to rent that car?"

Bill said he would not claim it against expenses. They were now carrying their wives' shopping bags. The Mercedes affair was nothing, Bill thought bitterly to himself, compared what their spouses had just spent on themselves. As they emerged on the ground floor, Sam spoke to Bill so that his wife could hear.

"Having fun is the money you don't spend, my friend."

He called someone on the intercom to order for the Mercedes to be taken back to the airport, without thinking that he would therefore end up having to pay for it himself.

*

Early morning, they returned to their car in front of the airport, slumped in the back of the same stretch limousine that had carried them before. They had slept the whole way except for a brief conversation as they drove away from the party venue in Central Park. Bill was reflecting.

"It's strange. The line dancing, I mean."

"So what?" said Catherine.

"This is the land of individualism, the land of freedom, and yet they seem to enjoy line dancing more than anywhere else."

"You've just noticed? Hasn't it struck you that Daniel will be saluting the flag every morning and reciting the pledge of allegiance?"

"But that's being patriotic. It brings them together."

"It's brainwashing!"

"I forgot to ask," said Bill. "How was Mrs. Rosenbaum?"

"She's adorable. I think he runs around her something awful," she said. "They spent a week in Japan Town in San Francisco a month ago. He had told her that all the beds had wooden pillows and she insisted he make a scene when they arrived to check in."

Bill grinned. He had never imagined that of his boss.

It was the monstrous surf-and-turf dinner that had so soon sent them to sleep. The lobsters must have grown next to a nuclear power station or a hormone factory, and the stakes had been abnormally inches thick, and there had been too much alcohol to drink as they had both resented all the ice that went with the soda alternative.

They had sat at a table with a French colleague of Sam's, one of Bill's former employers, together with one of her American assistants. At one point the conversation had turned to a slip-up the assistant had made while working on Bill's script. The Frenchwoman felt responsible and was evidently frustrated with what she saw as Bill's perfidious manner of avoiding confrontation.

"For God's sake tell me off and let's get it over with," she had said. "*Tell me off once and for all!*"

But Bill had obfuscated, and her Gallic roots could not take it anymore. She had turned instead on her assistant who had promptly got up to fetch her coat. On her way out, the assistant had taken her revenge by stopping in front of their table and saying that she had only worked for the Frenchwoman all those years by yessing her to death. They had never seen eye to eye, she shouted. She had stridden off in a tantrum, screaming that she would not be coming back to work in the morning. Ever!

Catherine had felt sorry for her.

"Does she have a husband who can support her?"

Catherine had imagined that she must have been a long-timer, perhaps a spinster in her mid-fifties, and challenged to find a similar job. Her pride had gotten the better of her, and clearly, she was not used to the aggressive Latin style of her boss.

"We don't ask that kind of question here," had come the reply. "There are Equal Opportunity laws!"

Catherine had looked puzzled. The French woman had sounded arrogant.

"The trouble is, Catherine, people make mistakes, especially Americans. The more of them you hire, the more mistakes you have to deal with."

Bill had whispered to Catherine that the assistant would gain from it all in the end. She had finally extricated herself from an unpleasant situation, and despite the problems, would feel freed. Everything in America eventually led to a land of Cockaigne.

The precariousness of employment featured in many of the conversations they had had during the rest of the evening. Sam had come over for a while and admitted to religiously lining up every morning at the bridge to Manhattan to pay for a single crossing. He could always have gotten an electronic pass or a reel of tokens, but he needed to feel goaded by a self-imposed last day mentality. Bill had taken note.

Sam had staged the party for his staff, and the venue was quite large with several rooms. On their way out at the end, there had been a Greek American marriage reception taking place in the next room. They had stopped for a while to sneak a view. The newly married couple had been dancing on their own to a bouzouki band, as dozens of guests threw dollar bills onto the floor, and two small children attempted to gather them up without getting their fingers trodden on.

"No-one throws money in Greece," the French colleague had pointed out.

She had followed up with some sort of sarcastic comment about adapting to a debased local culture. The great American taste for history and tradition, she had said, always gets compromised by the irresistible drive for money.

"And things too often get rushed as a result. It's a bit like their lack of care for quality. My assistant should have picked up on her error. They had to invent entire assurance systems here out of need. Just ask Ralph Nader. This is pure Darwinism."

Bill had had enough of her comments. He had recalled that when he had left the hotel for the last time they had checked out at the same time, and the receptionist had unwittingly switched their credit cards. When Bill had received his statement loaded with compromising items several weeks later, he had realized what had happened. He had had to build up courage before trading back the card to the woman's great embarrassment, but it had given him a great pleasure to have a lien had he ever needed one.

Bill and Catherine had then become distracted by the Latino music from a room further down. The doors had also been spread open for air, and they saw hundreds of colorfully dressed Puerto Ricans dancing to a wildly gyrating band on stage. There had been quite a few African Americans there too, dressed even more glamorously, but the fewer white people around had been more restrained. For a short while Bill and Catherine had been sorely tempted to go inside and join the fun, but they had passed by instead, trying to anticipate their next inebriated Wonderland experience.

The fourth room had turned out to be much quieter and sober. It had looked like a Baptist meeting, evidently suffering the noise filtering through from the adjoining rooms. Here had been only African Americans, every one of them exquisitely dressed in white, some with matching caps as well. The seated audience had been listening to a large bare-headed and bearded preacher who alternated between singing gospel and making his speech in a deep baritone voice, while a skinny man in a white fedora stood at the ready to his left, waiting to conduct a small choir.

The Frenchwoman had come up behind them and swiveled her eyes as the three of them pulled away and finally negotiated the front doors. Catherine had been on the edge and ready to punch her in the face once and for all. She had enjoyed the variety and liveliness and felt morose about returning to what she saw as their mono-cultural and relatively staid hometown up north.

"We must come back," she had said.

Bill and Catherine's driver, who had motored over from Broadacre for the pickup, had already spotted them in the emerging crowd and drawn up to the steps in time. Bill and Catherine had said goodbye to the others and climbed in, glad to get away.

He had been the same driver who had driven them before and motored everyone in Broadacre. In his first encounter with Bill, he had mentioned that he too had lived abroad, in West Africa, where he had regular dealings with a well-known local tyrant who was still in place. He had been obtruding about his experience and his religion, and Bill, concluding that he must have been either a spy or a missionary, and possibly both, had nicknamed him Channel Thirteen after the God channel they had discovered on the local cable television. Bill had already decided to write both career possibilities into his script, just as he would the ominous dark funnel clouds in an otherwise blue sky he had spotted over the Sound on the way to the airport. They had made him fear that the flight bringing Catherine and Daniel would find itself spinning to the ground.

Bill had fallen asleep well before Catherine. As usual, he had dreamed of permutations and distortions of all they had witnessed. He had gone through all the faces they had seen in New York. He always did that. When he had waited at the airport for Catherine and Daniel, he had passed the time by also looking at faces. He had calculated that one in twenty women who passed him were particularly attractive. It had always been the same tally in France.

They arrived at the small airport, and Channel Thirteen pulled up next to their car.

"Quieter now," Bill said.

He said what had happened the day before. Channel Thirteen confirmed he knew of the President's billionaire friend.

"You know his sister lives in Broadacre? Mary Dunne. I drive her every now and again. She once told me she had only ever met the President in bed."

Bill thought he was in for a treat.

"What do you mean?"

"Oh, he had come down with the flu while he was staying with her brother, and she came to visit."

"I guess she's someone you shouldn't cross," said Bill.

Little could he know.

8

They finally got home and slept until mid-morning, when it was time to retrieve Daniel for lunch. The Villeneuves lived in one of the grander mansions on South Street that contrasted with the highly visible Caterpillar that Josh kept in his large back yard, apparently for pleasure.

Bill and Catherine were looking forward to it. Josh Villeneuve practiced as a nose straightener to those who could afford him, and since many of his patients drove over from New York for an overnight stay, it meant that he mainly entertained at midday.

"Do you ever get called out for emergencies?" asked Bill as soon as they arrived.

Josh admitted that people's vanity meant that he was always in demand, rush or no rush.

Bill and Josh had spoken several times since the party. Josh had been pleasant enough to converse with in person, but over the phone he had the infuriating habit of constantly interrupting to take another call, and more than once Bill slammed the phone down in frustration. But Josh never took the hint. Someone needed to invent a suitable signal for the purpose.

Tom and Barbara had each separately talked about Josh. Tall, with a broad face, graying hair and in his sixties, born on the cusp of Gemini, he was an optimistic and broad-minded man of many interests, talents and different colors, 'multidimensional' as Barbara had described him. From time to time he was an amateur thespian at a theater in the main town, and his expressive manner of laughing or telling stories hinted of a tinge of pretense that no doubt derived from it, but he was far from glib. At home there were occasional telltale signs of strain between Josh and his strikingly beautiful wife, Emilia, with her long dark hair. All their close friends had frequently tried to delve further into the couple's relationship. Barbara recalled that when Josh once pulled out a cigarette for himself, his wife asked for one as well, and he literally threw it at her. Emilia was very effusive and opinionated, and a handful. She had a tendency to externalize problems. Her speech was always far from refrained, she interrupted constantly, and she took over any conversation and the surrounding people. She was also shrill and loud. God help him, thought Bill, if Catherine ever became like that.

The three of them had a great time despite all and, oddly but mercifully, the telephone never rang while they were there. Josh and Emilia described a European trip they had made during their halcyon days. They had rented a car in London in order to drive down to Switzerland for a week's vacation.

"We just loved your twisty roads," Josh admitted, "but driving on the right with an English car had meant that Emilia was constantly trying to slam on the brakes even though she was the passenger."

"Josh, what about what happened at the Swiss border?" said Emilia.

"Oh yes. They asked Emilia, not me, for her driver's license. And there I was sitting at the wheel, which was on the wrong side, so they ignored me despite her protests."

They then described how they had gotten stopped for speeding just outside a Swiss village by a mixture of French- and German-speaking policemen.

"They took us back to the main town and thank God the police chief was French and took a fancy to Emilia. It only cost us a bottle of wine! I wish our local cops were as human."

"The town as well," said Emilia.

Bill and Catherine disagreed. They found Broadacre as pleasant as any town they had ever lived in. The wooden houses brought so much character.

"I guess your impressions are not colored by what's going down in the background," said Josh.

Bill asked him what he meant.

"Oh, you'll eventually find out. They pretend this is the land of freedom and equality, but after you discover some of the politics and how this town is run, your overall impression is not so optimistic."

"You mean the Historical Commission?"

"That too," said Emilia. "They're always trying to turn back the clock."

"To bring in the tourists," said Josh.

During lunch, Catherine asked Josh about his patients. He described a mixed lot from many backgrounds and varying degrees of readiness to pay their debts. He had even developed a theory that predicted what would happen and consequently anticipated any risks by raising his fees for certain clients.

"Beware of anyone whose name ends with an 'o'."

This obviously useless guideline would somehow find its way into Bill's next morning's script all the same. He prayed Josh would not claim any copyright.

Josh asked Catherine if she worked. She told them of her court work in France before Daniel had been born.

"She has created a rogue's gallery," Bill said.

Josh said she should publish it, but Catherine said it was private.

"Will you draw *me*?" he asked.

Emilia looked on, just a little disapprovingly.

The occasion kept its distinctly desultory nature, and Josh played the piano after lunch while he and Bill continued to drink cognac and smoke illegal Cuban cigars. Bill noticed how the playing seemed to get better as time passed but was uncertain whether it was his alcohol-fueled perception or his host's lubrication that was most responsible. Emilia had originated from a Portuguese family, and she sang Fado, the first time Bill and Catherine had ever heard it.

They nearly had to confront disaster when Daniel, tired following a sleepless stay at the neighbors and now the strange music, slammed the piano lid down on Josh's fingers. Emilia abruptly stopped singing and looked shocked, and Bill and Catherine exploded with profuse apologies until Bill experienced a slither of schadenfreude when he remembered Josh's habit over the phone.

"Let's go to the Indian museum," said Josh

He got up from the piano, trying not to sandwich his aching fingers under his arms.

"*Indians? Here?*"

Daniel was excited. Catherine was concerned about Josh's state, his fingers, and his level of inebriation, but they took the Villeneuve's car all the same, and Josh insisted on driving.

The museum was situated over an hour's drive away towards the hilly northwest, through a forest, and deep inside miles of fields and woods the other side. Daniel had become alive again, and his brief shame over the piano incident had dissipated.

They pulled into the park and, to Daniel's delight, spread across the clearing before them were rather new-looking tepees and a large communal wooden hut that fertilized his imagination as much as intended.

"We used to bring our two daughters here all the time," Emilia recalled, explaining that both girls were now grown up and away at university.

A little later, they had escaped the excessive heat and humidity, inadequately masked by trees, and ended up at the small, air-conditioned souvenir shop in a main building. They were about to purchase some flints for Daniel to make arrows of his own. A middle-aged couple, hippies well past their due date, walked in behind them and straight up to the woman at the counter. They were shaking a bagful of flints that they had just recuperated from the woods. Once their murky business was concluded, Josh calculated the mark-up the museum was taking and promptly guided the four of them outside instead.

As they drove away, Josh felt he had to make up for the curtailment. They passed a sign indicating an Indian pow-wow in a local state park not far away. This, predicted Josh, would do more than enough. Daniel couldn't wait.

The large park parking lot was littered with trucks, trailers and vans with license plates from across the continent, from as far as New Mexico, Texas and Oregon. But as soon as Bill had volunteered the entrance fee, the stench of burning fat from the food stands turned out to be overwhelming. After watching a few rain dances dismally fail in the glowing sun, they collectively decided to return home instead. At least they had seen something new.

"What a shame," said Josh on their way back. "When they get on their horses, it's one hell of an entertainment.

Daniel got the grilling he deserved once they were back at the house, but he failed to explain his outburst at the piano. Catherine defensively put it down to his being tired. Bill, having gotten over the pleasurable side of the incident, blamed the Montessori school Catherine had insisted upon. From their very first visit he had observed the remarkably eerie calm there, nothing like the rowdier schools he had known himself. Bill thought of his meditating friends of the past. The children, he reasoned, would have to vent their pent-up energy elsewhere. For good measure, he hinted to Catherine that the piano incident might have been just a forewarning, but she was taking none of it.

That night, they experienced their first tornado alert. The siren complied with Harry's description, indicating that it was a weather event rather than the escaped convict they had first feared.

It was ten o'clock. They tugged Daniel out of bed and, in the oppressive humid warmth, scuttled around the outside of the house and into the storm cellar to sit it out until the all-clear.

The three of them waited anxiously for the wooden floor above them to cave upward and to be sucked away from their concrete-walled retreat. They apprehensively turned on the radio they had carried down with them. The emergency frequency had not yet been activated, but a weatherman on the regular station, who had a name that seemed a cross between a Hungarian composer and a hotel chain, delightedly informed listeners that the state had the fifth highest number of tornados in the country.

"*Oh, great!*" exclaimed Catherine.

Bill obstinately thought that they were too far north for that.

Daniel wanted to prop up one of the steel flaps to look outside but was instantly ordered to stay seated. While Catherine continued to imagine her son disappearing with a whoosh from the steps, the anticipation of Armageddon caused Bill to reflect. He was thinking about their stay so far.

He commented about how many things they were experiencing were continuing to influence his scripts. He wondered how far it would go. The boundary between real and imaginary was becoming worryingly blurred. He had never been so inspired.

"I can't believe it. Back in England and France, nothing happened for weeks on end. Here, not a moment goes by without an event that has to be retold or people recalled."

"What do you mean, Dad?"

"Just about everything. Funnel clouds, immigrants who can't help throwing their money on the floor, like smashing plates, everything and anyone that can be bought for a price, neighbors who know the president, and no restraint whatsoever in soliciting business, people like Channel Thirteen, Tom and his windmill, Mary Lou the frustrated attorney, Bohemian Barbara in her crazy walking boots and French cigarettes, Josh the nose-straightening actor, and his beautiful Emilia the singer, Sam the movie mogul who watches his money, and that scary Fritz Gargano. Who knows what he gets up to? And so it goes on. I can't see where it will ever stop."

"I didn't see most of that, Dad," said Daniel.

Catherine reacted angrily to Bill's naivety. She said that she was not surprised by any of it. There was something intrinsically wrong with everything and everyone around them. And then she let it all out. She talked about the dichotomy between appearances and the real life hiding behind them. She pointed out the obvious strains between Tom and Mary Lou, and Josh and Emilia. She recalled the multiculturalism they had witnessed at the dance in New York, people keeping to their own, in a country that professed to be a melting pot. She raged about the culture of grabbing they saw all around them, how every time they had hinted a need, a dozen hungry hands had appeared, and how it was clear to anyone that Fritz Gargano represented the very worst aspect of this. The more Harry had talked about his job, she said, the more she had recognized a police state.

"In this land of so-called freedom, the authorities seem permanently poised to come down heavily on anyone who stands beyond a conveniently invisible line. And woe-betide them if their politics, color or religion don't conform!"

Bill reacted to that.

"Come on Catherine!"

"If nothing else, the exploding prison population is proof."

She pointed towards the town center.

Saying nothing, Bill put her outburst down to atmospherics. She would surely have calmed down by the morning. His own view was quite the opposite; he saw everything as positive. The cup was more than half full. The words *no* or *can't* did not seem part of anyone's vocabulary here. Despite the line dancing, this country of generations of Italians, Germans, Jews, Latinos, Irish, ex-slaves and all the rest, reeked of individual freedom, which was right and natural. Every problem seemed to benefit from the mix of differing inbred mentalities facing it. And it was actually fun. Even the waitress at Sam's party had introduced herself as if she were mistress of ceremonies and had congratulated them on their choice of menu.

Catherine stuck to her guns.

"In the airport they had a gap of one foot under their loo doors, and the most religious people we meet are the biggest scoundrels."

Bill tired of her ranting.

"And don't forget that patriotism is the last refuge of a scoundrel."

Finally, she ceased, and they sat there in silence.

Apart from the humidity and warmth it was uncomfortable for sitting. Catherine asked how they were going to sleep, and Bill dismissively said to her that three hundred years ago people habitually slept sitting up. Daniel was already half asleep like that.

A mosquito put paid to it all. It must have gotten inside when they had put the light on before closing the hatch, but the sound of it drowned out by Catherine. Now it prevented any thought of sleep at all.

They were saved by the siren ten minutes after that. Assuming its continuous wail to be announcing the all-clear, they climbed out and headed back to the front. They saw that the threatening dark clouds above had been completely swept away and there were stars everywhere.

At breakfast a few hours later, the radio announced that a small town nearby had had its center flattened and that the National Guard were on their way. Abandoning the remains of their breakfast, the three of them rushed outside and jumped into the car in order to look.

The road out of town had been smothered with crisscrossed branches and hefty tree trunks from almost the start, but crews with chainsaws had already cleared through to the next small town. The damage was exceptional. They wound their way beyond, towards the pine forest higher in the hills they had crossed the day before with the Villeneuves. Everything within sight had been flattened, and the road ahead was still blocked. They could hear chainsaws buzzing away all around, many more than they could see. The view in front of them looked like a scene from the First World War.

Daniel pleaded that they wait to watch the National Guard arrive.

"Did the rain dances do this, do you think?"

Tom was hard at work on his windmill by the time they got back. He was frantically climbing up and down each of two tall ladders noisily hammering, sawing and cussing as usual.

After lunch he disappeared inside. The outsized pile of wood deposited by the local timber merchant before the party, and then replaced by Tom with a stack of offcuts, by now had completely gone. Barbara arrived mid-afternoon in a Jackson Pollock boiler suit and hard hat, and proceeded to apply a final coat of barn red. At least the color would blend in.

*

Two evenings later, Tom proudly knocked on the front door. Bill recognized the top of his baseball cap through the top window and opened up. As Catherine covered the portrait she was making of him, he invited the three of them over to inspect the windmill before it got dark. They would only be allowed one at a time, he warned, because of all the offcuts inside.

On the way over, Bill saw Tom was limping.

"What happened?"

Tom said he had been wearing safety shoes all day long but had dropped the kettle on his foot after he had changed to make coffee. Catherine chuckled and got a dirty look from Bill. Tom had fortunately not heard.

They found the offcuts were indeed sprawled everywhere inside, which didn't seem the point of it all. Catherine was struggling to get in without falling over in the descending dark.

"Are they for burning?" Bill asked.

Tom and Mary Lou had a wooden stove in the main house and had boasted about it. Outdoor bonfires were not allowed.

"Not these. They're treated with chemicals."

The arrival of complete dark pushed them into the main house. Tom invited them to stay for dinner to show how they otherwise lived. When Mary Lou screamed at the microwave, and then the smoke detector after it had gone off, Bill gave Catherine a telling smile which she duly rejected.

Tom said he was an amateur investor, and he showed them how he used the internet to spend hours poring over data and graphs related to prospective targets. If he was to be believed, his gains were huge, at least by Bill's and Catherine's standards.

He showed off his computer, many times more powerful than Bill's. From the kitchen, Mary Lou said how it had already taken him over, and how it seemed to her to create him work rather than save it. Catherine sympathized.

"It's rubbish what she says, of course," whispered Tom, "but it's not stupid."

He had opened Alta Vista to show off how fast it was. Daniel's school had warned of an upcoming class project on ancestors and origins. Catherine had characteristically commented that it appeared to be a shared obsession in their adopted country. Bill asked Tom to look for an aunt who had emigrated to Chappaquiddick decades ago and died there. She had something of a unique name and might provide some ideas for Daniel. Tom dialed it in while Daniel stood behind him and Bill went to serve himself a drink.

"Was she a musician?" Tom called across the room.

Bill knew nothing of the sort and returned to see for himself. It was probably her. Tom had fallen on something that showed that she seemed to have written some music during the war, and a copy of the score was available from an address in California. Bill noted down the telephone number and Daniel got excited. It was a coup. Daniel could sing the results of his efforts to his class. No-one else would do that.

After the quick meal, the three of them once again trod the lawn back home full of thought. Bill and Catherine joked about their newly discovered *DotTom*. Daniel was still thinking about the music score. Bill said how much he was wary about the amount of money Tom claimed he earned through playing the stock market and having started with nothing. He recalled that both Harry the trooper and Josh Villeneuve had talked about this land of opportunity and optimism with no losers ever to be found. A favorite local pastime, Tom had told them, was to drive over to the Indian casino on the south shore or fly from the local airport to Atlantic City. Even Jesus and Maria went by coach twice a year he had said. No-one ever lost money, so it seemed.

"So, who does?" quizzed Catherine, as Bill hunted his pockets for their front door key.

Bill kept turning it all over while trying to get to sleep. He was half thinking about the next day's script but trying not to. He thought of Tom. A call-in program on the radio he had listened to the day before had provided endless investment advice, and the astronomical sums banded around told of a separate world in which more seemed exponentially to beget yet more. While people like Jesus, Maria and Barbara were forced to hold down ever-increasing numbers of different occupations in order to stay afloat, and no doubt perceiving any gains they got as reductions of their debts, better-off others saw their savings grow beyond what fairness might have dictated. This dichotomy had to be further splitting a nation characterized by its vicissitudes, encouraging a sort of financial multiculturalism to add to all the rest.

He could not get to sleep. He thought of the parallel with the change-driven two-speed world once predicted by Alvin Toffler. But why on earth was there no talk of protest as there would be in any other part of the world? The strange thing seemed to be that even those left behind always remained permanently optimistic about their prospects, and promoted themselves at every opportunity, just like the waitress at the party. This was a different planet.

It was all excellent material, Bill thought, as he finally nodded off. He reminded himself that he had to get his aunt's score from California first thing to pacify Daniel. He would call early afternoon. He would ask Josh to interpret it for them once his fingers had returned to shape.

9

They were inebriated yet again. The heavily lubricated dinner at the *Equus* had been followed up at the bar a few doors away, where conversation had ceded to the sound of Texas rock. Talk didn't really matter. Their small company of superficial acquaintances didn't matter either.

As usual, Elliot and Susan Kaplan were impeccably dressed. They always stood out that way. But the initially impressed would soon discover their pathetic cyclic mood changes as inebriation wore on, obstreperousness metamorphosing into maudlin behavior, and vice versa. It was all very sad.

They had decided beforehand to crash at the cabin rather than risk an encounter with Elliot's mother, Anne Kaplan, not that she was ever in a position to moralize. Rosa had been forewarned to look after the boys.

Eventually, for the finale to their needless session of debauchery, they had somehow struggled into the open red Jeep and sped the entire distance to the cabin without even turning on the headlights. Their languid state upon arrival would have revolted anyone. Lucky to still be alive, Elliot was so far gone that he did not know which way to turn to deal with his poisoned insides, let alone how to rescue the cellphone that slipped out of his top pocket and into the bowl, filled with alcoholic remnants of Oyster Rockefeller. But it was he and Susan who needed rescuing the most.

Their marriage was equally lucky to still be alive, and yet they loved each other as they had since law school. It was the over-spoiled Elliot's self-destructiveness that had entrained his beautiful young wife towards a life that destroyed any trace of her once promising prospects of becoming a lawyer herself, bright and talented as she was. Because of their combination of moral and physical depravity together, she had long given up on trying to keep her husband in line in the way that wives normally did. Somehow the absence of having their own home, living off Anne with no project to break away, had added to their dissolute life and to her demotivation and encroaching deterioration. Their twin boys, both as ginger headed as she, had been born five months after their marriage, and ever since had kept her at home in the annex at Anne's, while Elliot practiced a second-rate profession as a very junior associate to Attorney Hughes. And although, to all extents and purposes, Susan had given up on Elliot, by some miracle she kept her energy for the twins, and they were both magnificent. When the three of them were alone together, she managed to pull together a regime of discipline that even impressed her mother-in-law. Anne secretly prayed that they would not one day discover that the dreaded faulty genes had been passed on. Ignorant of such looming threats, during the absence of her husband from the household, Susan bravely strove on. Toys were never left lying around, hands were properly dried, television was rationed, and the boys diligently collaborated to clear up their father's trails of mess from the night before, all the way down to routinely wiping his habitual black fingerprints from the refrigerator door.

Elliot knew that he only just hung on to the three of them. One day, Susan would snap out of the remaining withering bond between them and run away. She would discover plenty of suitors, and it would leave him destroyed for good. He had therefore resorted to spoiling her well beyond the means that his meagre job provided, and for this he relied on a combination of his mother's sagging generosity and a secret venture that he shared with Susan.

Their comportment together depressed Anne no end. She saw the ultimate train wreck hurtling forward and had confronted them. Too embarrassed to talk to Susan's family who lived up in Maine, too far away to call in on haphazardly, she had begun to believe that her only chance was to wean her son, getting them out of her house and away from her generosity, to give them both something more to live for, something that would keep them distracted and occupied. Knowing full well she would get nowhere with her son on this, she had planted the idea with her daughter-in-law instead.

The cabin had only recently become a regular escape, although it was unsuitable for living. It stood about half a mile inside the forest that bordered the town and sat among a thousand rugged acres belonging to Anne who never went there. Elliot had started to go there in his late teens during summer, inviting friends for wild partying and shooting sessions. He had brought back a string of girlfriends over the years, and this was how Susan, the most beautiful and unspoiled of them all, had gotten pregnant.

As for their secret venture, it was three years old. Through an old high school friend, Susan had been instrumental in getting Elliot to grow cannabis, although it had been he who had willingly and willfully taken it on. On a patch of almost inaccessible land thickly surrounded by trees some distance beyond the cabin, a succession of harvests had brought in even more money than he earned professionally. The friend had also introduced a dealer from Boston who took everything except the kilos they shared locally, including with some of the other parents at the boys' school.

Their escapes alone to the cabin had become facilitated by Rosa who had been taken on as daytime maid and cook for Anne. Anne had placed an unreasonably large advertisement in the local paper, and Rosa had turned up with excellent references from Boston, and a willingness to stay the night at short notice when needed.

Elliot rolled over and spooned Susan and woke her without intending to. They were both in too sorry a state to even think about making love, but that had become normal. He reached across her for the remote and switched on the small television they kept opposite the bed. Susan turned and sleepily asked what was on the other channel, as she always did. In reality, she would have preferred it off altogether. She still had last night's heavy music turning over in her head.

"Did you speak to your mother?"

He groaned, annoyingly blew onto her neck, and turned away again. Susan had given to pestering him about putting the money down on a house. It came on the heels of their buying a boat, which they kept on the south shore, once again to get away from Anne. That had started well. For a while Elliot had become an enthusiast, and they increasingly spent weekends down there with the twins. Then it strangely all came apart. Susan didn't know why. She suspected it was connected to his twice losing his way to the evening coastal navigation classes he had started at college there. He had admitted to becoming the butt of jokes from his classmates.

Elliot got up and slouched over to the stove to make coffee. He said he would talk to Anne when they went to recuperate the boys for a day back in the forest. He then ordered Susan to get up. Their visitor was due at ten.

It was already well past nine. Susan climbed out and dragged herself over to the cold shower before slipping back into jeans and a white tee-shirt. She energetically dried her long red hair with a towel and combed it as straight as she could while he tidied up the mess on the kitchen table. He then carried the bag of empty wine bottles out to the Jeep to dispose of at the recycling dump on their way in. Susan noticed, and it gave her a twinge of optimism. But the day would not end like that. It never did.

At a quarter to ten, they heard a car driving up the track. Elliot went outside and saw a battered blue Plymouth with Massachusetts plates arrive ahead of time.

A tall, short-haired and well-groomed young man wearing jeans, shorts and a light jacket got out and introduced himself as Winston. He appeared easy going and pleasant. Susan came out to join them and they shook hands and went inside. Winston had phoned a week before to say he was a friend of their friend from Boston, and that they had already met there, and that had been good enough.

Their cordial meeting lasted for less than half an hour. Winston said he was happy with the sample that Elliot showed him and made his offer for part of their crop, and they agreed.

Winston left the cabin and drove off. Elliot and Susan came out a minute later to close the shutters and lock the front door. They both looked happy. Winston would call them. Elliot had a few days at least to prepare the goods.

As Susan's long hair blew around in the wind, and they headed for the main road, the Jeep raised dust from the dirt track behind them as had the Plymouth before it, and then all went quiet in this deserted outpost.

Rosa spotted the Jeep turn into the driveway and called the twins. She was sitting opposite Anne drinking coffee while the boys were playing outside at the back. They both ran in and across to open the door, and while they were hugging Susan, Elliot announced a change of plan. They would head south to the shore instead. The boys ran around the room in excitement before Susan took them over to the annex to get prepared.

Rosa disappeared into the kitchen and Elliot used the opportunity to side up to his mother. He said how much Susan wanted their own home and was putting pressure on him.

"It's going to take time," she warned him, aggravated by his cowardice, but happy at the outcome, "but I will take care of it, don't worry, Elliot."

It would be her last financial effort to help him. She would call the realtors. She had sway. Elliot gave her a diplomatic kiss before joining Susan and the boys. He always did that to keep her at bay. Anne smiled to herself before Rosa reappeared. She was convinced that her son would soon jump into the much-needed distraction and would be off her hands at last.

Then she thought of a downside to her conniving. Much as she liked Susan around, she would miss the twins.

*

Mary Dunne decided to go in person to talk to the First Selectman on Anne Kaplan's behalf, but as usual refused to be seen at the town office. They said to meet at his home, and he dutifully but disgracefully dispatched his wife to the back yard before Mary arrived.

He waited for Mary. He was nervous. Would she repeat her habitual short shrift towards him? As he listened out for the gentle sound of her car drawing up outside, he checked himself out in the hall mirror in front of him.

He was in his forties, handsome, and, he believed, well-regarded in the community. He had lived in the town for thirty years, since his parents had moved there, and he owned the bookstore in the center which paid rent to Mary. Over the years, Mary had taken to her tenant as a prodigal son, as well as an opportunity, and had eventually encouraged him to join the board of selectmen. From there, as far as she had been concerned, it had been plain sailing.

He heard what he had been waiting for. He timely opened the door and spread his arms to greet his secret benefactor. Mary, holding a large paper carrier bag, tactically refused any contact and purposefully strode around him to take up position in the hallway while his hands awkwardly retracted. He pulled away to close the door and then led her to the living room which had its French windows opened to the garden.

"Is your wife here?"

He pointed her out toiling far away and Mary was relieved. It would allow her to descend into ribaldry, a privilege reserved for only a few select people, always those she dealt with.

"So how are we going to sort out this Commission mess?"

He knew all she would accept to hear would be solutions, but he still needed time. They talked a little about what needed to be achieved. When prodded by Mary about whatever she perceived as unsatisfactory, he said he did not think that any retroactive action would be either legally or politically acceptable. All they could do was to change the future, and that he would take care of.

Mary insisted.

"Time is of the essence. This f****d up idea of a windmill is going to spread."

He cynically wondered if she had shares in the power company. Her vision of binding the entire community into a set of rigid rules that would control how houses and properties could look and be modified, was the greater issue, and it had been dragging on for over a year.

He said to Mary that a referendum might be required once the Commission had decided its course of action.

"They'll be no talk of a referendum."

She asked who was doing the legwork for changing the rules. Was it the Town Clerk?

He had seen it coming. All she saw was a pallid, prosaic and somewhat obsequious character who stood for nothing. He thought the opposite.

"I'll keep a close eye on him. We'll have it ready by the end of the month. I won't let you down, Mary."

It was already midday, and she had unusually refrained from her first tipple of the day. She got up and walked towards the door without thanking him or shaking his hand. Then she turned around and placed the carrier bag on a vacant plinth next to him.

"There's one for each member. Make it work. We must move to phase two as soon as possible."

As her limousine pulled away, and while wishing she would disappear to Florida like most of her age, the First Selectman stared at the bag. Mary Dunne, the supposed leading angel of probity in Broadacre, was forcing him into bribery and he wanted no part of it. But he had no choice. If he ever lost her support, he stood little chance of surviving against the person she would then choose to succeed him, the one he badgered over the phone after a drink every night, and he would likely also lose the bookshop which he loved so dearly.

He closed the door and peered again at the carrier bag. He did not want to touch it and leave his fingerprints. He wondered if he should call her and remonstrate once she had gotten home. Then he thought of the positive side, phase two as she referred to it, of her secret ambition for a new village, and the credit he would ultimately take for it. Perhaps the bag was picayune by comparison. Yes, the risk was worth it.

He afforded himself a smile and propitiously picked up the phone to the Town Clerk.

"Get your butt over here right now!"

It would not do to be overheard at the office. He would spell out to his assistant exactly what had to be done and by when. It was the lore of hierarchy. Having just been subjected to his patron's treatment, he was about to do the same to the man whose career and salary he determined in turn, but in his case without the incentive of a carrier bag.

"And they call this democracy," the Town Clerk would bitterly complain once he too had left, even though he knew nothing of what was going on behind his back.

He went out into the garden, wondering what he would say to his wife. To hell with it, he needed as many views on the upcoming situation as he could get. Her discretion and help were free, and anyway she would soon pester him why he had so rapidly consigned her away from the house.

He walked up to her and asked if he could explain something important and get her advice before his assistant arrived. But she was having none of it. She said she was far too busy.

As soon as Mary got home, she called Anne Kaplan without mentioning the enticement. Anne thanked her and hung up. Rosa was not yet back from shopping, and she sat there on her patio, hungry for lunch and for the return of her two beloved grandsons. Her ginger rodents as she called them.

She had already called the realtors. There was nothing right now, but the lady there had described how Anne had just missed a golden opportunity sold to an English couple. Anne knew the property she had referred to. Its position and size would have been perfect. If it was a foreign couple that had taken it, perhaps it would sooner rather than later reappear for sale. The realtor lady had mentioned that it had been conveyed by Hughes.

Well, that was convenient, Anne had thought. Perhaps there's an opportunity. She would speak to Elliot for him to find out more from his senior partner.

10

Winston was free for another day. It was for work-release rather than parole, but it did not matter. It got him back into a positive-thinking environment.

As soon as the prison door closed behind him, he looked diagonally across to the two-story building where he would spend the day. They had told him it was a painting assignment and that he should report to someone called Barbara. Apparently, she and a builder called Tom were remodeling the Rodier dental practice, and the client wanted the disruption to finish early, before the change in the weather.

With release slip in hand, he breathed in the fresh air. Like his job at the cemetery, it would get him away from the claustrophobic Dickensian environment of the Broadacre prison, not to mention the oppressive behavior of the guards and fellow inmates that drove him insane.

He crossed the road diagonally, sprinting in order to avoid a pickup unwisely speeding in from the left, and arrived soon afterwards in front of his destination. As he entered the open doorway, a stranger came out of a back room where they were at work and asked Winston to fetch a carton of cigarettes from the automobile parked just in front.

Winston obliged. He opened the front door of the car, and then the glove box, and pulled out a brand-new carton. It looked foreign, and while out of curiosity he tried to decipher its origin, Harry the trooper happened to drive past.

Harry brought his cruiser to a screeching halt. He had recognized Barbara's vehicle, but not the clean-shaven man who was helping himself to something from it. Lights already flashing, he pressed his siren just once and wound down his window.

"Is that your car, Sir?"

Winston said it was not his car.

Leaving his roof lights flashing, Harry climbed out. He slid his baton into the holder in his belt and walked over.

"Do you know whose car this is?"

Winston realized the situation he had stumbled into. It was sadly typical. He briefly hesitated and then admitted that he did not know who the owner was.

"I see you are holding a pack of cigarettes, Sir. Is it *your* pack by any chance?"

Winston was already resigned to the fact that he was in trouble. He was cursed with the wrong profile, whatever that might be. Maybe it was his eyes. On seconds thoughts, perhaps it was a setup organized by one of the prison guards who had taken a dislike to him. There were more than a few.

His instincts came to the rescue. He was bound to lose this one. His frequent brushes with the law had taught him to be short on information when confronted in this way. Somehow people in authority always reacted badly to him. If they couldn't find an excuse to search him, they tried to be unpleasant instead. He remembered coming back from Mexico once and saying something to the uniformed immigration officer who had sarcastically asked if he was a diplomat. The guy could have had no idea that Winston had two thousand cigarettes stashed away under the door panels. He couldn't even wind down the window properly.

He had learned over time. Without trying to explain, Winston said that the pack was not his. Period.

Harry had heard enough. He warned his victim to stay where he was and went back to his double-parked cruiser to turn off the ignition. As irate traffic awkwardly diverted past the obstruction he had caused, he returned, reached out to force Winston over the hood of Barbara's car, and handcuffed him behind his back. He then pulled Winston upright and perp-walked him over to the building he had seen him emerge from.

Barbara appeared at the doorstep just in time.

"Harry, what's happening?"

"I caught this young gentleman helping himself to your car."

At that point Tom appeared behind Barbara, saw what had happened, and said to Barbara and Harry what he had asked Winston to do.

Harry looked at them both. He was in a quandary as to how to save face. For a minute it was touch and go whether he would release his prisoner at all, and people collected on the sidewalk to watch what was going down. In the end he reluctantly relented, removed the handcuffs and returned to his cruiser, trying to hide his frustration and humiliation.

Winston was free for a second time in a day, and it had only just begun. As Harry's cruiser pulled away, Barbara apologized to him, shook his hand, and led him inside to show what she required of him. If she was happy with his work, she said she would keep him on for the duration.

Inured to such ups and downs, Winston did not show any reaction to what Barbara had just said as he passed her his release slip. He felt relieved, however, that Harry seemed not to have pieced together where he had come from. Any brush at all with the law, whatever the rights or wrongs of the incident, was likely to spell trouble for him, and at the very least rob him of his precious day out. It had been close.

*

"Good morning, Father. It's Siegel."

Father Arnold was surprised by his equally ascetic associate in religion. He never called on Saturdays.

"Good morning, Rabbi. I hope it's nothing serious?"

Brushing off any hint of urgency, Rabbi Siegel asked how things were going. The clambake had been a great success, the priest said, and would see his finances through at least part of the winter, certainly well beyond Christmas.

"Good, good."

He regarded his colleague, as himself, as believing in the innate goodness of human beings. If it were not for them and their colleagues of the other denominations, Broadacre would be far from the same place. Their mutual challenge was the slow disengagement of their congregations ever since the nineteen-fifties. Even on holy days.

"Not enough *machers*, too many *schmoozers*," said Siegel.

Talking about the festive season, he said, he had been thinking of proposing an interdenominational celebration for around that time. Something to bring people together.

This instantly raised the hair on the Catholic priest's neck. It was not the smartest thing for Siegel to have come out with such an idea so soon. Only the year before, there had been an acidulous incident after he had positioned a Hanukkah menorah where the council had traditionally placed a Christmas tree for well over a century. His apparent confrontational and abstruse opportunism had created a fracas, aggravated even more by a combination of misleading and war-mongering reports in the local newspaper that had nothing better to print. The First Selectman had been called to adjudicate and had appealed to Attorney Hughes as a widely regarded and independent member of the community. Hughes had wisely delegated the task to his junior partner, Elliot Kaplan, who was light on work as always, and anyway could discreetly calm down the affair through his mother.

Meanwhile, the paper had persisted and only made things worse. The Jewish community, it had claimed, maintained that a menorah had as much right as a Christmas tree to be there. An embarrassed Siegel had promised to cede the space straight after Hanukkah. In the next edition, the Christian community had retorted that the tree was not a religious symbol, and if their opposite party wanted war, they would build a crib instead.

Elliot Kaplan had ended up doing a good job. He had persuaded the First Selectman to ordain that nine separate candles be placed next to each other on the tree. He could never advise them to ban the tree, he had said, because it had stood there every Christmas since well before anyone in the town had been born, and their parents as well. The paper had kept the story alive by making risky allusions to the fact that more people of stricter Jewish faith were settling in the town than ever before, and that long-established local traditions were being challenged as a result. It had gone on to announce that an application for opening a kosher butcher was expected within a year, and that Broadacre's planning committee would have to stand up against any partisan pressures and accept the need for equality.

Anne Kaplan had been embarrassed by it all as much as anyone. The trivial affair had stood to prejudice her relations, especially with Mary Dunne. Seeing it, as did her friend, as a distraction from pursuing the promotion of the town's traditions and reinforcing the Commission, she too had done everything possible to calm things down. The fiasco had evinced unusual and unwanted friction in the conservative community, and most had hoped that it would simply go away.

"Rabbi, I'm sure you didn't call me for that. What do you really want?"

Siegel promptly and surprisingly asked a series of questions about Bill and Catherine. He said he wanted to know which denomination they belonged to and if he should make an approach to them. Father Arnold recalled all that Bill had said and replied that the couple were not practicing. The rabbi hung up without saying a word more.

It had all sounded strange to Father Arnold. It was highly unusual for them to have compared notes in this way, and he could not figure out why his rabbi colleague might have done so. As he proceeded to make the usual preparations for the following day's Masses, his colleague's call refused to leave his mind. He even became intrigued. He decided to call Bill himself.

Bill was equally intrigued. The Rabbi's call had nothing to do with religion, and that someone had put him up to it. But who and why?

"I can't imagine," admitted Father Arnold.

"Me neither," said Bill.

Father Arnold described the feud from the previous Christmas, the intervention of the First Selectman, and the conciliatory advice that came from Hughes' law practice. It was the only lead he had.

"I'll speak to Attorney Hughes," said Bill.

Bill called Hughes the following Monday. The attorney was equally puzzled but said that it had been his associate who had dealt with the matter. The last thing he had wanted, he said, was to get embroiled in any local religious wars while he was so busy thinking about his approaching passage through what Father Arnold referred to as purgatory.

Bill laughed.

"I'm eighty-two, Bill. I really don't need any friction with Catholics or Jews. It's bad enough keeping peace with the Protestants around here."

He quoted someone who had said that time did not make people age but imposed on them disguises. His disguise involved avoiding any partisanship he might have once avidly adhered to. Then he said that Elliot Kaplan had not volunteered for the task, so he was unlikely to have motivated Siegel to make the call. Bill would have to look elsewhere.

"I assume this can remain between us," said Bill.

Hughes concurred. He would not even say anything to Elliot.

Bill called Father Arnold who said that his only course of action was to visit Siegel to find out more. He would get back to Bill within a day or two.

*

Anne Kaplan had counted on her rabbi. His absolute discretion in carrying out her delicate request meant that she took no risks in exposing either herself or her beloved wayward son over any interest in the house that Bill and Catherine had purchased. In fact, the Siegel front was so safe that she could afford to open a second one, confident that one or the other would bear fruit.

She thought about the ageing rabbi whom she had known ever since she lived there. His parents had been among those who had campaigned to colonize Macedonia instead of Palestine at the turn of the twentieth century, and for her, the eclipse of that movement had translated into an opportunistic feeling of superiority over their rabbi son.

She then turned to her Plan B.

Jesus, Maria and Yolanda were in the back garden pruning away, and Yolanda was once again pressing flowers on the side. Anne had provided a large amount of work over the years, and Jesus and Maria had become captive to her needs for which she considered she paid generously. They undoubtedly felt correspondingly loyal to her, and would remain discreet about anything she said, or they ever overheard.

She decided to approach Jesus while he was away from his partner whom, for no particular reason other than the look of her face, she trusted less. She opened the kitchen door and asked if he could come inside for a couple of minutes. The young Mexican obliged, as he always did for Anne.

"I have a very important and confidential task for you, Jesus. I need you to give me information on one of your other customers," she said. "Tell me about the new English couple you are working for."

"You mean Señor Bill and Señora Catherine, Señora Kaplan?"

"I don't know their names," Anne lied, "but they're the ones who moved into the small property in front of the builder and his lawyer wife. The ones with the pool."

It wasn't her style to want to appear too knowledgeable or interested in people below her status. She felt very uncomfortable indeed.

"But they don't have a pool," protested Jesus.

"Of course not. What do you know about them? The English couple, I mean."

Jesus described all the anodyne facts he knew about Bill and Catherine. They had a son who was seven years old and had started at the Montessori. They had moved from France. He was working for a film company in New York. They got on well with their neighbors.

"Are they happy with their house?"

"Oh, I think so, Señora Kaplan. They are talking to us about changes to their garden. The problem with the shed might give them a little more space for bushes…"

Anne reacted.

"What problem, Jesus? What shed?"

In just two minutes of conversation, she had made a discovery, and it could not have been more promising. She would contact Bill and Catherine's awkward neighbor right away.

But that was not the most important revelation. Her stupid son's senior partner had screwed up the conveyance right under her son Elliot's nose, and *she* had been the one to find out.

She thanked Jesus, saying to him not to talk to anyone, and rushed to the phone to call Elliot to come over right away.

It could not have come at a worse time. Elliot was over at the cabin hanging his crop to dry. But his mother rarely talked in such a tone, and so it had to be serious. Leaving everything hanging there in full view, he locked up and jumped into the Jeep, kicking up more dust than ever along the track to the main road.

Half an hour later, emerging from his mother's scalded but not completely burned alive, Elliot Kaplan drove back at half the speed at which he had come. He was busy turning over what she had told him. Yet again she had dispatched his mind to a completely different galaxy to where it had been. In a single stroke, his extra-curriculum venture had become irrelevant and unnecessarily risky. He had at long last been provided with a way of pushing his ageing senior partner out and taking over the practice. He would somehow get Hughes struck off for malpractice - conveying a property without a proper survey.

And because Elliot was his mother's son, he thought the same way that she had. He somehow also needed to get through to Bill and Catherine's litigious neighbor. Before Anne could protest, he had eagerly told her he would take on that task himself.

A flash of doubt came over him as he approached the turning to the cabin. Hughes was down to earth, practical, likeable, and very experienced, and his clients valued him for that. Elliot saw his own weaknesses all too well. He was too fresh out of law school and seen by many as a theoretically inclined greenhorn with a tendency towards idleness. His senior partner was always reticent in affairs, refraining from saying things before he had to, and disinclined to overexploit his clients' susceptibilities. Elliot, on the other hand, reacted to what he heard or saw. He blurted out anything that came to his mind and offered every service he could think of to extract more money. Hughes always held back and only went for the jugular when it was the right time to do so. Too often, Elliot precipitately latched onto what he then imagined being the truth. His elder partner had seen this and had memorably said to him that even top chess players needed ten thousand hours of practice to reach their level. Would Elliot's self-confessed impetuousness result in screwing up this golden opportunity?

He pulled up at the cabin. Anne's revelation had made him realize one important thing. It had been lurking in his subconscious since the very beginning. Everything he had done or thought since joining Hughes' practice had gone towards eventually seeing his senior partner taken out. How life was feral.

As he walked up to the cabin, he recalled Anne's second revelation that had stunned him almost as much as the news of his associate's slipup. She had sworn him to secrecy, even from Susan. She had told him about her plan for a grand model village with a historical theme, right there where he now stood. There would be hotels and homes for tourists to stay in, outlets where they could spend their money, and a giant parking lot for them to abandon their cars during their stay. Employees would dress up in eighteenth century clothes and ride horses and carts, and there would be enactments related to the lives of famous onetime residents of Broadacre. Hughes would fight against it if he remained active, but that could now be seen to. And, to top it all, Anne would have a big need for her son's services. This was a new world in the making. His fortune was on the way.

Elliot had been on his way out from Anne's when Rosa had appeared after shopping. She had just emptied the postbox on her way in. They greeted each other in passing, and then Rosa started to unload her car. On her second journey she inadvertently knocked over the bag that contained the letters. One content was a small inconspicuous bulging brown envelope that wedged itself out of sight between the back seat and the door of her Plymouth.

*

Elliot Kaplan only had a few hours left before the work was completed. Susan and the kids had gone to the south shore for the day. He had just made an important and inevitable decision given what his mother had told him. This had to be his very last harvest.

His mind turned to the secret patch in the forest where he grew his illegal crops. He would see to it straight away. He had to destroy any possibility that traces of its existence would ever be discovered.

He pulled the rotavator out from the lean-to and dragged it the two hundred yards to the patch, tugging frantically in order to free it past the closely knit trees and dense shrub along the way. It frustratingly took a long time. Once he got there, half exhausted, he fired up and went to work, systematically plowing in straight lines to ensure complete coverage of the ground, and then randomly in order to disguise any linear traces that would appear suspicious from the air. One never knew where threats might come from.

The weather had turned damp for several weeks, and so he hoped that, by the time anyone turned up, the overturned uprooted stems would have become unidentifiable mulch.

His resolve kept him going. It took over three hours. After he had returned the rotavator to the side of the cabin, he walked back through the forest to the nearest point of the stream that went up to the clearing in order to check from a different angle that he had done a good job. Satisfied, he came back via the route he had taken with the rotavator in order to ensure it too was fully disguised and covered over, pulling a few loose branches and dispersing them randomly along the way.

Exhausted, he went back to the cabin and grabbed the half-full bottle of bourbon that he and Susan had started a few days before. The sun was going down, and he took one last swig before a quick cold shower and change of clothes. Susan would be heading back with the twins to Anne's. He would have to inform her of his momentous decision and prayed that she would trust him enough to accept.

On the way back, Elliot called in on the off chance at the home of Peter Drake, Bill and Catherine's neighbor, to offer his services.

Peter Drake was more than surprised, and at first suspicious. He had spotted Elliot peering into his Corvette before knocking on the front door. He had forgotten to disconnect and hide the nitrous oxide canister leaning against the passenger seat.

Elliot said nothing about what he had just seen, but perhaps that helped to get his way. He neither mentioned that Bill and Catherine's attorney was his partner, and that certainly helped. Sensing the opportunist he was dealing with, Elliot told Drake that he had the golden opportunity to ask for an outrageous sum for the slither of land on which the two feet of his neighbor's shed had stood for forty years. The land would be no loss to Drake as it was the other side of his driveway. His neighbor's only alternative was to destroy the shed, which would cause the property a serious loss in appearance and monetary value.

"It's a win-win, Peter."

"How much are you asking for?"

Elliot gave a ridiculously low figure. It was almost a no-win no-fee solution. Relieved and delighted, Drake overcame his reticence, and they shook hands on the spot.

*

It was Friday, and they had just returned from school. Catherine opened the front door and let Daniel in ahead of her as she always did.

"Bill, hear this."

She asked Daniel to repeat to his father what he had told her on their way back in the car.

"You know the two red-headed boys in my class?"

Bill pretended he did.

"They said their dad is working for Mr. Drake over the potting shed business."

Bill put two and two together.

"You mean Elliot Kaplan?"

Catherine nodded.

That sounded odd. Kaplan's partner Hughes was already representing Bill and Catherine. And why would the two young boys know about that, or even want to mention such a thing to Daniel?

Daniel said the twins told him many things that went on in their lives. It had been their mother Susan who had mentioned Drake to them and hinted that she and Elliot were interested in Bill's and Catherine's house.

"Interested in our house? Are you sure?"

Daniel said that the twins had also talked about their stays at a cabin, and a secret garden in the forest their father tended to on his own without telling them. They looked forward to going there every weekend when they were not on their boat down south.

"They mentioned a nearby stream and lake where they fished and kept a small dinghy. I remember because they had said they would invite me to play 'Moses' there."

"Moses?"

"It sounds fantastic, Dad. One of them pushes the other away on a raft so that he disappears down the stream that runs down from the lake. Better than snowboarding!"

Bill looked at Catherine, wondering what all this added up to. After Daniel said the twins had boasted that their grandmother was a powerful local resident, and that she was going to make it difficult for Bill and Catherine to carry out modifications to the house, Bill sniffed a sizeable rat.

Daniel went outside to play. Catherine said she disbelieved it added up to anything, but Bill sensed she was as concerned as he.

"We don't know anyone well enough to find out what's going on."

Bill said that they should call Attorney Hughes. He got an appointment for Monday afternoon. That gave him enough time to see the surveyor first.

11

Fall had fledged. It was cold, windy and dark outside, but the rarity of clouds in the sky ensured that there would not be any rain, for a while at least. Just cold.

The early morning traffic had yet to congregate, and only the corner newspaper store was showing any signs of life. Its owner was carrying inside the bundles of newspapers that had been dropped on the sidewalk during the night.

Opposite, behind the grass verge backed by a few trees, stood Broadacre prison, its modest white portico and the tall, bricked front around it painted in dark red. The store owner looked up and noticed a battered Plymouth pull up opposite its entrance, dip its lights, and eventually extinguish them entirely, waiting there with the motor idling. But he had other things to do and went inside. Had he waited a little longer he might have observed in the increasing daylight that the Plymouth was blue and that it had Massachusetts license plates.

The car waited for ten minutes until the top of the hour. There was a metallic thud as the solenoids on the dented front door of the prison were jumped into action so that it could be pushed open from inside. In a brief second, a feeble overhead lamp lit up and the shadow of a young man appeared. He was on his own and clean cut, dressed in a heavy coat. He moved forward as the door slammed shut behind him and the light went out again, for all the good it had served.

The young man walked over to the waiting car. The person inside lowered the window to greet him with an embrace before opening the door and sliding over to the passenger seat. It was Rosa. Winston took off his coat and chucked it in the back. He spotted an envelope on the floor and instinctively picked it up and slid it into his back pocket. Rosa glanced at his clean white tee-shirt as he slid in next to her. She had lovingly kept the car warm for him.

Winston omitted to thank her for taking the day off for him. Instead, he rapidly threw the car into first, and then upward through fourth, speeding toward the isolated condo she rented three miles up the road.

"How long?" she asked.

"Back by five."

She was just making conversation. She already knew the answer and what it meant. It would be a day in bed, just like the last time, except for an hour or two. But his curfew meant he would not have time to get into the old bad habits he kept before he got locked up. She was glad of that. She could happily go on living with the day release program for the six months he had yet to serve.

As they passed the dentist's, he told her he had just got a job there with a refurbishment.

"Customer's a guy called Rodier. I'm helping two people called Barbara and Tom, a painter and a builder."

It added to the one-day-a-week job at the cemetery he had willingly grabbed when they had first started letting him out. She became happy thinking about it. He slid his hand inside his back pocket and felt the concealed envelope. There was something hard inside, perhaps a key.

They stopped at the supermarket to pick up some food. He hated this one, but there was no other in Broadacre. It went around the wrong way, and so he said he would wait in the car instead.

As soon as Rosa had disappeared inside, Winston pulled out the envelope and tore it open. The key was for a post box, and the post office was only a couple of minutes away on foot. He had time.

No-one noticed him as he located the box and opened it up. Customers lining up for service, and the clerks at the counter, were equally far too distracted to watch him pull out a thick package. It felt like a wad of bills.

By the time Winston had sneaked back to the car, Rosa had still not returned. He opened the package. They were brand new Benjamins. Lots of them. It was the first time he had seen so many, and he counted them, estimating how much they added up to.

He thought a while. The serial numbers on the notes were sequential. Without knowing why, he instinctively noted down the first and last of them on the back of the envelope. He slipped the protruding wad back inside with the key and hid it all under the seat. He then reached into the side pocket, found a few loose coins, and rushed to the phone kiosk in front of the supermarket to make a quick call.

"You've got something on your mind, haven't you," Rosa remarked after she had come back, and he had said nothing for several minutes.

It was unlike him. Winston was usually all over her long before they had turned into the small parking slot in front of the condo.

"Let's make it quick, hon. I've got something I have to do."

Two hours later, showered and in a fresh set of clothes, Winston drove to the cabin. He parked next to the red Jeep already there, grabbed the thick envelope, and got out in order to open the trunk for the empty backpack he kept at Rosa's. He then walked over into the forest towards the spot where Elliot Kaplan had said he would wait for him.

As he pushed aside the endless branches that tried to block his way, he thought about the time that he and Elliot had first met in a run-down bar in Boston, a year or two ago. It was around Thanksgiving and yet, despite the cold, everyone was as usual in tee-shirts under their coats. Elliot had said that he had been tipped off that it was a safe place to do business, and Winston had used a mutual friend to make the first contact. It had looked perfectly normal that a handsome and well-dressed man such as Elliot should pretend to hit on an attractive long-haired brunette in such a place. She was a friend of Winston's. They had walked out of the bar together and met Winston in an alley a hundred yards away, where she left Elliot and Winston to carry out their business.

But Winston had met trouble three days later. He had been stopped by a state trooper for speeding through roadworks on the main highway, and his aggressive behavior had led to the discovery of three bags of cannabis in his trunk. And if that had not been bad enough, one of his anonymous customers had gotten nabbed that same week, squealed for immunity, and then picked him out of a line-up.

Once he had been bailed, Winston got stung a third time, this time with dyed money that stained his fingers and got him arrested straight after a snatch. He had his three strikes. He was inside for sure. The world had it in for him.

He had been surprisingly sentenced to only three years, and by complete coincidence imprisoned in the same town that Elliot Kaplan lived, although he did not intend to give that away to his potential supplier. By the time he was allowed day release, he made sure that it occurred as early as possible in the morning, and that Rosa was there to whisk him away. If Elliot were to spot him around town well away from the prison, it would not matter at all.

Everything got a little more complicated when Rosa had taken the job at Anne Kaplan's. Winston gave her a rough time before realizing that it might somehow one day provide him with insurance. Anne was an important person in town, and her son Elliot had his own reputation to protect.

In prison, Winston had befriended several inmates but told them nothing. He had persuaded Rosa to find somewhere local to live. She had already looked after and cooked for several families in Boston and could not help spotting Anne's large advertisement in the local newspaper. Everything had worked out. Anne had taken to Rosa and being locked up in the center of town meant that Winston could watch and listen to people in the street, even if it was through iron bars. One of them was Rosa who would wiggle her derriere for him as she walked along the sidewalk in front. Things only got better once he became entitled to day release.

Winston found the spot next to the stream, but he did not need to call out. The instructions had been on the mark and Elliot was standing there, just a little further up. They walked together to the spot where Elliot had hidden the bales and made their exchange. With his extra money, Winston was laying his hands on far more produce than he had originally bargained for.

"You leave first," Elliot said.

Winston obligingly headed back to the Plymouth. The backpack was almost not large enough. By the time he reached the clearing he was tempted to stop for a quick smoke, but he knew he would be wiser to get out of there fast.

He thought a minute about Elliot Kaplan as he approached the Plymouth. He imagined the cannabis had been grown not far for where they had been. It would certainly have been near the stream. He envied Elliot. According to Rosa he had money, a boat, a permanent job, and a well-connected mother. Winston had no qualifications like Elliot and no such luck of circumstance. His greatest possessions were a lengthy rap sheet and dodgy friends. He so badly needed a regular job in which he could get interested.

He reminded himself of what he was carrying. Things would change. Soon he would be released on parole and making his fortune back in Boston.

He reached under the mat next to the passenger's seat before closing the car door. The key and emptied envelope were still there. He picked them up just to look again. In the envelope he felt a small card that he had missed. He pulled it out. It had a handwritten message asking to drop the key in the post office collection box when finished. He slipped them both back under the seat.

He thought about Rosa on the way back. He had met her in the same trailer park where his mom had lived after the divorce. Mom brought back dark memories. She used to beat him more often than his father ever had, but at least she was less effective. She would bind strips of wood together, thinking that the punishment would be worse. Rosa and her family took him in each time he ran away, which was often, and they were always good to him. Rosa had probably been faithful since, but he didn't think their relationship would last forever. He always needed to move on, and she had always wanted to settle down. Then again, maybe one of these days all that might change.

He thought about how he had at first planned to conceal the loaded backpack in Rosa's back yard. It had been a dumb idea. His day release job at the cemetery had allowed him to find a safer hiding place. It was a small building that stood alone next to the road for which only the town caretaker had keys to both doors, and by his own admission had not used either of them for years. It was a perfect solution.

He drove to the cemetery and parked out of sight at the back. No-one was around and it was the caretaker's day off. He lifted the backpack out of the trunk and wound his way through the graves down to the small building. He heard a vehicle approaching on the road and hid for a few seconds while it sped past. The copy of the key he had made two weeks before worked perfectly in the rear door away from the road, and he closed it behind him.

The small room felt musty despite the cold. The light switch failed. There was only a tiny slither of daylight coming through cracks next to the front and back doors, just enough to judge the layout. He felt shelves on either side and avoided disturbing the dust. They seemed empty. The cobbled floor meant that it would not be evident that he had disturbed any dust there either. With his foot he detected the grating of a drain. It was a chance.

He placed the backpack on the ground and got to his knees. The dark disorientated him. The grating had been somewhere to his right. It was difficult. He found it further away than he had remembered. He tugged on the iron grating. It refused to give. Perhaps he was wasting his time. He tugged twice again and finally succeeded. He lifted and dragged the heavy grating to one side and lowered his arm to its limit inside. With the tips of his fingers, he felt a small outlet down below. It was smaller than the bales. This was perfect. He unloaded the backpack, piling up each of the bales inside the deep pit.

*

The First Selectman simultaneously squinted and peered at each of the faces confronting him as the five other members of the Historical Commission took up their places around the long oak table that had served the town's administrators for over a hundred years. Although it only took seconds, his scan allowed him to place each of the potential obstacles before him into short-term memory. He had slept well. He still remembered the distracting smell of his latest amour's hair, sampled a mere two hours before. He felt in excellent form and ready for action.

They settled in. Some had not seen each other for weeks and decided to make up for lost time. As he patiently watched them and waited with his gavel poised, he briefly reflected his position, and himself, as he always did on such occasions.

His obsequiousness in front of Mary Dunne, and amenability to others, were ploys. He had far more substance to himself, so he believed, than she or they ever saw. He regarded himself as the consummate politician, to the point of keeping his genuine beliefs to himself. Overtly, he professed to believe in full and open democracy, of respect for the ideas of others, of alternation, of integrity, of suffering fools and meeting anyone with a smiling face and an open mind. Covertly, he was someone else, as his nightly phone calls to his opponent betrayed. He was far from bookish, as his second profession might have indicated. He had hardened once Mary has handed him his first opportunity, and he had had to deal with functionaries and think more about politics that worked. The frustrating process of ruling Broadacre had toughened him. It had caused him to become a closeted risk-taking anti-Leviathan Republican, the type that believed in a world of three-strikes rules and ruthless prison sentences to control the populace, in the right to shoot an unwelcome intruder as much as game in his back yard and on public lands, in a State that had the right to execute, and in the depressing realization that the vast majority of people were with no sort of ambition at all, and only deserved to be trickled on and kept away from any form of social leveling, or the tiniest thought of it.

The problem for him was that Broadacre presently found itself in a State and country controlled by Democrats, and so he had to tread carefully. He believed Republicans should rigidly stick to their beliefs without bending. Only Democrats bended and compromised.

Democrats! He detested everything they stood for. They were inclined towards dangerous and costly policies that enhanced bloat and sclerosis, smothering the poor and unworthy with unearned benefits and political correctness, a me-too culture, allowing too many immigrants, and propping up ideas that stole from progress.

He believed in the primeval world. He leaned towards the likes of Darwin, Leona Helmsley and B-1 Bob, and was appalled by interferers such as Keynes and Nader. People by nature needed a kick up the backside. A healthy unemployment level encouraged them to look for work. Those that forged ahead should be rewarded by being allowed to forge the world in turn and look to each other's interests at the same time. Taxes were for the underclass who contributed nothing. Those that inherited should be allowed to do what they wished without being penalized for it.

In other words, the First Selectman was a lot less amenable than everyone around him, including his wife, ever imagined.

He was primed, his mental Gatling gun at the ready. He was prepared to get what he wanted, to anticipate their moves, to sniff out his allies of the day, to issue the perfect retort to anyone attempting to undermine or challenge his authority. All executed politely, of course.

They finally quieted down on their own and he lowered his gavel to declare the last meeting of the year in session. The finalized proposal for extending the boundary was read out by the Town Clerk. The First Selectman looked at those around him he felt had been promoted to beyond their level of competence, wastes of space, frustrated middle aged or senior do-gooders who had failed in life and were now trying to at least leave their modest mark on their community before leaving this world. They made him angry and frustrated. They were an unresponsive lot. Most of them did not even bother to reply to his emails. So much for the art of getting things done when one had to deal with such rabble.

All except Anne Kaplan, of course.

The rest were no match for him. He always knew how to keep his lead and stay ahead. He was the first to know anything, and his position made it easy to be autocratic and take decisions on his own while those around him, reacting to being left behind, remained more focused on inventing issues that allowed them to keep their places. He could anticipate well ahead of them. He could take initiatives away from them. He could deliberately be overbearing to turn others off, or at least push them into behaving like weathervanes, constantly adjusting their position in his steady and uncompromising flow of demands so thinly disguised as suggestions. And the more he behaved like this, the weaker they became. Being the winner of most of the arguments, he discovered he could tailor history to his benefit. This was power, and he gloried in it.

But today was different, and he had to be wary and refrain from overconfidence. The broadening of the authority of the Commission raised new challenges he was less sure of. It was a major change that stood to invite resistance from people he did not yet control and who could try to influence the members before him. They could confront him with specialists, and clever people who conveniently made themselves experts. He hated such people. They were too often a danger unto themselves, and certainly a danger to progress. They had a tendency to confuse that which was possible with that which was practical. Only politicians, he believed, could make real progress. And he was the only genuine one around.

Today was critical. It was his first major change. It had taken over a year to get there, typical when matters required a committee. He had detested every frustrating minute of it. Each time they had met, they had endlessly argued in dilatory circles and bitched almost in order to use up their allotted time. Each time they had called in the lanky Town Attorney for advice, the man had sat there in his imperious manner, remaining deliberately unhelpful and evasive, in reality another shark waiting to unseat the First Selectman himself, even though he did not even live in Broadacre. The Town Clerk, meanwhile, had been just as bad. He had endlessly brown-nosed him in public, and had never taken a stand on anything, and yet when pressed for action never had time. His proven talent and valuable assistance constantly needed corralling.

He glanced at Anne Kaplan, Mary Dunne's friend. She was the only person in front of him for whom he had respect. She was a longtime member of the Committee who clearly had no peer. She could always be relied upon. He knew she would back the motion. What he could not know was that she would do this without even having seen the contents of the envelope he had anonymously made available to her, and then regretted as soon as he had done so. After all, Anne was far from in need of either the money or the persuasion.

His initial apprehension, his moment of paranoia, disappeared altogether once they had quieted down. Thanks to Mary Dunne, the wheels had been secretly greased for the right decision. The post box ploy had worked. Each of them had been anonymously handed one of Mary's packages a week before. The Town Clerk read out the articles of the revised rules of the Commission that would be extended to cover the entire community. Anyone intending to build or modify structures of any sort within the entire perimeter of Broadacre would have to apply to the Commission beforehand, and any rejection was enforceable by the law for which the old omnipresent prison and courthouse served as an excellent reminder.

The First Selectman took over. He read the magic bullet that would ensure the committee's support, even if Mary Dunne's little enticement had not already done so. In the interests of democracy, he announced, all six members sitting at each meeting would be drawn by lot from a pool of twelve candidates. All their deliberations would be broadcast on local television, but their faces would be covered, and their voices disguised. The First Selectman would be the seventh, present and in charge on every occasion.

"This will ensure that none of you become subjected to lobbying by vested interests," he said. "You will be able to make your decisions in the open without repercussions."

Whatever had been responsible for their positive reaction, it worked. They each nodded and the Town Clerk recorded the motion unanimously passed.

The meeting was declared ended. As they all either shook hands at the satisfaction of deciding their increased power over Broadacre, or reached for their cellphones to call home, the Town Clerk said he would have the resolution and new rules published by the end of the week.

"See you in hoods the next time," said the First Selectman to his unwitting acolytes.

Now would come that familiar feeling of emptiness that followed such a great success. It frustrated him that whenever something was driven by meetings, nothing ever happened in-between. Responsibility was a finite resource. The more one group took it, the less was left for others. But at least they had moved on, and the meeting had for once not been disrupted by someone on the phone or people in disagreement.

When he got back to his office, he called Mary Dunne.

"It's done."

*

Fritz Gargano had devised the perfect plan. There would be no need to get involved with Attorney Hughes after all. He wouldn't even set foot in Broadacre. He would do the necessary to curtail Bill's career from New York and speed up the screenwriter's departure by making an offer that Bill could not refuse for the house.

That left the business of the cemetery. There was always a chance the loot was there. He would get it checked out first. Lenny had always loved cemeteries, hadn't he?

Carmine and Gin Bottle were dispatched to sniff around a second time, and in particular to take a look at the small building that had raised their combined suspicions.

"And not a word," he said.

12

Attorney Hughes was dumbfounded by what Bill and Catherine had told him. After he announced he intended to ask questions, Bill asked him to be discreet until they were more certain of the facts.

Hughes was as perplexed as they were. Why was his junior associate representing the other side over the shed business, what on earth was this matter of a secret garden, and what was Anne Kaplan up to?

He said, all the same, that there was one thing he understood all too well - Bill's options over the shed were rapidly disappearing, as the voted boundary expansion by the Historical Commission was certain to complicate the option of pulling it down, which meant that he would have no choice but to pay for the extra land.

Although Bill was convinced that Hughes knew more about his associate and his mother than he was letting on, he was confident he would get the attorney's support. Hughes appeared with no doubt an honorable man.

"By the way, are you planning any modifications to the house?" the attorney asked in passing.

Bill and Catherine said they had no firm ideas yet. They wanted to see how Bill's employment worked out, but certainly the house needed work sooner rather than later. Hughes warned them that an expanded Historical Commission would certainly end up complicating such matters as well. But his priority concerned what they had just told him - it would be for later.

"Give me a few days."

The conversation then drifted, as it usually did in lawyers' offices. Catherine mentioned her court portrait experience and Hughes said he would speak to Judge Cipriano to see if her help might be useful locally.

Hughes sniffed loudly, as he appeared to do often. His prominent and slightly troubled nose led Bill to wonder if Josh Villeneuve had ever done work on it that had not quite succeeded.

Hughes talked about a local court case that the cable company was presently televising, and of which Bill and Catherine had caught wind. The broadcast was bringing the entire community to a daily standstill. Hughes admitted he had even started routinely to avoid any morning consultations in order to follow the latest events. People were openly discussing it all around town and he could afford time for the entertainment.

It concerned a once reputable local doctor, whose face one never saw during broadcasts. He had been accused of disposing of his wife in a wood chipper fifteen years before, after just being found out.

"Television is a very dangerous thing," Hughes said. "We'd be better without it."

But Bill was only half listening. He was distracted. His earlier mission to confront the surveyor who had misplaced their forty-year-old shed by two feet so many years before, and done nothing about it, had gone skew whiff and had to be aborted. The guilty man had not returned to his office as promised. It had been a wasted drive.

Hughes briefly returned to the case in hand. He would have a private word with the neighbor, Peter Drake, whose aggressive reputation had put Bill and Catherine off going to see him.

"I fought with you guys during the war," Hughes said.

They saw he was in his eighties, although that did not seem to stop him working over sixty hours a week in normal times, on top of hunting and going for walks when he could. During World War Two he had captained a submarine in the Atlantic and sailed alongside the Royal Navy. The sea pictures hanging on all four walls of his office proved that this had remained the major event of his colorful life.

Bill's distraction had been caused by something that had occurred just after he had parked his car and headed for the surveyor's office. He had spotted Mary Lou headed directly towards him on the crowded sidewalk. He swore she had just emerged from the hotel ahead of him. She had been on her own, this time wearing dark glasses and a black silk scarf around her head, once again swinging her hips. She had appeared preoccupied. He had braced himself, and at the very moment that he had opened his mouth to greet her, she had screwed up her face and looked up in the air, as if to ignore him.

He had been taken aback. Every thought imaginable had come to him at once. Had this been a deliberate insult, a wish to remain anonymous, or had their neighbor simply not seen him? He had not turned around after she had passed by, just in case she did the same. As he had firmly looked ahead, coming out from the same hotel, now just in front of him, had been a chubby man, but he had his back to him and disappeared down a side alley.

Heading back to Broadacre, Bill had turned the incident over in his mind and decided not to tell Catherine. It had reminded him of several days before when he had heard a noise in the porch and the outer wire-paneled door creak open. He had peered out over the top just in time to spot Mary Lou disappearing with Debra in her arms. Her daughter must have been hiding there and Bill had wondered why. Mary Lou seemed to have secret parts to her life.

Bill snapped back to the present. They prepared to leave. Catherine said that she had already grown attached to the shed. It so enhanced the property. Bill became embarrassed by her endless adulations that ensued. He irreverently thought of teasing her once they had gone away so that she could not run outside and check. He would use his computer to doctor a video to show it blowing up.

He returned to his senses. Hughes asked him if he had thought of moving the shed. After all, it was only a tiny distance. Bill confirmed it had been his first idea, but the structure had been literally built into its concrete foundations, and that it would be less complicated to rebuild it from scratch, which would still be expensive.

It was freezing cold and wet outside. They shook hands and climbed back into the car and drove the short distance towards the center. In front of the Rodier dental practice a fire truck had just pulled up. Then they heard a siren and a loud horn right behind them. A second truck had crept up on them.

Bill pulled over, and it overtook and dramatically skidded on the wet road in front of their eyes as it careened into position in front of the first.

Bill pulled over towards the center of the road. He glanced up when he saw the firefighters do the same and noticed a small plume of yellow-green smoke lazily trickling out of the stack on the roof above. A crowd had gathered and were looking up too.

"What on earth is that?" Catherine asked.

Despite the weather, Jesus and Maria were bravely pruning away in front of the house, but there was no Yolanda. Bill asked Maria. She appeared to get upset then shrugged her shoulders. Jesus walked around to the back and Bill followed him. He said that Maria had said nothing.

"It was terrible, Señor Bill."

"What happened?"

"They found her body on a beach on the south shore. Last week."

"Dead?"

"She had been cut to pieces, Señor Bill."

Bill was stunned. He winced before expressing his sorrow and condolences. There had been nothing on it in the papers. Perhaps it was because it had happened too far away. He had gotten used to the pretty gardener who pressed clients' flowers in the summer. He had more than once wondered if they would get offered her book.

He said nothing to the others, but how many more secrets would he have to keep from Catherine? While he was thinking of this unwelcome added burden, he also wondered why the young girl had been murdered. He knew it would have been unwise to ask.

*

The music score had just arrived from California, and they headed for the Villeneuve's for a sandwich lunch. The Rodiers were there too. Paul Rodier, who had glasses, a beaky face and bushy brown hair, talked a little of the refurbishments that Tom and Barbara were doing for his and his wife's practice.

Josh Villeneuve proudly showed Daniel that he had added brass locking nuts to the piano lid for when he needed them. Catherine blushed, but Daniel instantly reached for the lid and boldly tugged on it to check it out. Josh laughed while the lid held, and a frustrated Daniel insisted.

Bill handed over the score. Josh studiously put on his bifocals.

"Now let's have a look…"

He played a few notes and sang, and then he corrected himself a few times.

"I'll also have to remember the style. 1940s you say?"

After an hour during which the others talked, it had all become quite fluent. It almost sounded like an anthem.

"What a find, Bill. It gives me an idea."

He handed over the tape he had just made of his final rendering and declared that it had inspired him to think of a Broadacre music festival. He would invite neighbors to turn up with anything new or old that they or one of their relatives of friends might have written. Bill and Catherine were delighted. Paul Rodier said he could help. He knew the music teacher at the high school, as well as the local librarian who could print out posters and invitations worthy of such an event. Josh reminded them that his acting made him eligible for hosting such an event. Bill had already seen him perform on local television. His last Christmas bible reading to a throng of local children was being repeated daily on the local channel between showings of the court case. Even though he had inadvertently emphasized the word 'great' when describing Mary with child, no-one seemed to have noticed, and his performance appeared to have passed off well.

Bill noticed the front page of a copy of the local newspaper on a side table. There was a 1930s photograph of the Ku Klux Klan with a headline referring to the Historical Commission. He half remembered a bias incident he had experienced on Long Island but couldn't quite place it. Josh saw what had caught Bill's eye.

"Not what you might think, Bill. Someone has hit on a brilliant idea to preserve democracy in the Historical Commission."

He praised how the new decision-making process would work. People would be freed from the secret influences that permeated local affairs. Emilia looked skeptical.

"Are you sure about that, Josh?"

Paul Rodier joined in.

"Just wait and see what happens when they find someone who is causing them a problem. It will be as though they had *black* cloths over their heads."

"Before you know it, they'll be riding in the streets and forming lynch mobs," Emilia said.

Paul Rodier walked across to a side lamp and positioned his head over it.

"Horsemen of the Apocalypse!"
Bill and Catherine stayed out of taking sides.

*

Sunday was their first Halloween. Pre-warned by Daniel, Catherine had characteristically thought to purchase enough candy for a regiment. Bill, on the other hand, realized too late that he had equally characteristically forgotten to go to the store for it as promised. There were only minutes to go before the feared onslaught. Bill panicked.

"I could drive into town now."

"Closed early. Four o'clock."

Daniel protested he would be badgered at school for his parent's negligence. Catherine remembered that Paul Rodier had said that he handed out toothbrushes instead of candies. Daniel rejected the idea outright, and anyway, they had no such feasible substitutes.

"Dad, let's just pretend we've gone out."

It was a brilliant idea. As dark fell, they turned everything off, leaving only the porch light on as if to welcome their return at a later hour. The car stood in front of the garage, but being so close to the center of Broadacre, people would assume they had walked to their supposed destination. The three of them sat down and waited in silence.

Six o'clock, knocking hour, came and went. They sat there in the dark getting increasingly bored and frustrated by the minute. Perhaps they had overestimated the problem. Television was impossible as its flicker would have been an instant give-away.

They heard footsteps. The porch door opened with its habitual creak and the doorbell rang. Even in the total darkness Bill knew that Catherine and Daniel were looking at him. There was a second ring, and a frustrated knock on the door. Then silence.

They sat there motionless. Muffled voices outside betrayed a neighbor with her three-year-old son on his very first Halloween round. They had been talking about it for weeks. He was originally to be disguised as a stalwart of American democracy and founder of its values, firstly Johnny Appleseed, then Paul Revere on a horse, and finally a white hood and cape to better scare people into giving everything they had.

"What a pity! They must have gone out."

But it was too much for the child. He burst into tears. His endless wailing became unbearable for Catherine.

"We can't ignore them."

"*Yes we can!*"

"*Muum!*" appealed Daniel.

"Okay, *you* tell them we haven't any candies."

Catherine got up.

"I'm going to put the light on."

Bill and Daniel knew they had no choice. They got up and threw themselves onto Catherine, pinning her arms to the back of the couch. Bill thought she was going to scream. He grabbed a pillow with his spare hand and forced it against her mouth. Daniel said to him to make sure she could still breathe. His mother writhed and kicked her legs, but they held on until she gave in.

Silence resumed apart from Catherine gasping for breath. The neighbors were still there. They overheard the porch door opening again as the boy continuously cried with a drawn-out Mahlerian whine as he was reluctantly led back home.

No-one else came. As soon as it was safe to put the lights on and talk, Catherine swore at them both like she had never before and disappeared. Bill had to prepare stale cheese on toast for supper for Daniel and himself.

13

Paul Rodier had become Bill's dentist, and a close friend, which felt very odd when he presented such astronomical invoices after the torture he carried out on Bill's mouth. Paul was an avid trekker who sometimes accompanied Attorney Hughes. Although slight in build, he had served in the airborne forces before studying for dentistry.

One evening at dinner, he proposed that he and Bill head up to some falls on the state border and walk the fourteen miles west to where the three states met. They would exploit a combination of compasses and marker stones embedded along the route that delimited each border to find their way.

Bill was enamored at the thought of standing at the tripoint. It would surely have a magical effect. He would enjoy a moment of a triple personality born of the distinct differences he had already perceived between the inhabitants of each of the three states. The expedition was set for a Sunday.

They got up at four and picked up Paul's friend Eli Mendelsohn on the way. On their way north, Bill popped a question that was troubling him.

"Did you see the smoke coming out of your stack the other day?"

Paul said he only knew of it afterwards. They should have been evacuated, he said.

"In fact, the entire neighborhood should have been evacuated."

"What happened? What was it?"

It appeared that the yellow-green smoke was linked to a drum of cleaning solvent that Barbara was keeping on the worksite. Someone had not closed the bung properly, and vapors had escaped and traveled along the floor towards the boiler room at the back of the building which had been left open.

"It was a chlorinated solvent. If you know any chemistry, you can guess what was coming out of the stack."

Eli Mendelsohn described the effects it had produced during the First World War. Paul said Barbara was likely to be prosecuted for her lack of precautions, and that even the Fire Chief might lose his job for downplaying it afterwards.

"And what if any of it had seeped into the ground," said Paul. "I would be sitting on a Superfund site."

Bill thought of asking if he had thought of suing Barbara, but he held back.

They locked the car and started walking westwards along an endless carpet of golden red leaves that had ceded to the wear of weather and time. Eli Mendelsohn asked Bill if he and Catherine had yet visited Massachusetts to their right. Bill said they had been once.

"Catherine thinks the cops there look like the Gestapo. She blurted it out in front of *The Runaway* painting in Stockbridge. It caused a stir."

The others laughed. Eli offered to lend Bill a guidebook once they got back.

They finally got to their destination just after midday and broke open beer and sandwiches in celebration. Each of them stood in turn on the exact spot and was photographed by the other two while clutching a book of Paul's on multi-personality disorder brought along for the occasion. They then turned towards each state and ceremoniously compared and roasted its differences.

It started to drizzle, and Paul said they should head back.

It was late and silent when they finally approached Broadacre and took the back route into town. Paul warned them he often encountered deer crossing the road there and kept his eyes close to the windshield and headlights on full beam just in case.

"Doesn't that paralyze them?" asked Bill.

Eli spotted something. They were passing the cemetery to their left.

"Paul, pull up! Pull up!"

Bill saw why. At the front edge of the cemetery was a small, isolated building now thirty yards behind them. Through a crack next to the front door came an occasional flicker of light. Someone was inside, and yet it was supposed to be abandoned.

Eli told Paul to kill the headlights. They sat there with the motor running and saw it again. Paul turned off the engine, and they quietly got out in order to take a closer look. They crept back along the quiet and deserted road towards the building as silently as they could.

"I'll look behind," mouthed Paul.

He sneaked alongside the left side of the small building while Bill and Eli waited on the road in front. Eli pulled a flashlight from his pocket. When Paul appeared from the other side, Eli lit him up and he shrugged his shoulders as if to say nothing was there.

Eli went up to the door in front and tried the handle. Bill thought he heard a shuffle inside.

"Anyone there?" Paul called out.

Bill looked around. He could see light coming from the one or two houses way back beyond the swamp behind them, at least a quarter of a mile away, but otherwise there was no sign of life at all, and everything nearby was silent except for the occasional bullfrog and rustle in the wind. Eli tried the handle again and to push the door, but nothing gave. After a couple of minutes, they gave up and returned to the car.

Catherine was glad to overhear an exhausted Bill walk through the porch door as the car drove off. She had waited up. The boiler had broken down, and she had earlier called a handyman who would be there first thing. It would be a chilly night in bed, so they snuggled up together and Bill fell asleep right away.

*

Mario was chubby and cheerful, and he had been recommended by Tom and Mary Lou. After Catherine handed him a coffee and they started chatting, he said that his family had originated from the south of Italy between the wars. He lived in the main town, and it had a sizeable Italian population. He was one of the administrators of their club there, and evidently proud of it, and Bill was sufficiently interested that he offered to take him to see it afterwards. He said it served as a venue for marriages and Christmas parties, but on normal days it was a watering hole and summer bowling center for its members.

A couple of hours later, once Mario was done, he and Bill took off in Mario's pickup.

"Perhaps you will show me how real Italians eat spaghetti," said Bill on the way.

"They chop it up."

Bill asked him how he had come into his business. He employed several others.

"The army, Bill. All skills in America evolve from the military. They teach you to repair anything at all by numbers. Everything is laid out. It's a perfect training for the ham-fisted and dumb teenager that I was."

The town was ten miles away, and they passed one of those nostalgic 50s aluminum caravans on their left. Mario drove towards the popular end of town. For a few minutes they were the only whites around, which was the first time Bill had experienced any such thing there. It reminded him of once walking through Tokyo and encountering a sole white face in the subway, an only item of familiarity in a sea of strangers. He had wanted to smile and shake the man's hand, hoping his name would turn out to be Livingstone.

He then remembered the bias incident on Long Island. He had befriended a black replacement teacher at his hotel out on Long Island, and they had turned out blatantly to be made the very last to be served in a restaurant there. He had believed that this kind of thing only went on in the south and was too embarrassed to talk to his friend about it.

The street turned more Latino as they drove along. They passed more rows of deteriorated detached wooden houses with hubcaps and garbage strewn all around them behind collapsing rails and disintegrating wire mesh fences. Men and women were standing or sitting on their porches in heavy coats as if desperate to stay outside. All kinds of music streamed into the street from both sides and clashed in the center to create a confusing cacophony.

A fallen telegraph pole showed signs of having given way under the strain of all the cables mercilessly and carelessly attached to it. Two remaining poles suspended a traffic light precariously swinging in the wind. Beyond, stood the smooth edifice of the giant concrete shopping mall that Bill recognized from a different route into town. After all the symptoms of social chaos it was almost like a mirage.

Mario crossed and parked. He could have parked at the Club but wanted to show Bill the surroundings. Bill looked around. Car wrecks were everywhere. The store fronts were dirty, and their insides appeared empty. One short, skinny and bearded old man walked up to the curb beside them and weirdly pretended to change gear in order to cross. A woman further along had a bucket over her head but somehow managed to walk in a straight line and avoid the telephone poles.

Bill felt ill at ease. He also felt stiff after the long walk with Eli and Paul.

"This area used to be Italian twenty years ago," Mario sighed after guessing Bill's thoughts. "Now they've moved further out to larger properties."

The contrast with Broadacre was disturbing. It was as if a biblical level of change threatened their doorstep. Bill wondered which represented the future. He thought of people's troubled lives and pasts. He remembered his days in northwest London where his landlord and wife had been survivors from the Nazi death camps. They often talked about how it all might have been that much easier if they had each been on their own and not had someone else to worry about once they had been separated by the guards. When Bill had invited Indian friends to stay with him, the landlord and his wife were up in arms. Their extreme and open prejudice had surprised and disturbed him considerably. Such people should have been way above all that.

They sauntered half a mile down the quiet street, away from the mall, and came to an out-of-place grand gate fronting a long driveway.

Inside the club people were scarce, and they had a beer at the bar. Mario proudly offered to show Bill the club's most inner sanctuary, a room down a remote corridor accessed from behind the bar. It had a fireplace and was clearly a home from home normally out of bounds to strangers. There was an old man there on his own, but in a sufficiently unfit state to object to any outsider's presence.

Bill thanked Mario for the privilege as he looked around at the distinctly Italian style, decades-old, comfort. He glanced at the large portrait hanging over the mantelpiece and recognized the face at once.

"It can't be!"

"Oh, that!"

Mario chuckled. Bill said nothing more. It was Benito Mussolini. Was there hidden admiration for the dictator, or had it been a trophy brought back by one of the young men who had gone back during the war? Bill had heard of a small French club in a town further east and wondered what he might have discovered there.

Mario led the way out from the back of the building and, after rapidly showing him the bowling area, they headed to the pickup. There were two men in suits waiting for him there and he asked Bill for five minutes to talk to them.

It only took two. The strangers wound up their conversation and Mario waved Bill over and offered something to eat before heading back to Broadacre.

They pulled up at a Japanese restaurant with a large garden closer to the outskirts of town. Bill recognized the bumper sticker on one of the cars outside from Tom's Independence Day party.

At the next table, three customers had removed their jackets and were exposing holsters. After Bill looked uncomfortable, Mario said that the local police station was just around the corner.

A short, young and buxom Japanese girl announced she would be their waitress and gave them her unpronounceable name. Still getting used to the process of such rapid familiarity after all these months, Bill described to her how Chinese restaurants back home had a number for each item on the menu, and that Catherine had gone to their favorite one with a prepared list, only to discover too late that the menu had changed. The waitress looked perplexed and coldly declared that Japanese restaurants were not like that.

They ordered Kobe-style beef. While Bill was still dealing with the brush-off, Mario remembered that he needed a life insurance policy witnessed. He searched for it in his jacket pocket and pulled it out. Since Bill was not an American citizen, Mario called the waitress instead. She dutifully complied without asking what it was about.

The zaniness of the occasion persisted once they had ordered, and Bill left to go to the restroom. When he reemerged, the waitress was diligently standing there holding a small towel for him to dry his hands. Then, as he returned to Mario, there was a sudden sound of a train rushing past and the entire room appeared to shake. The waitress seemed very proud. Bill wondered what might come next. Mario laughed.

"I forgot to tell you, Bill. This is a converted rail station. The owner had the idea of creating the surprise. There hasn't been a train near this town for fifty years."

The meal was excellent, and Bill insisted on paying. They walked back out into the street, and he commented on the scruffy buildings they had seen near the mall, and so many people footling around in the streets as if life had no purpose.

"But islands of comfort inside many of those homes," said Mario.

Bill commented on the extremes they had witnessed. The Club was in a poverty-stricken area. Poverty had to attract crime. Mario said the local police knew how to control it. They siphoned off shady characters by deliberately never visiting certain venues so that they always knew where they were.

"This town has a tough reputation, especially since it lost most of its factories. But, in fact, the streets are quite safe except in a few isolated places. Don't rely on appearances, Bill. You really have to know where to find them."

As they drove back towards the road for Broadacre, Mario repeatedly pointed out how down-and-out areas often found themselves right next to overtly opulent ones.

"Remember what you saw in Manhattan. It's the same everywhere."

Everything seemed to thrive on contrasts. Mario's forbearance in avoiding controversial issues impressed Bill. What he had just lived through presented plenty more ideas for his scripts.

On the way back, Mario dropped Bill at Eli Mendelsohn's so that he could pick up the promised guidebook. Eli lived halfway between Bill's and Catherine's house and the town center. Bill surprised Eli with a dog on his lap in the back room, as if trying to unwind from the tensions of the week.

Eli's wife closed the door behind her and came out to welcome Bill. Eli appeared a minute later without the dog and announced that he trained young soccer enthusiasts on Saturday afternoons. He invited Bill along. Bill said he was still feeling energetic because of the Japanese coffee and needed the exercise after all the food.

Eli drove the two of them over to the playing fields on the edge of town. His colleague had failed to turn up, and he asked Bill if he would stand in for the occasion.

Bill wondered for a while whether he had been set up. It had been decades since he had been anywhere near a soccer ball. Apart from the difficulty of remembering some of the more complex rules and feeling distinctly gawky before it came back to him, he had a hard job getting used to the array of bossy mothers gesticulating and screaming along the touchline, or the mandatory group-hug required each time his team re-dispersed for action. Many of the kids had clearly been coerced to be there and cried endlessly while their budding bully colleagues were taking over the field.

Bill appreciated the exercise and his returning memories, but it was soon more than he could take, and he was glad when it finally ended. By the time, on their way back, Eli asked him if he would be interested in helping in the future, Bill had already decided that he would politely eschew this opportunity for the time being.

It was getting dark. Eli invited Bill in. His wife prepared coffee and Bill warned he had soon to be getting back to Catherine.

They talked for a while. Despite his commanding style on the pitch, Eli now showed himself more of a thinking person, even circumspect and introvert. Bill detected his nervous nature. He appeared diffident and, unlike Bill, always extra-focused on anything he looked at rather than skimming over it. Eli was clearly unlike the brash neighbors they otherwise had, someone more akin to Father Arnold.

Eli revealed he commuted to New York most weeks and stayed there for several days. He admitted that most of his work on inventions and patents was very boring except to the initiated specialist.

"And yet patents control our lives."

Bill knew nothing on the subject and wondered what was to come. Eli cogently talked about the conflict between the just rights from inventions and the undesirable monopolies that all too often came out of them. There was a power struggle taking place around the world, he warned, a Cold War, a Great Game, with multinationals and countries discreetly vying for control. States provided espionage in order to protect their largest companies and strategic industries. The activities of some of the historically more belligerent countries worried him most.

"Trust me, Bill. One day there will be a reckoning."

Bill found it fascinating but wondered if Eli had become a little too paranoid. He thanked them both and Eli handed him the book.

Eli's wife saw Bill out.

"He's going through a difficult phase, Bill. He's consumed by his daemons."

She said that whereas most people had their worst thoughts in the middle of the night, Eli seemed to be on a revolving clock.

"Waking up gets most of us out of our nightmares. Not Eli."

Bill repeated something Sam Rosenbaum had once told him. Every little difficultly people lived in their lives eventually came back repeatedly to haunt their dreams.

"You mean post-traumatic stress?"

"But apparently of relatively benign experiences as well," Bill said.

She said that for Eli it did not stop with the past.

"You should see how much he worries about the millennium bug. I'm dreading when he retires."

Bill thought about Eli on his way home on foot. He had also told Bill of his fascination for numbers, how he wrote everything down and looked for patterns in every aspect of his life. But nothing seemed to interest him more than patents because of the way they embodied progress. Bill guessed he had a point, but then again, even the boring game of golf became a life's passion to those who put their minds to it.

Once he had made peace with Catherine for his prolonged absence, Bill remembered the incident at the cemetery on the night of the trek. Since Hughes had lived in Broadacre longer than anyone else he knew, he called him at home and asked about the building in front of the cemetery. Hughes admitted he had no idea, he had never seen it used, and Bill then described what they thought they had seen.

Hughes was interested. He said that he often walked that way. He would investigate it for his personal interest.

No sooner than he had put down the phone, Bill thought about his trip with Mario that morning. Something had been preying on his mind ever since Mario had led the way out of the Club and restaurant, and now it came to him.

Bill was certain that Mario had been the man who had emerged from the hotel just after he had spotted Mary Lou.

14

The cannabis was good news, but it was far from gold. After ordering Carmine to go back for one last look, Fritz Gargano moved ahead with his plan to get Bill sent home and lay his hands on the house.

"I have good news, Boss," announced Carmine, hoping to rediscover favor.

Fritz grunted. Carmine constantly tried to make up for his shortcomings.

"Tell me you did that other thing."

Carmine smiled and imitated a pair of scissors with his fingers. It had been his own idea for expediting matters faster, and Fritz slapped him on the shoulder with his habitual primeval grin.

"But Boss, you'll never guess who owns the Broadacre car dealership."

Fritz had forgotten about finding someone local.

"Ray Bellicaso," Carmine announced.

Fritz grinned. It brought back memories of Sing Sing.

*

Josh Villeneuve was furious. Like everybody else, he had already received a circular from the Commission warning about the new rules and extended boundary and had thrown it away at once. But that morning he had received a second letter, this time addressed to him personally. It ordered him to place his Caterpillar out of sight because it was degrading the appearance of the neighborhood. If he intended to house it, he would have to apply for planning permission first. He had a month to put into action the solution he chose.

He called Attorney Hughes who said that there was nothing to be done as they were within their new rights. Josh asked how he could challenge the order, but Hughes warned him of the expense and uncertain outcome, risks that, in his view, far outweighed the cost and inconvenience of putting up a new building.

"You could buy time," Hughes said. "They can't prosecute you if you're going through the right motions."

Josh knew he was on his own. No-one was likely to join a cause over the simple toy he kept in his back yard. He would have to comply. Emilia said her Portuguese roots were more attuned to such domination by the authorities. Then it came to him he would find himself in front of Judge Cipriano. His name ended with the dreaded 'o'.

He had an idea, a brilliant idea. He went over to Tom's to congratulate him for getting his windmill through in time and asked him for the construction drawings. He would submit those to the Commission.

BAD DAYS IN BROADACRE

*

The weather closed in. The ginkgo biloba opposite Bill's and Catherine's had already shed its leaves in a day, with neighbors photographing themselves under its rain. Bill continued to do most of his work from home, with only the occasional visit to New York. It was still unclear how it would all come out, or even whether he would still have a job in a few months' time, but Sam seemed to remain optimistic, and encouraged him as before.

The exchanges with Tom and Mary Lou had slowed down since Labor Day, after their pool had been emptied and covered for winter. But the reason was not all one-sided. A cynic such as Catherine might have concluded that their neighbors' interest had equally waned once it had become clear to them that there would be no projects on the house for the time being.

The inclement weather kept them housebound under snowdrifts that almost extended their roof to the ground. Bill spotted Tom and Mary Lou peering out of their French windows as if waiting for life to return. Tom later emerged from the house on his own. It looked as though he had found himself something to do. Bill deciphered the equipment Tom was loading in the car.

"Looks like ice fishing."

But Catherine was more concerned about the privacy they had lost now that the leaves had fallen. Mary Lou was still there at the windows. Catherine felt they were being targeted.

"I'm going to plant a hedge in the Spring."

Daniel objected. He assumed the pool would be there for him in the summer.

"We'll have to walk around, Mum."

He was seeing snow for the first time, as he had grown up in France during successive mild years. It was a delight for Bill and Catherine to see him marvel at it all.

Bill caught on that they were not the object of prying eyes, at least not this time. Among the dark trees to their left, drifted a flock of dark wild turkeys, quite large, intermittently scraping up the fallen leaves while looking for worms and acorns in the snow.

"Daniel, something else I bet you've never seen before," Bill called out.

Daniel came over to look.

"Not as exciting as the deer the other day, Dad."

Catherine's mouth dropped. She asked him what he meant.

"Two of them, Mum."

He proudly pointed to where he had spotted them.

"Eating your plants over there, Mum."

She hastily put on her boots, coat, hat and gloves and stormed out of the house, calling out on the way that she was off to Barbara's, but without explaining why.

Two hours later she was back. Bill and Daniel were already starving.

"I thought it was going to be quick," Bill said.

"She kept talking and talking. She wanted company, I guess."

"Well?"

"You won't see any more deer from now on."

Daniel groaned over his loose tongue as Catherine grabbed the keys to drive into town. They would have to starve a little longer.

The next morning, Daniel came back into the house after snowballing Jack and Debra. As he sat down in the hall to remove his boots, Bill grimaced. He had whiffed his son.

"It must be what mum put down. It stinks outside. I can't stay there."

"This is terrible," Bill said. "We might as well live in the prison!"

Catherine came in from the back and said that she had been careful where she had put down Barbara's magic potion. While she said that, they heard a strange grating noise coming from the side of the house and rushed over to the window. Someone had a snow thrower out. It was spreading yellow snow everywhere.

"Harry!" said Catherine.

*

It was bitterly cold outside, and Bill's fingers burned like never. Winter had arrived with a vengeance, although everyone still said that the snow had always been much deeper back in the old days.

"When they were all smaller," had said Catherine.

Bill, Catherine and Daniel struggled their way to a school event at the town hall to celebrate the finale of an anti-drugs campaign laid on for Daniel's class. It had been led by a colleague of Harry's, and Bill had recognized her. It was she who had rescued him the week before.

There had been no-one else around. It had been an icy bend on a quiet road lined by tall snow-clad fir trees that shielded the sun, not that it counted for anything. He had already unbuckled, bumped his head on the upside-down roof and emerged from the car by the time he spotted her cruiser pulling up behind.

Ice and snow had been everywhere. The bright blue sky had hidden the sober reality. He had felt relieved after recalling the frightening drive between massive trucks and trailers in a snowstorm out on the main highway the night before. It could have been far worse.

He had smiled to himself. It had been his first such encounter and his imagination had taken off. She could not order him to stay inside with his hands on the dashboard as she might have done. Not upside down.

"I've located the driver, code ten."

The radio had squawked unintelligibly from the other end before she had announced "White Caucasian male, six foot two, beard. It'll be a thirty-six."

Bill had walked back toward her unmarked cruiser as she sat there with her window down. How she had thought she knew his age had been a complete mystery. Anyway, she had flattered him by more than a few years.

"You were driving too fast for conditions, Sir."

She climbed out and pushed her baton into its holder, irritated that he had dared to walk up to her. The sound of her voice had been strangely dampened by the snow all around.

Bill had had a sudden flashback to a similar accident he had had in France. It had been a winter night and the village gendarme had to turn out while quite drunk, but at least he had looked to expedite matters quickly and avoid trouble. His ploy had nearly come unstuck when half the village had appeared in their pajamas to shake hands with their beleaguered English acquaintance who had just been upside down.

"Can you take me home?"

"I sure can, Sir."

She had first gone to check out the car with its wheels in the air and Bill had followed.

"Where are you from, Sir?"

"I'm British."

She had briefly stared at him

"Your guys killed two of my family during the Revolution. But I think I can forgive you for that now."

The atmosphere had changed for the better. Bill had felt relieved. Like all her colleagues, she had at first looked menacing. He had prepared himself to be hit on the head or worse for careless driving and taking up her time. He had timidly opened the passenger side of her giant cruiser and sank into the seat. Before they had pulled away, she had said something about a seventy-three into her radio.

On the way home to Broadacre, and after he had announced that he knew Harry, everything about the incident had been mentally registered for Bill's next-day's script.

An earlier message of hers had been playing on his mind.

"How did you know my age?" he had asked her.

"I have no idea of your age, Sir!" she had retorted.

In the morning, Bill completed his script quota for the day before heading for the garage in Catherine's car. Ray Bellicaso admitted he had tears in his eyes when the rescue truck had pulled in with Bill's severely battered car. It seemed to count against the success of its original sale only months before.

Bill remembered the occasion. Congratulating them for their choice, as everyone seemed to do for anything he or Catherine purchased, Bellicaso had sworn that, thanks to Catherine's brinkmanship, he had lost his shirt when he sold it to Bill in the first place.

And now this.

Bill and Catherine had joked about Bellicaso afterwards. He had a balding head and black thick-rimmed spectacles that were trademarks in his ads on local television. He was an impressive and tall man who either enjoyed an incredible physique or was packing, or possibly both, according to Josh, who reminded Bill that his name also ended with his dreaded 'o'.

Bellicaso had let Bill borrow a stripped-down Bronco for the time it would take to bash the Camry back into shape.

The Bronco instantly became Bill's pride and joy. The car's only entertainment came from a stuck Bowie tape that played whether Bill liked it or not. The driver's window constantly needed forcing, so Bill opened up the panel to discover a clutch of suspicious leafy material.

Catherine and Daniel joined him for a ride after lunch. She was at first alarmed by Bill's wild driving while the three of them sat side by side on the front seat, singing along with the tape. She appeared to enjoy the higher ride, but she constantly stopped singing to issue warnings.

"*You can collect as many red lights as you like,*" she quoted, "*but never white canes.*"

Daniel was perplexed.

"You mean blind men, Mum?"

And so, despite Daniel's protests, Bill slowed down until she complained no more, and in town they felt as if they were permanently following a funeral procession.

They had fun all the same. The next day Bill drove the three of them singing into snowy climbs in the countryside around that he would normally have avoided.

They did that several times again over the following days and weeks. One by one they negotiated each of the high points of the state parks within thirty miles to gaze at the scenery. Each time they ended up sitting together on the warm hood to watch the winter sunset with Bowie blasting in the background as Catherine sketched away. All Bill missed was a six-pack to enjoy the part to the full. Why on earth had he not rented a log cabin up there in the wilds instead of the tame strait-laced and run-down house the entire world seemed to covet?

They were presently in the park that offered the most spectacular climb and view at the end. Daniel stepped forward to throw snowballs into the ravine, fronted by a flimsy ice-cold steel fence. Catherine and Bill were on the hood as usual and looking alternately at the thick snow around them and the reddening sun on the horizon directly in front. Catherine broke the silence.

"Remember that boy Daniel has been clearing driveways with?"

Bill vaguely nodded. He was busy admiring the scenery.

"He has just been sent to reform school."

"What for?"

"His mother didn't say. He was in the Junior High Band."

"We have to be careful about his friends," Bill said, "but there seemed to be nothing wrong with that boy."

Eli's wife had called about the snow clearing. The boys had taken to asking for money before the first snowflakes had fallen. They targeted old ladies, and Daniel was netting forty bucks a day. Bill reminded Catherine, and she instantly became protective.

"How could you think such a thing of him?"

Bill had forgotten all about it and never told Catherine.

"One lady had complained to the town office."

"Where on earth did you hear that?"

"Eli Mendelsohn had mentioned that one. He heard it from the Sheriff."

"They don't have sheriffs here," Catherine retorted, as if it disproved the story altogether.

"There *is* a sheriff," Bill said. "He transports prisoners, and he has a black and white van. It's parked outside the post office. The kids had knocked on his door."

He thought back to his walks to the post office in the summer and having to line up behind countless tall octogenarians with their knee-length pants and spindly legs, impatiently spooning each other to get to the counter. The Sheriff's van was always parked there. His first wild thought had been that it was there to guard the institution that Tom and everyone else seemed to regard as damning proof against all federal institutions, and the suspected quasi-communist leanings of the state.

"So, you believe about Daniel, after all?" Catherine asked.

"No, I know there actually is a sheriff."

They looked down into the valley, the river that flowed from left to right, the covered bridge that looked distinctively more orange than they normally did, the large expanse of flat grassy land to the right strewn with small huts spaced about twenty yards with shivering calves pegged in front of them, and then the large hill behind it all about to be attacked by the falling sun. Bill grabbed Catherine's arm.

"Look at that!"

As the sun gradually followed the exact line predicted by the shape of the side of the hill, its blaze seemed to set light to the naked trees on the way down. Catherine had been distracted by an old rail siding far away to the right where Daniel had once climbed aboard the carriages that had become museum pieces. She looked up and saw the miracle being performed on the hillside.

"We thought we were coming to a land of chance, of uncontrolled events, of chaos even," said Bill. "Instead, we discover a strange certainty about everything. The falling sun is painting the landscape as routinely as people go to church, as they dance in weird straight lines, obey their absurd speed limits, and as the weather is guaranteed to fall apart straight after Labor Day."

"And as much as they try to chase us out of our house and prey on each other!"

But Bill dreamed on.

The boiler was making unusual noises when they got back, and Bill could not get hold of Mario. It had been a while since they had last seen him, and Bill suspected that he would have migrated to Florida like so many others. But his license plates were local. He gave up trying and Catherine asked him to walk over to the store for some cooking oil.

"The green one," she said.

She was always explicit on colors. It was the artist in her. When they were driving together, and she was navigating from a printed map, she would tell him to take the red road rather than the yellow one. Whenever they visited a town, she would always somehow discern its predominant color, ochre, white, gray and so-on.

At the store, Bill spotted Mario's face splashed over the front page of the morning newspaper. He picked up a copy and read it on the spot. Mario had been shot in his bed and his wife had been arrested. Bill hurried to the shelves, grabbed the oil and paid and rushed home.

"I said the green one."

He had mistakenly picked up a bottle which had a yellower tinge to it. He offered to go back but there was no time left, so the meal would be ruined instead, she declared.

Bill read the rest of the article while they ate. Catherine hated it when he did that, but the situation was exceptional, so he gave himself permission. Mario had apparently been killed with his own shotgun. His wife had owned up, accusing her husband of forcing her to do strange things with other people. Bill quizzically looked at Catherine but said nothing. The newspaper said no more, which made the story even more enticing.

"Mario *d-e-a-d*?" mouthed Catherine for Daniel's sake after Bill had told her. "It's not possible."

He had waited until he had read the entire article. Catherine could be merciless for details. The story had a sort of double that occurred to Bill. The last time they had met, Mario had told Bill about how he had just fired an assistant who had later turned out to be a wanted murderer. The police had come to see Mario to warn him, and they had left a guard at his house for several weeks. Bill had thought that linked to the two suits who had met Mario near the club.

Josh called.

"Have you heard?"

Josh said he had told Barbara and that he had just decided another of his schemes. One of his many occupations on the side, he said, was to organize the annual house tour in the early fall. Visitors would purchase tickets to see how a dozen of their more interesting neighbors lived, and there was always a great competition to be on the list.

Bill and Catherine had visited on the last one and had found it peculiar encountering one of their affluent neighbors quite out of context, babysitting someone else's house during the visits. But there was a lot to learn, and Catherine had come out of each house partly scorning and partly bundled with ideas.

"I'm thinking of adding Mario's house to next year's list," Josh said. "It will be a sell-out."

Bill was appalled at his opportunism.

*

It was eleven thirty. Catherine had gone to bed and Bill was sitting at his desk finishing up the script destined for Sam in the morning.

His cellphone went. It was unusual at that hour.

"Bill?"

It was Attorney Hughes, sounding excited. Bill stood up out of respect, but Hughes hung up. Bill waited for a couple of minutes and then tried to call back. It rang forever. There was no answer.

*

Catherine arrived with Daniel from school just before five the next day.

"Something's going on at the cemetery. There are police cruisers and vans everywhere."

Bill's instinct told him to go out there right away. He drove the already warm Bronco the short distance along the back road. One of Harry the trooper's colleagues was standing in the road with his arm up.

"That's negatory, Sir. You can't go any further. Try going by South Street."

"What's going on?"

"An incident, Sir."

Bill thought of driving over to see Harry but decided against the risk of wasting his time. Anyway, as local state trooper he would have deployed himself to somewhere nearby.

He got back to find Catherine putting down the phone. Her face was pale and severe.

"It was Hughes' secretary. He can't see us in the morning."

She had difficulty following on. Bill assumed it had been the reason for the call of the night before.

"They found him in the cemetery this afternoon. He was unconscious."

Bill could not believe it and felt uneasy. Apparently, Hughes had not returned the night before and his wife had alerted the barracks in the morning. It was the town caretaker who had stumbled on him near the small cemetery building at midday.

The telephone went again.

"Bill?"

It was Ray Bellicaso.

"It what's left of your car. There's something you need to look at."

Bill said he would be over right away.

Bellicaso was waiting for him on the forecourt. He looked quite agitated.

"You need to see this, Bill."

He led Bill to the Camry which was up on the hoist. Bellicaso helped himself to a flashlight, and they crouched underneath.

"Look right there."

Bill asked for an explanation.

"Bill, it looks to me that someone had tampered with your brakes."

Bill took a hard look again and now understood.

"I just want to give you a heads up, Bill. I've informed the police."

Bill was surprised he should do that on his behalf.

"It's an issue of liability. Should they succeed next time around."

Bill thought long and hard on his way home. He couldn't tell Catherine and yet he needed her. Her cynical take on things might help to figure out who might have been motivated to do such a thing. His natural myopia could only think that it was linked to the shed business.

15

Harry the trooper came to see Bill the next morning. He had called in at the garage on the way and accepted Bellicaso's diagnosis. Bill said he could not imagine anyone wanting him dead. Harry said they were in an impossible situation, because frankly all they could do was to wait for the next incident. He told Bill to be on the lookout, have his house alarm and car regularly checked, and warn him if anything else suspicious occurred or if he remembered anything.

Saying that he never believed in coincidences, he turned to the subject of Hughes. It looked as though the attorney had slipped and fallen about fifteen feet from the small building at the front of the cemetery, but they were keeping an open mind over the cause. They had found his cellphone and confirmed the time of the call to Bill. For the time being, Harry would wrap both incidents together.

"Bill, why would Hughes have called you then?"

Bill had already thought long and hard over how much he should say. He had even discussed it with Catherine. They had said that the Elliot Kaplan business had yet to be proven and bringing it up now could get them into trouble if the police handled it badly or turned out to be under some form of influence. So, Bill limited himself to the night of the return from the trek with Paul and Eli and what they had seen, and how Hughes had taken interest.

Harry took out his address book and dialed a number from his phone but got nowhere.

"We'll get the caretaker to show us that building."

Before they left, he pulled out a large photograph from the leather case he was carrying. Bill recognized Hughes lying on his side with one arm outstretched.

"Look around his hand," Harry said.

Hughes seemed to have been making signs in the mud.

"Any ideas?"

Bill asked if he could borrow it. Harry said no. Bill said he would keep it to himself, and if he ever discovered anything ensure that Harry took credit.

"It's strictly between us, Bill."

They found the caretaker at the edge of the cemetery, positioning wooden beams over a newly dug grave. Harry asked Bill to recount what had happened on the night in question. The caretaker shrugged his shoulders and reluctantly went off to fetch the keys from the town office.

He returned fifteen minutes later and led them to the front of the small building.

"It's never used," he said.

The largest in the bunch of keys proved how old the lock was.

"This is the first time I've touched this one in years."

While he was telling Harry that he kept the key in a locked cupboard at the town hall, he inserted it and opened up. The door gave easily, and they went inside.

The caretaker tried the light switch, but it failed. Inside, it was completely empty and smelled musty, but everywhere was clean except for a coating of dust. The floor was cobbled and there was another door on the cemetery side. He said that the building had once been used to stage coffins before burial, and the only reason it was still standing was that it had been decided that it had some historical value. Not that he knew why.

"You see. There's no reason anyone would come in here."

Harry thanked him and they drove back to Bill's house. On the way, he said that the caretaker was a general handyman and looking after the cemetery formed only a small part of his duties.

"But you've got me interested, Bill. I'll keep an eye out. You never know."

Harry said he had known Hughes to be interested in wildlife and walking in his spare time, often at night. His proximity to the wildlife sanctuary at the time was entirely understandable, and the cemetery was just next to it. He talked for a while about him. The much-respected attorney had always been seen as a great civilizing influence on Broadacre.

"Hopefully he'll come around soon so that we can get to the bottom of it all."

With that, Harry drove off.

Bill told Catherine he wondered whether Hughes had discovered something. He needed to discover more about what the attorney had been up to.

He walked over to Hughes' office. The secretary was alone, which was convenient. He asked her if Hughes kept a notebook or diary, but she said he was such an old-timer that everything always remained in his head, adding that Harry had already asked. Bill apologized for his intrusion and left.

He knew he would invite trouble if he tried the same on Hughes' wife. He thought about the building. Perhaps Harry was not as perseverant as he should have been. The small building needed a more thorough search.

Bill ran into Harry again just outside the post office. He made conversation by asking about his colleague who had organized the anti-drug campaign and rescued him after the accident. He had not seen her for a while.

"Oh, she's gone. She had an accident."

"Car accident?"

Bill was thinking of her massive cruiser which should have been far safer than any car it encountered.

"No, no, nothing as serious as that. She fell over at the barracks just after your business and went on sick leave."

Bill asked how she was.

"Well, it's a long story, Bill. They've been cracking down on insurance fraud in the force, and they found her with her boyfriend in Florida water-skiing when she was supposed to have been laid up. She'll be lucky to get off lightly."

Harry's news astonished Bill. He had developed the impression that most people didn't take vacations, let alone try to cheat the system. This was a revelation to him.

The radio from Harry's cruiser made a noise. Harry said that an inmate of the new old people's home had disappeared and that a helicopter and search volunteers were on their way to search the swamp nearby. Since the old man had been physically fit and only suffered from amnesia, they had housed him on the ground floor which made it easier for him to escape and wander off.

"After the Hughes incident and what happened to you, we're on edge more than ever."

Bill walked back to the house. It felt like spring. The birds had come to life and were making a racket. He spotted Catherine in the front garden with a golf club, something she had never held before, let alone possessed.

He deliberately looked twice to be sure. She seemed to be putting small white objects deep into the gap under the back of the wooden garage. Her strange behavior gave him a fright.

"I bought it. It's second hand."

She coolly went on putting. Bill wondered if this was some side effect of winter claustrophobia and if his health insurance would cover her malaise. Perhaps she'd been drinking. Everyone he knew seemed to be falling like flies.

"Bill! *Please*. Can't you see what I'm doing?"

He picked up one of the white pellets. It was a moth tablet.

"*Why?*"

"To scare off the skunks, of course."

They were news to him, but he did not want to be accused of being unobservant or deaf. She came to his rescue.

"The one I saw going under there this morning. They're making a nest there, I know it."

A family of skunks living within spraying distance of the front door was worse than the snow-throwing incident. Their home would be placed in quarantine. Catherine had rightly passed to action, and Bill apologized.

"Why should you apologize?"

"Oh, never mind."

"You never take me seriously. Do you realize what will happen to us?"

A helicopter passed overhead and hovered over the other side of Tom and Mary Lou's. Bill repeated what Harry had said.

He went inside and saw that Catherine had not yet opened the mail. He picked up an envelope that had Hughes' office address on the front. The letter was from Elliot Kaplan, declaring that he was representing their neighbor Peter Drake. It demanded twenty thousand dollars for the slither of land which covered the two feet over which the shed had trespassed. Bill froze. It was well over twenty times what Hughes had predicted. Should he hide the letter from Catherine?

A second envelope had come from the Historical Commission, the same that everyone else had complained about days ago, which told Bill that he and Catherine had been an afterthought, perhaps because of their recent arrival. It announced that from now on any plan to alter the external appearance of their house and outbuildings would have to be submitted for approval. The letter was signed by both the First Selectman and the Town Clerk.

Bill took the news in his stride. However, he hated it when people did not have the courage of their convictions to sign on their own.

*

Catherine's brave efforts seemed in vain. Two days later they found themselves forced to call the skunk man. Tom, nervous about an invasion, put them on to someone called Randy.

Randy turned out to be the incarnate of the great American tradition of becoming enthusiastic and truly expert at something in their spare time. Bill had seen it with several of the people they had already met. This nation of amateurs, in the best sense of the word, he thought, proved itself prepared to jump onto anything and see it through with unparalleled gusto. Randy was one of them. Apparently from early boyhood he had taken to skunks. Since there were quite a few to be found around Broadacre, he had made a successful side career of it.

Bill and Catherine liked Randy from the start, despite his frowsy appearance. Keeping his distance, Daniel tried to figure him out. They had just rented a film in which Clint Eastwood had to steal a prototype Russian jet fighter; an aircraft so sophisticated that in order to fly it he had to think in Russian. It was a bit like driving in a foreign country with the GPS deliberately set to the local language - it was the only way of attuning to other drivers' quirks in order to predict their behavior. Randy was no Clint Eastwood, but he read skunks, and both Bill and Catherine knew what he was about when he walked through the door. He furtively tiptoed into the house and introduced himself, keeping so close to the wall that Catherine had to pull him away from it.

The strange man standing in front of them described the habits of his subjects with clarity and adoring that instantly enthralled. His audience of three assimilated in their minds the sorry life of a pregnant female discovering that human beings had taken over the territory that her ancestors had roamed unhindered for millennia, bravely finding the perfect refuge to give birth in safety, in their case the deep underside of a garage with its back on stilts.

Daniel pored over the idea of using what he was hearing for his next school project. Catherine was nearly in tears. Bill discreetly gulped.

Randy then described his traps. Daniel recovered from his dreams.

"How do you kill them?"

Randy glanced furtively at each of them.

"You don't have to worry about that, folks. I will take her away. The rest is my business."

Catherine regained her cool.

"How do you lure her?"

"With cheese."

"How much do you need, Randy?" Bill asked.

"A hundred bucks a head."

That seemed a lot of cheese to Bill. Catherine nodded her agreement. Bill prayed that their unwelcomed visitor had turned up alone and had not yet given birth.

In the end, Randy caught two adults, each as keen on gooey American Cheddar as the other. He drove off with them in his battered high-heeled four-by-four, his pockets stuffed with Bill's hard-earned greenbacks he had to draw from the bank to avoid any trace of transaction. Catherine pulled out a sketch that she had made of their visitor and Bill laughed. Randy was indeed the living image of Strewell Peter.

While they were placing netting around the base of the garage, Catherine wondered aloud what would turn up next. Daniel, some way off, had overheard.

"Squirrels!"

In fact, apart from their perpetual barking, and never standing still as they chased up and down their trees after tasting apples that must have turned alcoholic long ago, squirrels remained a footnote. A more regal visitor was a solitary, cheeky-looking groundhog that would lie on the back lawn, only when it was sunny, with its hind legs ungracefully spread out behind it. It lay there for hours and would not even budge when Bill went outside to investigate. He once drew up his chair at a safe distance, sat down, and stared at it with an occasional deliberate wink. The groundhog soon developed a corresponding twitch, but steadfastly refused to budge.

Then, a week later, the twitching visitor had become history. It had been seen off by Oswald, Tom's and Mary Lou's overweight black and white tomcat that turned out to be terrorizing the neighborhood. Oswald was a full-time predator, without the usual endearing feline occupations of purring, meowing, flinching in his sleep, or leaving trophies. The only exception was that he had the habit of putting his paws to his mouth each time he yawned while flat out on the lawn in the summer. When he was not stalking one of the other neighbors' pets, Oswald needed the same spot as the groundhog in order to eye the cardinals busily visiting Bill's and Catherine's bird feeder, a handy flight away from Tom and Mary Lou's small pond at the front of their garden.

*

Bill finally plucked up enough courage to tell Catherine about Elliot Kaplan's demand. There was no ultimatum provided, so they had time to figure out what to do. At the back of their minds was the possibility that they might have to move back to Europe, and so there was no point in wasting money. Bill suspected that a solution might become apparent if he found out more about Elliot Kaplan and his secret life. But how could he do it?

He peered out of the window and spotted Oswald yawning. The cat was a mess. He had very untidy split whiskers. He had snored loudly when out on Bill and Catherine's warm patio in the summer. Daniel had once pointed him out walking along the street, hobbling along two feet up on the sidewalk and two down on the road. Tom and Mary Lou would have been ashamed had they known.

Was Oswald a harbinger to the surrounding reality? Perhaps Catherine had always been right. Maybe the world they were in really *was* crazy, or gradually becoming so. And with the skunk affair, Catherine herself had started to follow suit.

*

The next day, Attorney Hughes' secretary called. Bill had expected good news and that the attorney would fully recover and place his partner in check. It was not to be. Hughes had died under intensive care without regaining consciousness.

16

It was Saturday morning. According to habit, Father Arnold was seated in his confessional. The resurgent icy wind that highlighted the limber of the smaller trees in front of his church had already delivered a succession of six ardent and rueful repenters, one of whom had begged for forgiveness for taking a bribe, something he rarely heard.

Was this a sign of sins to follow? He hated the long, drawn-out winters that seemed to bring out the worst in people. Time had flown faster since he had aged, but winters seemed to take longer.

He was contemplating the possibility of another surge in the devil's ways in Broadacre when his seventh and the last of his visitors crept inside. He recognized her pungent perfume straight away.

"Forgive me, Father, for I have sinned…"

She then appeared hesitant. It made him impatient.

"What's on your mind, my child?"

He felt stupid because he knew her so well, and she knew he knew who she was, or she thought he did.

And then came the sort of news that he dreaded hearing and had always feared. She had committed sin behind her husband's back, behind the very man who had rebuilt the church's altar two years ago. How could she?

"Do you still love him?"

"Why yes, of course, Father."

It was a relief. It had been a question of instantaneous carnal desire, she admitted, when both parties had felt the same. She painfully described a libidinous moment of impossible pressures, created by the opportunity of the attentions of a man to whom she had always been physically attracted, but with whom she had nothing else in common.

Father Arnold realized she had arduously prepared her exposé.

"I now have a burden to carry, Father."

He encouraged her to put it behind her. She should move on. Forget the distraction. Return full-time to her devoted husband.

"But Father, it has led to the man's death."

At first, he did not know what to say. He reminded her that if she had not had a direct hand in the person's demise, she had nothing to reproach herself.

"Thank you, Father."

The confession went on to other more anodyne matters and she serenely took her leave. He felt as relieved having escaped her perfume as much as her disrupting news.

Father Arnold's demeanor for the rest of the morning was far from serene. He remained erratic and distracted. Like the typical policeman who had never used his gun in anger, it was the very first time in over forty years of hearing confessions that murder had been mentioned in one of his confessionals. He assumed she had meant murder.

But what made it worse, much worse, was that he had recognized Mary Lou's voice from the start, and that he had assumed that she was talking about Attorney Hughes.

In the afternoon, it became time for the second part of his duties of the day before the Sabbath. As he walked over to the prison, he thought again about what the morning had yielded, what the wind had blown into his holy confessional. Hughes had been too old for Mary Lou. Could his associate have somehow been involved? Why would he think that?

He knocked on the front door and glanced upward at the closed-circuit camera before the buzzer went. An overweight guard greeted him inside and, after absolving him from the customary pat down, led the way through two successive caged doors which he unlocked and relocked and finally to the small white-tiled and camera-less interview room that Father Arnold always used.

He had been doing this for many years. Each of his inmate sessions was divided into three roughly equal parts; acclimatization and lowering of guards, both physically and metaphorically, then the real business of the day, and finally careful preparation before returning to the harsh and uncivilized environment that the prisoner had all too briefly escaped. These represented Father Arnold's delicate mastering of his so-called processes of refraction, reflection and, last of all, re-infliction.

Winston was first, but it was not his first visit. He was led in and uncuffed and, more for the prisoner's sake, the guard said to Father Arnold that he would remain on duty just outside if needed.

He had always done his best in order to tread into Winston's selectively remembered world. Once he had successfully peeled away the bundles of protective layers, Winston would tell him almost everything, as if he had to. On each previous occasion, Father Arnold discovered yet another human being who had gotten himself into a perpetual whirlwind of trouble by creating one problem to solve another. It was always like that. Like the old lady who swallowed a fly.

This occasion was no different, and they became at ease with each other faster than usual. Father Arnold asked how things were.

"I get by. I read books from the library. I'm trying to better myself."

Winston talked especially about his work release and parole days, and how they were helping him to get through his sentence.

Then Father Arnold heard Winston's confession. Winston said little, except to admit that he had always all too easily fallen by the wayside. He made an offhand reference to a current business deal that might get him into trouble.

Father Arnold assumed it involved drugs. It was not as though it took much guessing. He said that Winston should walk away. He deserved better. Winston said he had missed his chance, as he always did. The deal was done, but the dangers had not gone away. He twice used the phrase "someone who should know better".

And so, in the second most notable incident of the day, Father Arnold figured out that Winston must have purchased drugs from someone local and important.

There were others to see. It was six o'clock by the time he was finished. Father Arnold returned home wondering who Winston had dealt with. He ran through in his mind all the confessions he had heard of late. There existed likely candidates he knew of. Then he reminded himself that he was crossing the line. It was not his business to know more.

He had another of his dreams that night. Sometimes he felt that there were now too many of them. The multiple lives he had lived for so long through his parishioners, especially the troubled ones, regularly came back to haunt him in permutations and combinations of nightmares with familiar bits to them, sorts of traumatic passages created from an alphabet soup of life experiences. Tough cases became impossible, endless and crazy, and defied any small amount of logic he clung on to while awake. The only way to escape was to wake up.

Not for the first time he wished he had never taken on his calling. More and more often the distorted aberrations of reality had invaded his mind even when he was awake. He wanted to reach out, but in the end, despite their many troubles, his fickle flock rarely needed him beyond the confessional. And yet for once he wanted to do something useful. Things had become too serious. Enough was enough.

While he lay there in the final stages of waking up, he realized that there was one person he could safely confide in. It was Rabbi Siegel.

As soon as the hour was decent enough, he called his colleague in God and asked to see him straight away. At ten o'clock, between Masses, Father Arnold climbed into his truck and drove over.

"I have a delicate matter to discuss with you, Rabbi."

Glad to have the attention, Siegel warmly said that he was all ears. Whatever his opposite said would absolutely remain between them.

"Rabbi, I learn that someone prominent here might be dealing in drugs."

"What are your thoughts, Father?"

"It is our duty to stop whoever this pernicious person is."

They said to keep each other informed over their common intent and then parted their ways.

Rabbi Siegel thought long and hard about what his Catholic colleague had told him. It could hardly be specious. Over the years, the people of Broadacre had always shown respect for the status quo. It was equally rare that they sneaked on each other behind their backs. This was a proper neighborhood.

He concluded that the source of Father Arnold's story had to be someone from the outside, someone who was at a loss at how to deal with the town's establishment. A stranger. Wait! A foreigner. Of course, a foreigner! There was only one possibility, or rather two. Father Arnold had to be talking about Bill and Catherine.

Without thinking where this was leading, he sycophantically called Anne Kaplan who said to come over straight away.

Anne was happy to see him. They sat down for coffee served by a taciturn Rosa who promptly left to continue her work in the kitchen, not completely out of hearing. Rabbi Siegel asked Anne if she had ever found out anything more about Bill and Catherine.

"That's what *you* were going to do."

He then bluntly asked if she had ever heard anything about drugs.

Anne sat up. She was shocked. She begged to hear more, but the rabbi said his lips were sealed. Anne announced she would do everything in her power to see to hell anyone caught dealing in drugs in her town. Rabbi Siegel insisted he had only posed a question, and that he wanted Anne's assurance that she would speak to no-one.

After half an hour on trivia he left, wondering if he might not have gone a little too far.

He had. Anne called Elliot.

"I may have something more on that English couple."

*

Spring sped up. It invaded their life with a cloying vengeance. Early one Saturday morning, Catherine thought that the hot water had started to boil in the pipes. Bill jumped out of bed and ran to check. It was a false alarm, and the noise stopped, so he climbed back in. Catherine was of another mind.

"Stay near the boiler until it starts again."

Bill obediently got up again, made himself a cup of coffee, and reluctantly drew up a chair in order to listen through the wall. He thought about poor Mario instead.

"Bill, quick!"

"Dad!" shouted Daniel from his room. "What the heck is that?"

Bill rushed to join Catherine, still in bed.

"It's coming from up there!"

In fact, it was coming from outside. Their roof sounded as though it was being machine-gunned. It was the wrong side to be the windmill. Bill put on his dressing gown and overcoat, unlocked the front door, and encountered Oswald who had cunningly opened the outer wire-paneled door with his paw and was sitting next to his shoes. As Bill walked along the side of the house, he felt the wet penetrate his socks and heard a gentle squidging. He looked behind and spotted Oswald bolting in the opposite direction. He would deal with him later.

He arrived under the roof just above the bedroom and looked up. There was not a sound.

Suddenly, a vicious tap-tapping started up from the stop sign just across the road, next to the ginkgo biloba. He turned to look. The sound was metallic. He spotted a tiny dark green object with a bright red and white streak on his head. The bird was perched on top of the sign, leaning over to make its infernal din incommensurate with the size of its body. Clearly it had just found a better percussion to attract a mate, and not even the nearby presence of the cat had been a deterrent.

"At least all the other invaders were quiet," moaned Catherine who had unwisely forced the window open and was still looking out when he returned to the bedroom having forgotten to doff his coat.

She pulled down the window and sniffed.

"Did you step in something?"

Bill looked down and remembered his wet sock.

"This is our *worse pain*," sighed Catherine.

Bill understood right away what she meant. They had just bought a comedy tape in which Mel Brooks describes how he had found the secret of how to make a terrible pain go away.

"How?" asks Carl Reiner

"You create another one, much worse, somewhere else."

But Bill was thinking of Dorothy Parker instead. She had been on the money when she had written how much she hated spring.

*

The large, lifeless and deserted pond down the road, where Jesus had once deposited the performing frogs, had iced over for the winter and had been great fun for skating. Catherine had almost disastrously attempted a modest somersault there.

After the thaw that followed, a flock of some thirty Canada geese had arrived on their way back north. Their game plan had been to resume their journey in a couple of months, having done what they normally do to add to their numbers. They had paired off and disappeared into the remote long grass on the other side, their stationary heads from time to time visible during the long business of incubation.

One fine sunny day, dozens of goslings had appeared on the small rocks at the side of the pond and negotiated the limpid water ahead of their proud waddling and fattened parents. The nasty black water snakes, which had no doubt turned up to feast on goose eggs, disappeared for good. Bill and Catherine, together with Daniel at weekends, had taken up going to watch in the morning. Each of the families had dedicated themselves to flight practice. At first, only the parents, once they had slimmed down from walking around, took off, leaving their young ones gaping in awe as their elders made a circuit in full view and landed back on the lake with a skid, ever more graceful as time wore on.

Before long, the youngsters were trying it as well, and after a few hard weeks they looked as professional as their elders. All the geese practiced their fly arounds almost continuously. They adorned the circular surrounds of the pond with a growing carpet of irremovable acidic droppings. Skeins now crossed the house at low altitude, coming in to land with a dramatic coordinated series of splashes and skids. Every now and again they would take off almost straight away, a frantic go-around, only just missing the roofs of the houses nearby.

Canada had finally beckoned. The geese had left by the time Bill, Catherine and Daniel were routinely waking up to the sound of woodpeckers. They could at last go to the pond without being threatened, and they walked over after breakfast. Apart from the brief appearance of an aggressive snapper turtle, the only other visitor they watched was an otter which regularly slid into the water from the woods on the other side in order to catch fish. Catherine stayed and sketched as it noisily crunched its catch while lazing on a protruding rock surrounded by water. Daniel got bored and went on one of his amphibian collecting expeditions. He returned with a frog in each pocket and nearly smuggled them into the house had it not been for Catherine's keen eye as she followed him in.

*

Bill was seated behind the large, opened bay window that looked out towards the pond. He was at his script, and every now and again looked up. Catherine was at the back microtoming her mahonia. A burly blackbird stood on the lawn and emitted a pathetic tweet before moving on. Pigeons up on the roof were again failing to finish their sentences. Oswald appeared, and they hurriedly took off with a flamenco clapping of their wings.

Bill's confidence remained boosted. The script was going well and, from all that had happened in Broadacre, he had plenty of ideas to spare. The car business at the back of his mind, he thought of notables who had migrated and lent their names to American culture - Dvorak, Einstein, Hitchcock, and presently Tracey Ullman. Would he ever follow?

Although the success of the pilot, due to be launched in September, would be the ultimate test, even Catherine had become as optimistic as their neighbors were about everything else in life.

Summer was not far off, and times looked good.

17

Leaves had started to appear. The beauty of Broadacre was about to be enhanced by a brand-new costume of green, and its denizens reinvigorated. All except the usually optimistic Bill. Looming in the background of all this beauty, hiding among some of stubbornly less attractive features of all that was around them, existed a predatory world that could descend on them at any time. There were the dramas of Hughes, Mario and Yolanda. And the Peter Drake and Elliot Kaplan business was also part of it, gnawing its way around Bill's subconscious. Perhaps the brakes business was connected. He could only continue to ignore it all at his peril. And he knew he had to be proactive. He had to do whatever necessary to make any real threat to their lives go away forever. But for this he needed to find out more.

It started with the Kaplan cabin. From what Daniel had been told, it took a drive to get there. Bill had to be careful about to whom he spoke. There were bound to be hidden alliances in Broadacre as there were anywhere. Going to the Town Clerk's office to study land ownership would be risky. There would have to be another way.

He thought he had a stroke of luck when the red Jeep shot past just as he was pulling out of the gas station. He chased after it. After ten frantic minutes it had escaped, and anyway, it looked as though it was headed south to the shore instead.

He could not rely on chance. He had to plan his moves. Elliot Kaplan was most likely in the habit of taking his family to the cabin on Friday nights or Saturday mornings. That would narrow the time Bill would have to lie in wait. But he had to be cleverer than that. Then he remembered the twins' mention of a stream and a lake, and it gave him an idea.

The first day of the trout season had taken him by surprise. He had woken up to discover cars and trucks bumper to bumper out on the normally empty road outside. Some of them were violating the grassy verges. Luckily the ginkgo biloba was being left alone.

He got dressed and went outside. There was a deathly quiet. He walked towards the pond and saw a bizarre continuous sea of faces adjoined to all manner of hats, scarves and coats protecting motionless bodies from the early morning misty cold. Every foot of the pond's bank had been infested with freshly minted anglers, shoulder to shoulder, resigned to their object of enthusiasm. To a man or woman, they were flouting their latest purchase of fluorescent rods which had surely emptied their pockets, let alone the old timber game store just outside town.

Bill had spotted Tom standing and watching from his garden and walked over. His neighbor assured him that the craze would wane during the following days, and that within a week the pond and roadside would be back to their haunted selves until the following spring. Bill wondered whether the expected hiatus would be because of attention deficit or a depleted stock of fish. There surely had to be more anglers around the pond than fish inside it.

Tom was also dazzled by the ghastly fluorescence.

"And by next year, the cane fashion will have changed, and they will all have purchased new ones."

What Tom had said sounded right. Bill thought of the shopping he and Catherine did at the empty mall ten miles away. Catherine had already been caught out and frustrated by winter clothes being sold out by the end of summer, and now summer clothes no longer being available as the season approached. In fact, he thought, the new batch of canes would be obsolescent even before they were used.

Bill returned home. There were things to do. Catherine had said that she needed something from the store for lunch. In the afternoon they were headed to a school fundraising event where Bill would set in motion his plan for effortlessly tracking down the Kaplan cabin. He had developed the plan when he had first heard about the event.

It was to be a display of paintings by a local artist. Bill knew he had to apply all that he had learned so far about the American psyche. He persuaded Josh Villeneuve to advertise a painting competition at the event due to take place on Memorial Day. The prize would be one of the displayed paintings that Bill would purchase ahead of time.

As eager as always, Josh had jumped at the opportunity without delving into Bill's motivation. Children would be challenged to paint whatever they had caught and present their works at a second event in a few weeks' time, willingly held by the school. Bill calculated the Kaplans would take the bait like everyone else and head off to their private lake straight away, gloriously unaware of who was on their tail.

On his way back from the store, Bill ran into Father Arnold, and they chatted about the geese and the anglers. They were walking together under the maples, along the empty grass-lined sidewalk with the large properties to their right.

The priest seemed distracted.

"Have they found out anything about Hughes?"

Bill was surprised. He had always imagined Father Arnold to have been one of the first to have heard something.

"I suppose the practice will be taken over by his associate."

"Unfortunately," said Bill.

His negative reply provoked Father Arnold's surprise, and he asked why Bill felt that way. Bill said what had happened over the potting shed and the exorbitant demand. Father Arnold asked Bill what he knew of Elliot Kaplan. Bill said that he knew very little, but that he had some suspicions that he was following up. The priest said nothing about his own suspicions of the junior attorney's links with the Hughes affair, Mary Lou and, come to think of it, what Winston had been trying to tell him.

Josh Villeneuve was at work in his front garden and greeted them. They entered though the small gate in the low, white wooden fence and shook hands. They were joined almost immediately by Eli Mendelsohn who had returned early from New York and was there to borrow a hacksaw.

Bill asked them if they knew Elliot Kaplan and explained his conundrum with the shed. Both were equally surprised as Father Arnold that Hughes had allowed his partner to get involved. But in the end, all they really knew about Elliot Kaplan concerned his mother and how influential she was.

This was an opportunity for Josh to gripe about his problem with the Commission and the Caterpillar.

"You can bet the Kaplan woman has something to do with it."

"Be careful, Bill," said Eli.

Father Arnold accompanied Bill over to the pond to watch what was going on. They stopped for a while.

"Bill, remember that Rabbi Siegel had once been asking about you."

It had been odd. Given the various allegiances and connections around, his interest might just have been connected to something else. One never knew.

They spent fifteen minutes in front of the pond before going their separate ways.

Bill went alone early to the fund-raising exhibition to be among the first through the door. He purchased a painting of a local river scene and asked for it to be hung next to Josh's broadsheet advertising the competition.

Half an hour later, in the descending dark, Bill parked fifty yards from Anne's house where he could see the gates. It did not take long before the red Jeep arrived from the direction of the school and pulled into the driveway.

He waited one, two, three hours but nothing happened. He feared he had been wasting his time, or perhaps they were going to leave in the morning instead. Then, the lights in front of the garage doors lit up, the front gates opened, and the Jeep moved about in the driveway. The Kaplans were on the move.

His heart was racing. Would he keep up this time? He could not believe his luck when the Jeep shot past with a boat in tow. The Kaplans had fallen for his trap, literally hook, line and sinker, and the vessel would slow them down all the way to their destination.

They headed west, but they always remained within sight. How far would it be?

Once on the open road, Bill had to rely on tracking the Jeep's beams and confusing double pair of taillights that bounced from side to side behind them. The Jeep turned right off the main road and headed northwards. They were still close to Broadacre.

Bill hung on. He sensed they were getting close to the final destination. About three miles further on, the slight incline rapidly turned into a dip and they disappeared. He accelerated, and once over the top he saw the lights ahead, just before they approached a bend. As soon as they were out of sight Bill accelerated again. He did not see the lights again after the bend. He accelerated even more, and still no lights. They must have turned off onto a sidetrack.

He pulled over to the right and did a U-turn across the deserted road, scanning both sides for a turnoff. Half a mile later, there was a track to the left. He went a little further but there was nothing else either side, so he doubled back. Then, high on the right he spotted the telltale flickering of lights traveling through trees less than half a mile ahead. He knew he had found what he had been looking for. It was good enough for now.

He drove back home cogitating his next move. He would wait until the middle of the week.

*

It was Wednesday. Bill left the house sufficiently early in order to be turning onto the track before daylight. The first thing he spotted was a sign announcing that the land was posted. He could not afford to get caught, but fortunately he still had the Bronco that would muddy the waters if he were spotted.

By the time he had wound his way up to the cabin, it had become light enough for him to find a good place to hide the truck. He retraced his route towards the road, and after a hundred yards found just what he needed.

It started to drizzle, but he was protected. He walked to the cabin. The empty trailer was there. The shutters were open. He tried the door. It was locked tight, as were the windows and lean-to.

He looked around. The land behind him was too sloped, he thought, to lead to a lake. He went ahead instead.

As he approached the trees, he spotted a pathway. He saw the marks. It must have been this way that they had dragged the boat. He followed the beaten track several hundred yards and fell on a lake surrounded by daffodils and trees only feet behind.

Pulled up onto a shallow bank nearby was the boat. He walked around the perimeter of the lake. It would take him about a quarter of an hour. Three quarters of the way around, he stumbled on the escaping stream. Water was trickling away down the slope, and he followed it.

Twenty minutes later, he found himself in another much smaller clearing. He recognized at once what he had found, but he had to find proof, and it would be months after the last harvest in the fall.

The soil had been plowed over. He picked up a branch, broke off three or four feet, and fumbled around in the dirt. He pushed the branch well into the ground and felt gravel. He worked in different directions. The gravel appeared to occupy about two or three feet square. In the dirt he had disturbed were withered and moldy clumps of vegetation. He cleaned one of them up with his fingers and slid it into his coat pocket.

He headed back up the stream to the lake and retraced his way to the cabin. The sun was now quite high, and before he entered the clearing he looked around. The Kaplans had a fine spot here, and he envied them.

He walked over to behind the cabin and used his branch to smash one window at the back. He reached in, unhooked the latch and climbed inside.

Everything was tidy. He had to be quick. He looked upward and saw the open beams that crossed from one side to the next. They were lined with hooks. He rifled each of the cupboards and drawers until he arrived at a locked cupboard in the main bedroom. He forced it open and fumbled around but there was nothing of any interest. He pulled the cupboard away from the wall to see if anything had been hidden behind. Something light fell to the floor. It must have been wedged or sitting on the rear edge of the cupboard. It was a withered and dried out leaf with some form of fruit. He grabbed a couple of polythene bags from the kitchen and filled them with what he had found so far.

He gave one last look around. There was nothing else to be discovered there, and he made his way back to the window.

On the way to Broadacre, Bill thought about what to do with his discovery. It did not take long to reach a decision. He remembered Harry admitting that most of his police work came through anonymous tip-offs.

The following morning, Bill drove all the way to the main town to post the two polythene bags and their contents. In the envelope he added a small note with a sketched map of the land indicating where the samples had been found and who the land belonged to. He handed the parcel in, taking the precaution of using the same gloves that he had used at the cabin and to handle the note.

*

Harry the trooper looked at the post mark, and then in vain for the sender's address. He opened the package and emptied the two polythene bags onto his desk. Using the blunted end of his pen, he edged out the small note and read it before picking up the telephone to the state police laboratories.

Three days later, getting the warrant was a cakewalk. Judge Cipriano did not hesitate after reading the results of the chemical analysis. Twenty state troopers descended on the Kaplan cabin, and Elliot's home, while Harry went to the practice.

"You say the son of the woman who virtually owns the place is about to take over the dead man's law practice and has been growing cannabis at the same time? Why the hell would he need to do that?"

Sam announced they should now refocus on business.

"But this is business, Sam. What Bill is telling us is what he's putting into the script."

Fritz was still ranting on about how he liked to get involved with his investments when Bill interrupted him with a surprise.

"Oh, I almost forgot. Someone tampered with my car. I had a nasty somersault."

Sam was alarmed.

"*When?* Was it linked with the drugs find?"

Bill said that it had happened back in the winter and the police had gotten involved but it had gone nowhere.

Fritz, showing no sign of discomfort, asked how Bill knew it was tampering. Bill said it had been the garage owner who had spotted it.

"And who might that be?"

"Another character I have borrowed from. Ray Bellicaso."

On the way back to the office, Bill asked Sam if he could take a couple of months off before production started. Suitably primed by the lunch, Sam said yes. Of course, Bill could take a well-earned vacation.

After Fritz Gargano had left, Sam apologized for loading him onto Bill without notice, but Bill shrugged it off, his mood now conditioned by the thought of escape.

*

It was warm enough for Jesus to sit in the rocking chair on his small porch. His rented ground-floor apartment stood just off Main Street in the town ten miles from Broadacre. The busy narrow side street in front provided plenty of entertainment from passing cars and pedestrians.

His wife sat next to him. In front of them, their youngest daughter was crawling across the floor like a sea lion. Most of the surrounding houses were rented by Latinos from Puerto Rico, and they would regularly gather and play in the street to escape their doleful homes, especially during hot summer weekends. Sometimes the police would arrive and insist they leave the roadway free. It almost created a riot on each occasion.

He was waiting for his partner who lived half a mile away. She always walked over. Maria had been his wife when they first came to America, and until they got their green cards, but for the last fifteen years she lived with another man and between them they now had four children. A fifth had died last year. She had only been two years old, and they were still getting over it. The memories of following the tiny coffin and seeing it perched so timidly on its catafalque still flashed through Jesus's mind every day, even though the kid was not his own.

The death of Yolanda had still not been resolved. The south shore police had intimated that she had frequented dubious characters and places around there, but Jesus was far from persuaded that either had been responsible. She had been far from a slut. In fact, he was worried. Something told him that her death had been a message destined for himself and Maria, possibly a warning against taking on a third partner. It was as if someone was eying their business.

It had been a long time coming. He and Maria had brought it upon themselves with the tactics they had employed to get to where they were. They almost had a monopoly over in Broadacre, but they had never exploited it. Their rock-bottom prices were because of their customers, especially the richest of them, who would complain about being hard up. Many would quibble over the smallest invoice, conveniently forgetting that they were getting a bargain. Jesus and Maria complied in order to continue to work. They were never that hungry for extra money. Maria sometimes said that it was slavery. Jesus retorted each time that at least slaves had a job for life.

Jesus had always called the tunes. He had originated from a reasonably well-to-do family. His father, until he had been assassinated in the street in front of his office, had been the deputy police chief in their small and indigent eastern town an hour from the Texas border. There was talk of corruption and drug money like everywhere.

No-one was prepared to hire Jesus after that. He became a liability. All that was left for him to do was to escape across the border. People who had known joked about it. He used to play the pan flute at parties and marriages, and the joke went around that someone had bundled him across so that they would never have to hear him again.

His arrival in Texas had not started well. He stole a car and was stopped while taking shelter under a bridge during a hailstorm. Luckily the cop received an emergency call and had left abruptly, but Jesus was stopped a second time near Philadelphia for erratic driving after nearly falling asleep at the wheel. He was ordered to provide a urine sample. When they saw it was purple, they told him to leave, frightened that they would face liability for the rough treatment they had given him. Jesus had been saved by the blueberry cakes served at breakfast at the motel of the night before.

The further north he traveled, the more gringos he spotted cleaning the streets. He was unused to such sights but realized that this somehow spelled opportunity for himself. He arrived in New England and ditched the car and was joined by Maria soon after he had rented the same apartment in which she lived now. They found work with a man who gardened in Broadacre and broke away two years later to never look back. Gradually climbing higher up their hierarchy of needs for their own survival, they undercut their previous employer into extinction with their better and cheaper service.

Jesus thought about it. Perhaps it was this man's family who had taken its revenge on Yolanda.

Maria had still not arrived, but she was not yet late. Jesus wondered when to talk to her about his present worries, or whether to just keep quiet.

But Yolanda was only part of his concerns. While working at Anne Kaplan's, he had overheard a conversation about a new project that would bring hundreds of new properties to Broadacre. After initially thinking it would bring more opportunities to them, he now had second thoughts. Any substantial building project in Broadacre was bound to introduce competition, and someone could easily do to them what they had done to their old employer.

This was horticultural Darwinism. He had no choice. He had to speak to his partner so that they could decide a plan of defense.

*

A startled Peter Drake spilled his coffee over the table. He nervously straightened his hair as if in a febrile and craven trance before reading the article a second time. His lawyer was headed for prison when he needed him most. It was no longer greed. The twenty thousand dollars would get him out of debt.

He decided to call Elliot Kaplan. Elliot was too preoccupied to give it any serious thought on the spot. He apologized for the situation which he assured was bound to be sorted out in his favor and asked for his client's forbearance.

But Peter Drake was worried that Bill and Catherine would go public over the affair. He could be up for extortion and his reputation sullied.

Elliot tried to put him at ease.

"It may be considered gouging, but there's no risk of legal prosecution. Don't worry about it."

"I know that, Elliot. It's my reputation that I'm worried about."

Elliot slammed down the telephone.

Peter Drake knew he had to silence his neighbors in time. He had hoped that Elliot could dig up a little dirt to hold against Bill and Catherine. He left to consult his rabbi.

Siegel greeted him inside the synagogue and, noticing that he looked troubled, stepped down from his dais to talk to him in private.

"I know you too well, Peter."

And then, by chance, he asked what turned out to be the golden question.

"Neighbor problems, Peter?"

It had not been specifically intended. It was one of several standard formulae that Rabbi Siegel used with his parishioners in order to get them to open up.

"Well, as a matter of fact..."

He talked about Bill and Catherine and the shed problem.

"Is there any way I can help you?"

It could not have been a more convenient offer. Peter Drake asked Rabbi Siegel if he knew anything about his neighbors. The rabbi denied knowing anything but rumors.

Peter Drake had second thoughts. On his way home he realized he would get himself into a quagmire. He had to live in peace with his neighbors. He had to clear the air as quickly as possible and reach a compromise with Bill. To hell with the money!

It couldn't have been a more dramatic decision. He picked up the telephone and Catherine answered. He asked for Bill. She said he was out and offered for him to call back.

But Peter Drake had fatally put down the phone before saying who he was. Bill was just that minute entering the newspaper offices to show them Elliot Kaplan's letter.

*

Jesus finally spilled the beans to Maria while they were taking a break in Mary Dunne's garden. They were sitting on a bench overlooking a small pond and looking out to beyond the property. It was their favorite view.

Maria had also overheard about the new village. She asked what they should do.

"We have to fight it," he said.

Neither of them believed that the residents of Broadacre would want an addition to their beautiful town. But no-one other than Anne Kaplan or Mary Dunne had talked about the plan, as if it were still a secret.

Jesus and Maria said that their best chance would be to speak to some of their other customers as soon as possible.

"We're at the Villeneuves tomorrow."

"Let's start there," said Jesus.

19

Bill and Catherine held a dinner party before their departure on vacation. It turned out to be fun. Barbara soon showed how esoteric and interesting she was behind her rougher edges, but still presented herself in walking boots. One of her passions turned out to be Egyptian antiquities, and instead of bringing wine like the others she turned up with a scarab for Daniel.

Catherine noticed how Paul Rodier appeared distinctly disheveled and peevish when he and his dentist wife stood at the front door in the dark. It pushed her to ask how things were, but Paul said everything was just great.

"They probably left their house on fire," she whispered to Bill as she followed them in to the others. "They all say that."

She had been percipient, but she always said it. Bill took up the challenge and insisted. Paul eventually caved in and admitted that he had nearly not made it because of a threat from the Fire Chief.

Everyone stopped talking.

They all knew about the remodeling. It had turned out that someone had accidentally disconnected the telephone line reserved for the fire alarm, the alarm company had seen fit to tell the fire department first, and the Chief had turned up in his massive red four-by-four to confront Paul in person with a full-page warrant.

Paul had it with him. Josh Villeneuve read it out aloud. It threatened Paul with a ten thousand dollar fine or six months in jail if he left the premises before the line was reconnected.

"You can't imagine the language he used when he called the alarm company," Paul's wife said.

But Paul was serious and upset. His integrity had been insulted.

"The Chief lectured me on how many buildings were burned down in order to collect on insurance. Hell! I pay through the nose for his extortionate salary, and he insults me like that!"

While his fulminations persisted, Catherine caught herself edging up to the window to see if anyone was arriving outside.

Josh asked Bill how the business of the shed was going on.

"It's extortion!" Josh exclaimed.

"He's a parasite!" Barbara said.

"He's a troll!" Eli Mendelsohn said.

That sounded odd. Bill asked Eli what he had meant.

"I confront them all the time. In my case it's patents. They buy up them up solely to make money out of infringers. They are predators of the worst kind. It's all malarkey."

"I think you should do something about it," said Barbara to Bill. "People should know."

Josh said to speak directly to Peter Drake. Bill said he had already spoken to a reporter. That seemed to go down well with everyone.

"You'll be glad you're escaping from New to Old England," quipped Josh.

"And talking about local scandals, what about your Caterpillar?" Bill asked him.

Barbara laughed. She would have loved a toy like that. Josh said that he understood the Commission's point of view, but they were infringing on his rights.

"Have they replied yet?" asked Paul.

"I think I've successfully got them bamboozled," he said.

Emilia Villeneuve did not laugh. She found it all futile.

"Hey, Paul," Eli asked, "did you ever get to the bottom of that yellow-green smoke?"

Barbara volunteered that she had been held responsible for storing hazardous chemicals and not training her assistants. The Fire Chief could be in trouble for letting the incident slide.

"It's the chlorinated solvent that was the problem," she admitted. "It's dreadful stuff. It's not inflammable, but it gives one hell of a kick in the throat if you're smoking."

"Even more than those Stukas you smoke?" said Josh.

His mother's family had experienced them during the war.

"We have our air conditioning inlet up there on the roof," Paul said. "Had it been summer we'd have all been dead."

Paul and Barbara put their arms around each other and said they had made peace. It had been an honest oversight.

Eli recounted the story of a friend who had been experimenting with micronized opium for medical research and had opened a container near an air-conditioning vent in his hotel room. By the time he had closed the container it had been too late. The top layer of the extra fine powder had literally been sucked out, and he had run down into the restaurant downstairs terrified he would see everyone wobbling out of control.

The discussion moved on to a debate about air pollution in general. Catherine argued polluters should be made to pay. She scowled about the evils of the profit motive and obsession with growth.

"I don't think the profit motive drives most people," Eli argued. "It's usually only a small part of doing business. Most people are fighting for survival. That's what drives them. To avoid a downward curve inevitably means you must go upward, be obsessed with novelty. That's growth."

"Has anyone heard any news on the Attorney Hughes case?" asked Bill.

No-one had. Bill admitted he had spoken to Hughes about the cemetery building incident.

"It's guaranteed he would look," said Paul who knew him as well as anyone.

Bill could not hold back. He went over to his desk and pulled out Harry's state police photograph. Catherine was shocked that he had kept it from her, and annoyed that he was now betraying a confidence.

"Harry and I think Hughes was trying to pass a message. Any ideas?"

Paul wondered if they should take another look themselves. They should walk over there in the morning.

Josh asked Bill how his work was going. Bill talked about his visits to New York to meet a sinister backer who fitted his script better than anyone. As Bill pursued his story Eli looked uncomfortable. Then Bill came to the gold chain.

"You wouldn't be talking about a Fritz Gargano, by any chance?" Eli asked.

Bill stopped dead, embarrassed at his indiscretion, and then horrified that the ogre could be closer to home than he had imagined.

"You know him, Eli?"

"I met him a few times. I told him everything I knew about patent trolling, and he's made millions out of it. He's the prime example of what I was talking about."

Bill asked him what he knew about Gargano.

"A dangerous man. That's why I stayed out of it."

Bill asked how he had come to that conclusion.

"His daughter had been one of our interns for a while, but I only found out they were related afterwards. Turns out he had spent half his life in prison and was looking for a safer way to make money."

Bill was dumbfounded. Should he say anything to Sam and risk jeopardizing the project that kept him in such good employment?

But what Josh said next swept everything that had preceded it from their minds.

"Have you heard about the new village project?" he asked.

No-one had, just as he had expected. Without mentioning his source, Josh talked of a plot to convert a thousand acres owned by Anne Kaplan. The land lay right next to Broadacre, so the town would grow by half in one fell swoop.

"As I understand it," Josh said with a grim face, "it's part of a plan to convert Broadacre into a tawdry historical village infested by tourists."

He mentioned all the hotels. When everyone unanimously discounted the possibility of it ever happening, he stopped them dead in their tracks.

"That's why they expanded the Historical Commission," he warned them.

Bill guessed right away that Josh was talking about the land where the cabin stood but he said nothing.

*

The First Selectman declared the meeting open to one of the three television cameras that surrounded them. In a slow-paced declaration worthy of a Roosevelt fireside chat, he explained for the sake of any first-time audience that it was assisting a new age of democracy. Members of the Commission would discuss and vote entirely anonymously and after being randomly selected.

He solemnly asked the Town Clerk, the only other unmasked person there, to read out the minutes of their previous session and someone seconded them. Then he attacked the first item on the new agenda. It was the Caterpillar case. The six hooded members were brought up to speed, although Josh was not named. A windmill was unacceptable. This was a direct confrontation to their authority, they said. One of them said they should call the culprit in.

Anne, her voice electronically disguised and head covered just like the others, snapped back that the subject had probably already told many people about what he had done. He was in danger of playing to be a martyr.

"No," she declared, "the Commission has no choice but to come down hard on the person involved. We should give him a week to come up with something acceptable."

The First Selectman pointed out that a week was absurdly short for drawing up new plans. Anne conceded.

"Alright a month. But there should be a threat of prosecution if this person continues to pursue the same line."

They called in the Town Attorney who, like the other officials, appeared with his head uncovered. The lawyer looked neither happy nor enthusiastic about giving advice. He had already privately thought that the entire proceedings were barmy, and he intended to hand in his demission once the meeting was over.

His face changed once he spotted an opportunity to sow trouble.

"Of course, you should prosecute. Threaten him with a fine and a jail sentence."

The haphazard movements of the hooded heads seemed to show that they were surprised by his comments made so openly on television. Overlooking this, Anne felt he had provided their wishes on a plate and was not prepared to spoil the opportunity. She looked sternly towards the First Selectman.

"So, we are all agreed?" he asked.

And vocal answer came there none. Instead, each of the six hooded members silently nodded in agreement. The First Selectman resumed.

"We now have our second item on the agenda."

He looked over at the Town Clerk who glanced at his notes and tried to disguise his gulp of anticipation.

"The plan for the new model working village," he read.

The First Selectman cut him off.

"I would remind you that this represents a vital commercial venture intended to attract more visitors to our town."

"The increased tourism will bring benefits for everybody," the town Clerk said.

There was no discussion. It had already taken place off-camera just before the meeting. Each of the six firmly nodded. The matter was carried, and luckily for all those present, the broadcast would only go out the following day.

*

"Sam, this is Fritz."

He rarely called. Sam Rosenbaum was welcoming as usual and asked the reason for his call. Fritz Gargano descended into such an obdurate diatribe over the quality of the script he was receiving regularly that Sam knew that there had to be an ulterior motive.

"I guess you think little of our Englishman, Fritz."

Fritz complained about the credibility of the plot and each of the main characters, but he did not suggest any alternatives. Sam asked him to go into detail, but Fritz only retorted that he knew a bad script when he read one, and that his daughter had agreed. Sam coldly reminded him that their contract forbade him to show the script to anyone else.

"What do you want me to do, Fritz?" Sam asked.

The answer came without hesitation. Fritz insisted that Bill be sacked and sent home. He was so convinced of it he was prepared to meet all the expenses related to such an action.

Now Sam was convinced more than ever of his initial reaction, but he could not for the life of him imagine what Fritz's agenda might be. He told him that the other investors had said nothing, and that he personally, with his years of experience, was confident in Bill's work. Fritz was therefore in a minority of one.

Fritz threatened he would withdraw his investment. After Sam warned him what it would cost to break the contract, Fritz slammed down the phone.

*

Bill, Eli Mendelsohn, Josh Villeneuve and Paul Rodier met up at ten and walked towards the cemetery. They happened to be passing the drive that led to Peter

Drake's house, set far back. Josh reported nothing had yet appeared in the paper.

"Did anyone see the Commission meeting on television this morning?" Eli called out.

No-one else had. Even Josh had missed it, although he had expected his case to come up. Eli confirmed it had. He told them that the new village project had been confirmed and predicted that the town would have to raise a new tax to cover its expenses.

Peter Drake appeared in front of them by pure coincidence. He had been jogging from the cemetery. They each tried to figure out how to react to his presence.

"My friend Bill!"

Drake walked over and graciously shook Bill's hand. They all watched in astonishment. Drake's blatant hypocrisy tortured Bill, as it did the others, but he recognized that this might be a positive sign.

"Oh, Bill," Drake said, "can we talk sometime?"

Bill replied in the affirmative, without mentioning their impending departure.

Once the perfidious neighbor was out of hearing, Josh commented he must be petrified of destroying his reputation.

"You'd better call that reporter."

They arrived at the small cemetery building next to the road and tried the front door. It was firmly locked. They scouted around where Hughes had been found, and then Josh eyed the second door facing the cemetery. It opened up with no effort. The lock looked irreparably damaged, but the deformed door had wedged itself in place inside its frame. Bill admitted that neither the caretaker nor Harry had tried it.

They filed inside. Eli held the door open as the others fumbled around. The walls were smooth, there was nothing on the shelves, and the only other feature of note was a drain in the cobbled floor. Bill bent over and tugged on the grating, and it lifted, but there was nothing to see underneath except an empty pit that led to an evacuation pipe in the ground.

It was Winston's day at the cemetery, and from the other end he had spotted the four of them. When one of them opened the near door, he walked over. Paul recognized him as one of Barbara's assistants and introduced him to the others. Winston asked if they had the caretaker's permission.

"We're just looking."

Winston nervously glanced at the damaged lock but said nothing. He had already come to the dramatic conclusion that someone had helped himself to his cannabis.

Bill called Harry from his cellphone to tell him about the door. Winston discreetly retired to where he had been working. The last thing he needed was a second encounter with the cop.

The cruiser drew up fifteen minutes later. The caretaker stepped out from the passenger side and regretted not having tried the door the last time. Bill pointed out the drain. They said that if there had ever been anything hidden there, it would have been inside the drain.

Just as they were preparing to disperse, Harry turned to Paul and pulled him aside. He pulled out a sheet of paper and showed it to him. Paul was visibly upset.

"What's going on?" asked Josh.

Before Harry could reply that it was a private matter, Paul volunteered Harry had been on his way to arrest him for leaving his premises after the Fire Chief's visit.

"The man's saving face," accused Eli.

But Eli's gesture achieved nothing. Paul accompanied Harry back to the barracks, and the other three headed home, discussing between them what might happen to their friend.

Nearer to home, Bill walked on ahead. He was still agonizing over what Eli had said about Fritz Gargano, and whether he should tell Sam. Eli caught up with him.

"Bill. I'm good at recognizing patterns."

He was talking about the photograph. They went inside and Bill handed it over to him.

"Keep it to yourself, Eli. You promise?"

*

Winston stood there in the cemetery getting increasingly angry with himself. He had squandered the unexpected opportunity. The only good the whole affair had brought to him was that he had not had to tap into Rosa's stash for the meagre amount of cannabis he had originally planned to purchase.

But who had gotten to his hiding place? He wondered if someone had spotted him. Had it been the caretaker who had gone to check him out on his day off? Had Elliot Kaplan himself followed him there? Could he trust Rosa?

Yet again the entire world seemed against him. It was becoming a disaster. He was almost better off staying inside.

*

Josh Villeneuve called Bill in the evening. He had just seen the repeat broadcast and was furious. He knew he stood to get little sympathy for the Caterpillar, but the new historical village was out of the question. It was a boondoggle by people with time on their hands and nothing better to do, and they needed to protest right away. Bill said he was on board with the idea but regrettably he, Catherine and Daniel were flying in the morning.

Josh called Father Arnold and got permission for the church hall. He would call it a "Meat Meet" to attract hungry numbers and rouse them into an opposition.

Josh mobilized friends. Tom the builder eagerly drove up into the hills to bag what he could find, while Josh, Emilia and the others spent all day decorating the hall with posters. Josh planned to use the piano installed there to play Bill's aunt's music which everyone said could be altered into the perfect rousing anthem needed for their movement.

To drum up yet more support, Josh spent the entire day on his cellphone, juggling several calls at a time and driving everyone insane as they were repeatedly put on hold.

Mary Lou offered to be the group's lawyer. Tom printed off some posters to line the hall while Father Arnold looked on, delighted because it gave him an excuse to stay around without appearing to take sides.

The motley crowd started arriving early. The meat was already cooking over oil drums cut in two, perched on the lawn outside, and the smoke and odor had permeated the streets around. Randy the skunk catcher had provided three of his captives that he had skinned and gutted to disguise what they were. Tom ended up bagging a goose, two squirrels and an opossum, and Debra and Jack had caught three frogs near the pond. At least one family had gone looking for the hated Oswald for all the birds he had eaten and other cats he had attacked, but for once the tomcat was nowhere to be found.

Josh addressed the rambunctious audience of about a hundred.

"Back to nature! Everything is edible. If the Historical Commission wants to take us into the past, we'll do it better than they can!"

Inside, Josh played the piano to Emilia's singing while everyone ate, and afterwards he gave a screed from Hamlet that added to the general atmosphere, but no-one seemed to listen to. For the lesser highbrowed, Tom more successfully organized a spaghetti eating contest where knives were not allowed, and it was all followed by line dancing where spectators were encouraged to throw dollar bills beneath their feet. Because it was the church hall, everyone respectfully brought bottles and cans of beer and wine hidden in brown paper bags so that the statues and paintings all around, and Father Arnold for that matter, were spared the sight.

Finally, it came to speeches. Emilia, inebriated, addressed the confused audience.

"We don't kill bulls in Portugal, but we sure know how to immobilize them. It just needs enough of us."

Josh gave an electrifying and declamatory speech in which he explained how anyone who had ever been underemployed knew of its destructiveness. That was just how the Commission was behaving.

"Let's apply that same principle to democracy! Let's harness all the energy we apply to our individual interests and focus it on improving our life together!"

Everyone roared enough for him to be encouraged to go on. He lapped it up and responded.

"We have an intolerant and destructive force in front of us that masquerades as democracy. Let's take it on. Let's pool our talents together."

Barbara, sitting next to Mary Lou who was looking glamorous, stood up and said that if they all repeated enough what they wanted, eventually it had to become a reality inculcated into everyone's mind. Her speech sounded as slurred as its predecessors.

"This is *their* cynical take on democracy. They are compensating for their feeling of incompetence. We only hold the ball for a while. Let's now show them our game."

Everyone continued applauding, even though only she had understood exactly what she had meant. Josh summed up in a manner worthy of an orator.

"Never forget how much we all exist on a knife edge. Nuremburg, Kosovo, Rwanda; they could all happen here. Right now, the enemy is the Broadacre Historical Commission!"

After the rousing anthem, the crowd had dispersed. Across the road, Rabbi Siegel had been joined by Anne Kaplan. They watched people briskly heading home in the dark.

"I just wonder what lies were said in there," she said.

Siegel was angry at his over-munificent Catholic colleague. He considered he should support the entire community and not just one of its factions.

*

Mary Dunne was horrified when Anne Kaplan called her. She was even more disgusted when she heard that Father Arnold had so readily lent them the hall in the first place, but she stopped short of asking Anne to request the equivalent from Rabbi Siegel for retaliation.

Anne suggested the golf club for a meeting. It would keep out the riffraff.

"Some of us should stay in the shadows," advised Mary.

Anne privately swore at her friend and what she regarded as her cowardly warm weather tactics.

*

Channel Thirteen had deposited them on time at Kennedy. As they sat in the waiting lounge, Bill, Catherine and Daniel each reflected in their own way on their first year in America, blissfully ignorant of the latest stirrings in Broadacre.

"One thing we can agree on," said Bill, "is how exciting a year it has been."

The other two said nothing, but they agreed.

Little could any of them even imagine was what was about to happen during their absence.

20

Eli Mendelsohn's comfort zone was uncomfortable. For example, he was one of those unfortunate beings who always had to count and track the paving stones on which he trod, the fence posts he passed, the books he read, the petrol he consumed, the calories he absorbed or expelled, and the money he earned and spent, in other words every single quantifiable feature of his troubled life.

The arrival of his first computer, which he had naively expected would provide relief, had unsurprisingly only made it all worse. Now he had the power to crunch those numbers he so carefully collected. The blank screen with its ominous flashing DOS hyphen heralded fathomless power to make him become even more of a basket case than he already was.

He fully understood his infliction. He even called it his *cartesia*, his Sisyphean obsession that naturally led to a need for order. He could not go to bed unless his slippers had been precisely positioned for the next morning. He wore his watch in bed. He became irate if the mail did not arrive on time, or if meals were served outside schedule. Those meals that followed had to be back on time whatever his appetite. And so it went on for every facet of his existence.

But ironically, his obsession with schedules led him to distrust them, or more precisely to distrust his own or others' ability to respect them, and so he turned up for everything well before time, which was hardly in keeping with his philosophy.

He never voluntarily spoke to anyone about it, although his wife had caught on ever since their marriage. She had even confronted him over it. He blamed it all on his mother, who had never erred from her rigid routine for anything at all. He blamed it on his childhood schools that had colluded with his mother's ways. He imagined it came from the post-war environment in which he had grown up, the need to restore order from chaos. It had crept up on him in his teens. He remembered spending countless hours trying to link prime numbers, to discover patterns and trends from all his experiments at school and work, to dig, drill and map any data he unearthed.

Today was no different. It was early morning, and even his drive back from New York was the object of an experiment, one that he had been repeating for months already. Ignoring the honking cars behind him, he checked the speedometer. It had to be fifty-five.

He pulled up in front of the house, reached for the pad he kept in the glove box, and religiously noted the fuel consumption and outside temperature.

His mind turned to the upcoming Saturday soccer practice, and he smiled. He had to avoid watching sports like the plague but keeping busy by playing was a rare and welcome escape from his obsession.

As soon as he got through the door, the telephone rang, and his wife picked up. He overheard a female voice. His wife assumed it was one of his assistants and passed the receiver. Little could she suspect it was the secret apple of her husband's eye, Tanya Gargano. It was a rare call, and of course he counted every one of them.

"Eli, you remember me?" Tanya asked excitedly.

"Of course I do, Tanya."

Eli turned his back to his wife in order to hide his sultry glee. His wife left the room.

"It's my father," Tanya said. "I think he's up to something in Broadacre and I'm worried."

"Broadacre? Well, that's news to me, Tanya. Are you sure?"

"So, it isn't you?"

She almost sounded disappointed, or so he imagined. She insisted she had overheard her father talking about the town with one of his lieutenants.

Eli said he would find out more. Much as it made his day to have heard her sweet voice after so long and hurt him so much to sense her unrequited feelings, the news that Tanya's father was likely to be anywhere near his life again was little short of traumatic.

He decided to go and see Harry the trooper right away and give him the heads up.

Harry was circumspect. He had nothing to work on. The danger was undefined. Eli did not help by refusing to say where he had heard the rumor, claiming that his Long Island source was in permanent danger. Harry pulled up the federal data on Fritz on his screen, and saw who he was dealing with, but said nothing to Eli about it.

"Let me speak to New York," Harry offered, hoping that would placate his departing visitor.

He reached for the telephone and then hesitated. He needed those people. His ability to get their attention in the future would be compromised if they ever saw him as being too jumpy. Anyway, these types of affairs always became clearer with time if left alone.

Eli headed home certain that Harry would sit on it. He had to find out for himself. He had to detect a pattern. Why on earth would Fritz Gargano involve himself with Broadacre? The man was a monster. The reason had to be big. He dismissed the deaths, the drugs and the cemetery incident. They were all peccadillos for Fritz. There was only one thing that made sense. Gargano had to be involved in the new village project. It was the biggest thing around.

He remembered he had Bill's photograph. Those apparent signs Harry had asked about and that he intended to work on. Could there be a link? Could it lead to a clue?

He rushed upstairs and pulled the photograph out from his top drawer. This was what he lived for. He studied the random marks in the mud. He traced them onto a blank sheet of paper. But however he looked at them they made no sense at all.

He took out an eyeglass. At the extreme edge he spotted something that looked like a tiny flat pebble with patterns on it. Its remote position meant that the police photographer had either not spotted it or felt it relevant. Eli looked at it from different distances. It was out of focus. There appeared to be many colors. It could even be a distorted flag. He picked up the photograph and took it downstairs, covering the part that showed the body. He needed some lateral thinking.

Eli's wife didn't hesitate.

"It's a veteran's badge."

Eli kissed her and ran back upstairs. He called Hughes' secretary, whom he knew much better than the attorney's widow, and asked if he had ever worn a badge.

"Never, Eli. Why do you ask?"

He didn't have an answer to give her. He could never admit what he was up to. He feebly said that he had wondered if his attachment to the navy had ever led him to wear such a thing.

"The only veteran's badges I've seen of late," said Hughes' secretary, "were worn by two visitors who came here a few months ago."

Eli's face lit up as she described the two Gargano employees and their strange questions about Bill and Catherine's house. She recalled she had mentioned it to Hughes just afterwards.

"Did you mention the buttons, by any chance?"

She said it was exactly that she had meant. Eli thanked her and hung up, his mind buzzing. He thought about the implications of what he had learned. Hughes had called Bill just before he had the fall. Had he not already told Bill about the Gargano enquiries about the house? Had he spotted the badge on the ground and thought to call Bill on the spur of the moment before he forgot? An old man would have done just that. It didn't seem crazy, but he had no proof. If there was any evidence to be had it lay in the marks of the ground by Hughes' hand.

Tanya called in the morning and asked if he had discovered anything. He was in a predicament. The last thing in the world he wanted was to put her off.

"There's a grand new village project worth millions, Tanya. Maybe he's somehow involved."

Tanya reacted at once.

"I'm coming over. I'll call you when I'm at the hotel."

Eli slowly put down the receiver. He was shaking. He might have misled her, but he had never been so excited. While he impatiently waited for her call, he whiled away the hours trying to decide about what to say. He couldn't leave her empty handed.

By the time Tanya called in the evening, he had decided on showing her the photograph. It was all he had, and he would explain that there were no signs of a struggle. It would keep her guessing. They arranged to meet for breakfast.

Eli went to the hotel ahead of time and ordered pancakes which he drowned in maple syrup. His wife had always refused to make them, and he had been mulling them for hours. Tanya appeared looking ravishing and embraced him when he got up. She ordered the same to be followed by fried eggs. She didn't yet have to worry about her figure.

"Sunny side up," she said to the waitress.

They got down to business right away. She studied the photograph while he explained it. With no prompting she spotted the badge, declaring that it was familiar to her.

"He's been sending his men up here," she said.

Eli was not going to mention or challenge her about the marks in the mud. He wanted to keep that part to himself.

"But how could that relate to the village project you talked about, Eli?"

He admitted he had no idea yet. He had hoped she might fill the gap.

"I'm afraid, Eli, Dad has said nothing about this, so I have to be worried. But it would be worse to confront him without more."

Eli said that her father's interest might be innocuous, but it could spell complications for anyone who did not want the village, and that could lead to trouble.

"Thank you, Eli."

She put her hands across his and squeezed.

"Thanks to you my father had been behaving himself for years. I can't let him destroy both our lives."

She said she would call him. They finished with a second round of coffee poured by the waitress. Tanya picked up her overnight bag from the floor and carried it to the open sports car outside with Eli in tow. She embraced him once again and took off with a wave and a peer through her rear-view mirror. Eli sighed when he saw her hair in the wind created by her rapid acceleration, less than five seconds to sixty.

Their brief encounter had goaded him as intended. He returned home to continue working on the photograph. Against all the rules of objectivity, he decided to approach it with the assumption that it was indeed a message about Fritz Gargano destined for Bill. It was a risk worth taking.

He was at it all day long. The marks had to be words, but the lines did not seem to constitute letters or even parts of letters, or numbers for that matter. What might Hughes have wanted to say? *WARNING GARGANO AFTER VILLAGE. GARGANO WANTS IN ON VILLAGE. GARGANO DANGEROUS*, and so-on. At least one word needed to refer to Gargano, or perhaps *FRITZ*, or perhaps even *FG* or, more obscurely, *GA*, but when he tried to overlay any of these phrases over the marks nothing corresponded.

He thought of asking his wife, but by this time she was already fast asleep.

He worked through the night, but his ideas only became increasingly stupid. There were not that many marks in the mud that were discernible, which might rule out longer phrases. He thought of codes, but then Bill would have had to have known the key beforehand, which was unlikely. He sketched a map with Bill's house in position, but neither that gave a clue. He thought of puns, of synonyms, of rhymes.

First traces of daylight appeared through the blind in front of him. He had gone completely off course. The answer had to be much simpler, but he had exhausted himself and was wasting time. He went downstairs and turned on the television. It was an old war film. He turned off the sound so as not to wake his wife and promptly fell asleep next to the dog.

He woke up catching himself snoring, his head keeled backward over the rim of the couch. His wife had still not appeared. The film was still running. It was showing two cruisers and a submarine, they were sending messages…

Of course!

Hughes would have used Morse code. He went back upstairs and pulled up an alphabet on the computer screen. Nothing fit. Of course, it wouldn't! The marks were too elongated and went in all directions… Stupid again!

Then he thought of semaphore.

Eli's wife came down to breakfast to find her husband already there. He was dressed and smiling from one ear to the next, which was unusual for him, especially so early.

Eli explained his discovery. It was obvious now that he thought of it. The marks were scrapes and were not absolutely clear because of the circumstances, but an educated guess was possible now that he was on the right track. What Hughes had written, Eli announced, was *FGAFTERVI*. This was momentous, and it happened to be exactly what he had said to Tanya, although that part he did not mention.

Josh Villeneuve said he was free for an hour. Eli went over to test out his theory. Eli showed his traces over the photograph to prove his point.

"It's much worse than we ever imagined. Fritz Gargano is getting involved in the historical village affair. Attorney Hughes found out and tried to warn us."

Josh ended up agreeing with Eli's findings. He had already heard enough about Gargano to be worried. Of course, they could say nothing, but it meant that they now had to fight the project with everything they had.

What neither of them realized, not that it would turn out to matter, was that Eli had gotten the end of the message critically wrong. Hughes had indeed got out only two letters of the last word. But what Eli had found to be *VI* was in fact *YO*, whose semaphore positions would be very close for a man in the process of losing consciousness and the control of his finger. Hughes had instead been warning Bill that Gargano was after him.

*

Fritz Gargano became visceral. His voracious appetite had been whetted, but he had gotten nowhere in getting Bill sacked or bumped off. He decided to activate a plan which had been maturing in his mind for some time.

During his latest fruitless meeting with Sam, he had deviously persuaded him to lend him the Italian flying robot. After Sam mentioned that Bill and his family were about to leave for a few weeks, Fritz saw his chance. He called his old acquaintance Ray Bellicaso. After what Bill had told them, he considered Bellicaso owed him a favor.

"I had no idea, Fritz," the garage owner had sworn.

Gargano brushed it aside. It had led to nothing. Everything would be forgotten if Bellicaso could get layout plans of the Broadacre prison.

"You got a friend inside?" had asked the garage owner, become worried. "I've been straight for years, Fritz!"

Fritz had insisted and then got angry. Three days later a set of perfect drawings had arrived in the mail.

21

The second day of protests was nearing its end. Tailed by Harry the trooper with flashing lights, about fifty people had marched for both days around the center of Broadacre, alternately up and down North Street and South Street, around the Green, and a mile each eastward and westward. Many of the demonstrators carried Tom the builder's colorful placards designed by Barbara that displayed such emotive words as 'tyranny', 'fake democracy', 'corruption', and even 'KKK'. The inmates of the prison, situated as it was at the crossroads, had been provided with the most entertainment and some of them mooned their support in return.

"Puerile neophytes," had said Rabbi Siegel in an irate call to Anne Kaplan while spying on the procession through his hall window.

Members of the expanded Historical Commission kept in touch with each other but remained as yet unperturbed by any of this. Ignoring the complaints, and believing that any opposition would soon subside, they were due to convene just before dusk.

When the time came, they would follow the newly established procedure. The twelve candidates for the committee would arrive by the back door after parking in the unfenced lot behind. In the ground floor room used for municipal voting, they would go inside their separate cubicles and don their white capes and hoods before proceeding to a smaller room next door. Here straws would be drawn in order to select the six of them who would serve upstairs while their hooded colleagues remained below.

*

Maria the gardener had heard that Josh Villeneuve had become the Commission's first target, and she mentioned it to her partner Jesus. They were finishing up work in a garden just down the road, having been distracted each time the protestors paraded past and, when Josh came home, Jesus slipped out to see him. He said he imagined bad things about the Commission.

"They are carrying out a coup," he warned him. "Where I come from, we see that kind of thing all the time."

At first Josh was skeptical, but Jesus had already tipped him off about the new village and so he lent him an ear. When Jesus started talking about his and Maria's concerns, Josh realized he had gained a useful ally, someone who represented a special kind of unifying thread in the community. They talked about how they could launch what Josh called a counter-revolution and Jesus a revolution, and how to put the blame squarely on the other side.

After a brief space of time, Josh picked up his phone and called Barbara, Paul Rodier, Tom the builder, and Eli Mendelsohn, to come over right away to discuss an idea.

Emilia Villeneuve prepared something for them to consume. They talked about for how long the protest should be sustained. Josh warned that time was running out. They had to do something soon that would attract more interest from those who had not yet committed. Then he said what he and Jesus had just come up with.

"We must muscle in on tonight's Committee meeting."

There was total silence. It sounded violent. The others thought the idea unnecessarily confrontational and risky. They would be seen to be no better than extremists, and they would lose any claim to moral high ground.

Eli Mendelsohn was an exception. He wanted to find a way to ridicule the Commission meeting. After Paul Rodier jokingly suggested feeding nitrous oxide into the room, Eli reminded them of his friend and the micronized opium. They collectively brainstormed for a better solution on the same lines.

Josh Villeneuve grew impatient.

"Listen guys. You're either at the table or on the menu. You choose which."

Emilia brought in the food and drink. She had been listening to their discussion and said that it had to be subtle. In any case, she said, the whole point was that the meeting should still be broadcast so that people could see what was being tried on them. Publicity was their greatest arm. They would need to stir up more action once the broadcast had gone out in the morning.

"Not this time," said Tom. "The cable station has announced that it's going out live."

They said they should put the word around ahead of time to have people in the street. Jesus reminisced about the white hoods. They reminded him of Holy Week at home. It was while he was talking about it that Barbara lit up and spread her arms to be heard.

"I know what we need to do, but I'm dammed if I know how."

Everyone stopped talking to hear her through.

"No-one will know who is under those hoods. We need to infiltrate the committee to speak on television."

They cheered. They called her brilliant. But how could it be done?

"Remember what the Russians did to their writers, Napoleon did in Paris, and the Romans before him," warned Eli Mendelsohn, who was something of a history buff. "They used to exile people who gave them trouble."

No-one took any notice. Everyone had heard a little about how the committee was to convene. They went through the routine step by step. Although the six committee members were not known in advance, they would all recognize each other before they donned their hoods, but not afterwards. That was when a switch had to be made.

They discussed the voting room where they changed. Tom had built and installed the cubicles a long time ago and he described them and drew a layout. They were quite large. If someone could sneak into one of them beforehand, perhaps it would be possible to neutralize the arriving member and proceed to the next room without being detected.

Eli grinned with satisfaction. One project he was presently working on concerned a patent for noiseless duct tape. He already had samples at home.

"Give me a couple of minutes."

*

Twelve prospective committee members arrived at the town hall, locked their cars, and went into the voting room. The Town Clerk had already placed their gowns and hoods inside each of the cubicles.

Outside, the noise of the protestors had become infernal. The crowd had started using loudhailers hastily rounded up by Tom from the main town up the road.

Upstairs, the First Selectman was already at his place at the head of the table and wondering if they could ever hear themselves. A cameraman was checking his equipment for the last time.

Downstairs, in the voting room, the noise from outside completely drowned the brief scuffles inside three of the cubicles, followed by the deployment of special low-noise duct tape. Miraculously, no-one was alerted to the brief smell of ether.

A short while later, in the room next door, twelve anonymous figures dressed in white assembled in a line after drawing their numbers. The six with the highest numbers were directed upstairs.

*

In the descending dark, Fritz Gargano assembled fifteen of his closest accomplices, men he had known and served time with. On his lawn overlooking the Sound, he announced the plan. They were to drive up to Broadacre and arrive there after midnight. Fritz would personally oversee the entire operation. Gin Bottle was to lead the raid on the prison with the flying robot he had been practicing with all afternoon. Carmine would profit from the chaos from the prison to descend on Bill's and Catherine's property with a combination of military-grade metal detectors he had just laid his hands on, together with the Caterpillar they would steal from down the road.

Carmine reminded Fritz that there was no moon. How could they communicate in the dark?

Fritz had the answer.

"Establish a password."

Carmine said that two of the men stuttered.

"So, give some f***ing time before whacking them!"

Two hours later, the convoy rubbernecked across Throgs Neck Bridge to attract the least attention possible. In the trunks of the five cars was an assortment of shotguns, rifles, handguns with silencers, a couple of Uzis, plenty of stun grenades, along with the detectors and C4, courtesy of a last-minute raid on the nearby barracks belonging to the local National Guard. Behind the leading car was a stolen U-Haul trailer carrying the flying robot with its remote console equipped with a video monitor.

Fritz's plan was to get as many prisoners to escape as possible in order to create havoc and distract the few police who might be around. Gin Bottle was to first use the flying robot to cut the wires leading to the prison siren. Then he would direct it over the prison yard and drop the C4 charge in a narrow alley between the building and the outside wall. They had enough explosive to blow both simultaneously so that the inmates would have a free walk from their cells to the outside.

Carmine shoved his handkerchief into his mouth when they passed both MacDonalds without stopping. Fritz would have none of it. Gin Bottle, meanwhile, felt that he was the man of the day. He was supremely confident after all the branches and apples he had robotically removed all afternoon from the hated tree on Fritz's lawn.

"You know, Boss, this will be the first time a robot will do our work. Shouldn't we be worried for our future?"

Fritz was delighted to be consulted for his wisdom.

"Not at all, Gin Bottle. Robots need people to train and manage them. We will all become managers of robots. Call it intelligent crime."

Gin Bottle sat back and glanced at Carmine with satisfaction and pride.

*

They had pulled it off. Eli Mendelsohn and Barbara had made it into the committee meeting, but on the way, it had been a close shave and they had left Tom behind among those who had not been selected. As the other four hooded members of the committee settled in, they each discreetly tried to figure out the special devices in front of them that would disguise their voices.

The meeting got underway as the last time. After five minutes of introductory remarks, one of the hooded members raised their hand. The First Selectman invited them to speak.

"In view of the greater activity of the Historical Commission," the voice said, "the challenges of enforcement for the much greater area, and all the planning work we shall carry out regarding the new village, I propose an increase of local taxes to accommodate the expense."

The First Selectman was taken by surprise. This had not been on the agenda, and anyway it was council business, not the Commission's. As he prepared to intervene, the other five members moved their heads while they quietly deliberated between them. Just as he was about to speak, one of the other members loudly announced that they seconded the idea.

It was too late. He hoped it had not been Anne Kaplan. The cameras were there. The dramatic motion had been rendered public, and to make matters worse, the remaining hooded members of the committee were now nodding that they agreed.

The proposer suggested a vote, and that too was seconded by the same other member as before. The First Selectman looked in dismay as he saw the six hands raised in the air. This could spell disaster.

The six members of the committee who had remained downstairs filed over to the small coffee machine and helped themselves to donuts nearby. They drank and nibbled in silence, lifting the bottoms of their hoods to do so. As they each found a chair and sat down, some of them upped their wrists to check the time, thereby giving away their gender, if not a little more. Others, aware of this, contented themselves by looking up to the clock on the wall. Every room in America had its clock.

They sat there in silence for half an hour until they heard the scraping of chairs coming from the meeting room floor above them. One of them nodded it was time. As the first of them filed back into the voting room, they spotted the bound feet of three of their colleagues under the curtains of their cubicles.

There was an instant uproar. All semblance of secrecy was abandoned as they rushed in, threw their hoods to the ground and removed the curiously silent tape from the mouths and limbs of the three captives. One of them called Harry the trooper on his cellphone to alert him. In the commotion, none of them noticed Tom sneaking off through the back door as he tore off his cloak and hood and threw them to the ground.

As soon as she was released, Anne Kaplan angrily strode out to her car and called Mary Dunne before turning the ignition. Mary was horrified and then livid. Things were getting out of control. Negatives were trumping the positives. She imagined protestors invading her property and dragging her out into the street like Marie Antoinette. She said she would call her brother right away, straight after hiding her jewelry in the trash bin, a ruse she had learned from her impoverished mother.

Still in her white cloak, Anne released the park brake and tried to move out, but nothing happened. She checked she had properly put the car in gear. She tried again and accelerated, but the car stood frustratingly still. She had to get away.

The man in the next car seemed to have the same trouble. He got out and was first to see what had happened. He tapped on Anne's window and said that their cars had been lifted off the ground and placed on pedestals. It must have taken dozens of people to have pulled it off. Both cars weighed tons.

Anne thanked him and sat there for a while thinking about what to do. After the man left on foot, she did the same. She reached for the coat that she had left on the back seat. It moved. She screamed and turned her head. She was looking straight into the tail end of a skunk.

*

As the television crew packed up their gear, keen to get to base to report on what had happened during the meeting, the First Selectman looked down onto the street. There were hundreds of noisy protestors out there, more than ever before, and others were joining them from all directions.

A stone smashed the window just above his head. The remaining cameraman shrugged his shoulders and said that he did not have his floodlights to film the riot.

*

Eli Mendelsohn and Barbara caught up with Tom as he briskly headed to Josh Villeneuve's. The diversion created in the parking lot had allowed them to escape. Barbara uncharacteristically offered a high five.

"We did it!"

Tom congratulated them on hearing their news. When Josh opened his front door, everyone inside lifted their glasses. Emilia had taped the broadcast so that they could all watch together while they got drunk. The voice boxes turned out to be so effective that the others argued between them which hood had belonged to Eli or Barbara.

Josh was pouring another round of drinks when there was a knock on the door. Everyone stopped talking. Josh went over half expecting to see Harry and a few of his colleagues, so the others rushed to the kitchen to hide.

It was Jesus. He had decided to stay in the town center before joining them. He was grinning and had been ring leading the protests.

"It's a full riot. Everyone is out in the street and they're blocking all the main roads. The police have disappeared."

22

The red light on the emergency telephone flashed. The sound of the Governor's voice provoked an instant type-one reaction born of decades of training and forty postings around the world: Major General Eugene V. Borto stoically stood to attention.

The Governor sounded as though he had gone off the wall. It fell under Borto's definition of a hot situation, something for which his psychological immune system was prepared. While he hung onto his supreme confidence, the general's fortitude and experience told him what to do. The last crisis had been the tornado that had ravaged the small town next to Broadacre a few months back. The emergency plans they had used had been reviewed and updated during the torpid months that had followed. Those were the plans he would now put into action.

He ordered ten platoons of reservists to report to the barracks right away. He had the appropriate number of trucks started up and driven out onto the floodlit marshaling area.

They had to get to the trouble spot as fast as possible. It would take time for the men to jump into their fatigues and race from their homes scattered over at least fifteen miles. He glanced out of his second-floor window. National Guardsmen who had already been manning the base overnight scurried around. They piled provisions and equipment into the rear truck and drove into place the four Humvees that Borto and his staff would use to lead the convoy.

Borto knew the muster would take about an hour, and perhaps another hour to get to Broadacre. The plans included sending a firm signal to the town ahead of their arrival. A great believer in shock and awe, he initiated the second action on the itemized list before him.

Two Warthogs from the Air National Guard nearby were scrambled to fly over Broadacre and make as much noise as possible. A couple of armed helicopters would accompany the convoy itself and, shortly before its arrival, fly ahead to replace the fighters and gather the latest intelligence.

Borto moved to action number three, his very own idea. The rioters were certain to hamper his vehicles inside the town. They had probably already constructed barriers. He would therefore surprise them by substituting horses for Humvees once his troops were in place. Horses could cross fences, and private property, and jump over obstacles in the road. They would unsettle a population over-conditioned by vehicles. Horses would be unexpected and scare the citizens of Broadacre into compliance.

He grabbed the telephone and ordered equine transport to be ready to follow in the morning. The horses themselves were to be requisitioned from the surrounding farms that had already been lined up on a reserve list.

Finally, he called home and asked his eldest son to hook up his personal box to the family four-by-four and saddle up Bucephalus right away.

"And make sure those darned stirrups are not caught up again!" he ordered.

"Yessir!" replied Junior, praying he would be allowed to drive.

"And come over to the barracks as soon as you're done, Junior. Bring an overnight bag and tell your mother."

"*Yessir!*"

Beth, Borto's priceless factotum, briskly arrived with her somewhat obtuse husband who acted Second-in-Command. As she diligently prepared their coffee flasks, the two men went over what they already knew.

"Eugene, do you want your milk and sugar already in or separate?"

"I've got a hunch about this one," the general growled.

"General?"

"Beth, get me the State Police barracks at Broadacre."

The switchboard at the barracks patched through to Harry the trooper who was standing with a shotgun next to his cruiser in front of the prison. Borto advised him what was about to go down.

"What happened, Harry?" asked the Second-in-Command.

"General?" said Beth.

"Yes, put them both in, for Christ's sake!"

Borto glanced apologetically at her husband. Harry meanwhile informed them that an explosive charge had been detonated inside the prison wall three hours ago and that prisoners had escaped. They had even stolen the sheriff's van parked next to the post office.

"They have something small that flies," Harry said.

While they were still grasping to understand, Harry said he had gotten there half an hour later with four colleagues who had been on night call. The rioters had long gone home. The town was now quiet apart from strange noises about a quarter a mile south of them.

Harry was standing next to the Warden.

"Any idea why someone would want to do this, Warden?" asked Borto.

The Warden said he was mystified. There were no prisoners of serious value except for the wood-chipper doctor. For the time being, they were assuming there had to be a connection with the protests. The prisoners were probably hiding all over town.

"And those strange noises?"

"We don't know yet, General," said Harry. "We have our shotguns on the jail in case anyone inside is armed, but no-one is shooting right now."

Borto asked about the First Selectman, but Harry said he had not been answering his calls.

"Beth dear, get me the First Selectman at Broadacre," her husband asked after Harry was done.

She found the number and dialed. After about two dozen rings on the second attempt, a voice finally answered. Borto was abrupt.

"Who's that?"

"This is the First Selectman. Who are you?"

"Borto, National Guard! What's going on in your town? I've had orders to send in troops."

They overheard the First Selectman shuffle around and then his wife shaking him to come to his senses.

"*You* tell *me*, General!" he finally replied.

"A hundred escaped prisoners for a start!"

"A hundred! The entire prison! But there was no alarm."

"First Selectman, you'd better get your butt over to your office and call in your team. Make sure you're protected and pull up the emergency procedures, the new ones. We're in touch with the State Police."

"Harry?"

"Affirmative. He's outside the prison with four colleagues and the Warden and waiting for us. You'll hear our air support any minute now."

At that point Borto slammed down the telephone in disgust. Beth came back from the storeroom and handed them maps and more copies of the procedures, along with the coffee flasks discreetly laced with brandy.

"We have some brownies in the fridge," she said. "Shall I put them in your case?"

"Beth, you'd better come with us, Beth."

"But I'm not packed! I…"

"Honey," the Second-in-Command interrupted, "go back home and put together what you need for a few days. We'll be leaving in about half an hour."

She glared at him. He knew very well she needed much more time than that, and anyway she had to fetch the cat in. He relented.

"Alright, we'll think about all that tomorrow."

Borto got up and headed for the private bathroom that adjoined his wood-paneled office that only he, and Beth when he was away, could use. He locked the door and eyed himself in the large mirror that served before parades. His very short crewcut made sure that there was no loose hair to put back in place. The eyebrows that had grown bushier since he had turned sixty made him suitably fearsome. His prominent jaw still looked reasonably shaven since the morning, and anyway a bit of rough there would do no harm, and the fatigues he had just put on over his broad and muscular torso were well-ironed by Junior's mother. They made him look in full health and as ready as ever for action.

He only had to control the nervous tic he had developed of late, but no-one knew about that.

As he reached for the door handle, his self-aimed grin gave away that he fancied himself. He had always believed that he looked a bit like that handsome portrait he had seen at the Italian club in the main town near Broadacre.

He spread his hand and moved it across his skull, wondering if he should shave it just a little more to encourage even more resemblance to give his men and town of Broadacre a suspicion of *déja vu*. Then he got distracted by his missing finger, his only war wound from thirty years ago, and gave up the thought altogether. He would shake everybody's hands there instead. That scared.

Beth and her husband had disappeared down the corridor, also wood-paneled, by the time he re-entered his office. He had more precious minutes to himself. He mulled the upcoming thrills, marinated his thoughts before the grand mustering outside. His tic had predicated what might become his last hurrah, and by God he was going to live it to the full!

He thought about the reception he would get in Broadacre. Most of his fellow countrymen had a pathological hatred for anyone in authority and power. Their ardent anti-federalism would barely help a general from the National Guard, even if he was local. He would argue that he was there for the public good, but politicians had said that so many times before, over the heads of their electorate, that such an argument had long worn thin. His only recourse was to be seen to be fair, independent and tough. He could not afford to be afraid of smoothing or smothering feathers to get what was needed.

He had to resist the onslaught of influence peddling that would begin as soon as he put foot in the community. He had to put a brake on the opinion-makers who would conspire to spread inaccurate information to get their way. Opinions were free, but facts were priceless and needed to be controlled. He had to neuter the local press and people's means to produce leaflets. There would be no Russian *samizdat* under his rule. He would cut off the paper supply; he had already learned that one to his cost elsewhere.

And then there was idleness. It would bring evil. It would creep up on them after a few days. He had to keep everyone on their toes, especially his own forces. No-one could be allowed to make mistakes. They had to be forced to think before reacting. They had to search for what had not been thought of. They had to apply his beloved pre-mortems to predict why ideas might fail. Rather than being afraid of inaction, they had to take over Broadacre with their brains.

He was afraid of his own mistakes as much as anyone's. Everyone had to watch each other. Subordinates had metaphorically to sleep outside the doors of their superiors to think like them, understand their myopias, predict their errors and, especially with the higher ranks, grow to anticipate their wasteful petty schemes.

He knew everyone hated being told what to do, and that would include the citizens of Broadacre. People always preferred to act on their own. If he imposed himself too much on others, micromanaged or bullied them, they would soon develop the habit of telling him what he wanted to hear. He had no choice but to trust, delegate and hold accountable, and nurture their ambitions by keeping them in need.

He smiled to himself again. He loved every minute of the challenge, and his mission to Broadacre would be exemplary.

He went downstairs and outside to the muster area. Its axle-busting uneven slabs of concrete and potholes had needed attention for decades. Uniformed men continued to turn in from the main road and park in the secured lot next door.

Borto and his Second-in-Command took position side by side in the the leading Humvee. Beth diligently climbed aboard with her camouflaged backpack.

Reservists ran up and were handed their rifles and ammunition before clambering into their assigned trucks. Two Warthogs roared overhead, only just missing the tops of the trees. The platoon commanders each confirmed their troops present and accounted for and the convoy rolled. They accelerated past the lone sentry at the gate, distracted by the arrival of the helicopters overhead before being overcome by the cloud of stinking diesel fumes that emanated from the departing vehicles of war.

*

The distant explosion had woken Tom up. He was still lying there, trying to figure it out, when he thought he heard a digger start up nearby. He had to be hallucinating. It was the middle of the night. He leaped out of bed and rushed downstairs to the French windows to check. Mary Lou came running in and asked what was happening.

"They're shadows walking around outside Bill's and Catherine's," he said. "And a searchlight over by the potting shed."

He strained to make it all out.

"Isn't that Josh's Caterpillar?"

None of this made sense. Why so many people, and what were they up to?

Mary Lou remembered the binoculars and fetched them from the coat cupboard. She peered towards the light on the Caterpillar. The surrounding men seemed to walk around with...

"Metal detectors!"

"Something's wrong."

Tom grabbed his cellphone and dialed 911. The operator took the message and said she would send a cruiser right away.

*

Tom's call was intercepted by Borto's communications team in the second Humvee. With headlights blazing, the convoy headed along the main road that would take them directly to Broadacre. The helicopters reported that the route ahead was clear.

At the back of his leading Humvee, Borto was reading the map that Beth illuminated for him. He called out instructions over the radio to each of the platoon commanders. They would disperse at the last minute in order to approach the town from different directions. While two platoons would accompany him to the center of town and the prison, the rest would take up positions to form a ring around the outskirts. Arms, he ordered, could be used for semi-automatic warning shots, but under no circumstances were they to be aimed without a direct order.

*

It was totally dark. They were lying on the floor. Josh Villeneuve and his wife Emilia came too and felt their aches and pains at the same time. They had each been coshed, tied up and gagged, and as far as they could tell they had been locked inside the downstairs utility room.

Josh remembered what had happened. They had held him down and threatened Emilia if he did not hand over the keys to the Caterpillar. For some crazy reason he had thought that this was a coup arranged by the Historical Commission. For Emilia's sake he had given in straight away.

But why this?

He tried to sit up. He could not move. His sleeves were pinned down with nails longer than he had ever seen. This was like a horror movie.

*

There was a frantic knock at the door. Barbara had been in a deep sleep. She got up, put on her dressing gown and peered through the glass. For some reason she expected to see the long-missing pensioner from the old people's home. It was Winston instead, and he was in his prison uniform.

"What on earth...!"

"Barbara, please, let me in!"

She did so without hesitating. He said that the prison had been liberated, and he had run straight over.

"But you can't stay here. If it weren't for the way they were behaving yesterday, I should call the police."

Winston insisted. He had to stay out of sight. Barbara sighed, re-locked behind him, and led the way to the kitchen. She sorted out something to eat and a soda from the refrigerator and they talked standing up.

Winston described all that had happened at the prison. He was near the end of his sentence, and he now wanted to live locally with Rosa. He didn't want to put it all in jeopardy.

Between bouts of trying to encourage him to let her walk him back, Barbara explained everything that had been going on in town and what they had pulled off against Anne Kaplan and other members of the committee.

When he heard Anne's name Winston's ears pricked up.

"Rosa works for her. She's strange."

"Why do you say that, Winston?"

He had never intended to talk about it, but he thought that in offering information now she would feel bound to help him. He told her about the cannabis deal and how he had found the huge amount of money and noted the numbers before handing it over to Anne's son Elliot.

"And this key was meant for Anne Kaplan?"

Winston saw he was getting her on his side.

"All we need to do is to find out who reserved the post box."

Barbara asked where the key and envelope were. Winston said she should hike over to Rosa's in the morning and make a pretense on behalf of Winston to search under the car mat.

Barbara persuaded Winston to go back to the prison once she had collected the key and envelope.

"I'll drop off the key at the same time. The post office will never say to whom they had given it."

But Winston said to her to keep hold of it. Not that he knew why, it might somehow provide him with an opportunity for immunity.

*

Eli Mendelsohn had heard the Caterpillar at the back. Through his blind he saw it move towards the front of Josh Villeneuve's house. What was Josh up to? Could it be a protest?

He was about to go outside when he started to wonder whether Josh had lost it. Perhaps he had gotten drunk. He decided just to watch in the dark. The juggernaut awkwardly drove down South Street away from the center.

It was too early to call any of the neighbors. He thought of calling the police but instead decided to try to ascertain where it was headed.

The phone rang. He rushed back inside to grab it before it woke his wife. It was Barbara, who had spotted him moving around. She provided a running commentary. The Caterpillar had arrived in their street and slipped into Bill's and Catherine's garden.

"Should we call the police?" she asked.

They did not know if it was really Josh at the wheel. Perhaps he was doing something for Bill and Catherine while they were away and got impatient. Sometimes he was like that.

"Never at this time of night," said Barbara.

Then she asked if she had only imagined the explosion before the Caterpillar. Eli had had the television on. He couldn't sleep.

It was too early to go looking. There might be police on the streets after the riots. Eli said they should wait until daylight to find out.

*

The troops arrived via the different routes as planned. General Borto and his contingent crawled along the deserted road towards the prison. They could see ahead of them the flashing lights and headlights from the center of Broadacre.

They approached the cruisers. Harry the trooper and the others were standing behind them and the prison was lit up. Borto's Second-in-Command was the first to spot the dark breach and gasped. His instinct made him estimate the charge that had been used.

"We'll need that repaired," said Borto. "Get a builder in first thing."

They came to a full halt when Harry and the Warden stepped into their beam. Borto was the first to get out. He walked up to Harry and shook his hand before the others. After he had recovered from his miniscule reaction to the missing finger, Harry told him that nothing had happened for an hour, but they were concerned about the noise from down the road. People had called 911. Something strange was going on over there.

Borto confirmed they had intercepted the calls on the way. He looked around in the dark. He told his Second-in-Command to organize a couple of squads to investigate. He asked Beth to step out and said to her that her priority was to set up a headquarters.

The First Selectman said that all the buildings around were too small, and that the only suitable candidate close to the center would be the Catholic hall. Harry recalled that it had served for the protest meetings. It might symbolically be a terrible choice.

"What's that?"

Borto was pointing to the Jewish hall further down the road. He ordered twenty men and a lieutenant to accompany Beth and the First Selectman to go over there and clear inside. He turned to the First Selectman.

"Bring anything you need from your office. I think you should be there with us."

"What about getting into the hall, General?" asked Beth.

The First Selectman confirmed that Rabbi Siegel lived next to his hall. Borto ordered that, if he did not answer, the hall door should be broken in. He then turned to Harry and the Warden, and with several troops ahead of them they went to inspect the prison.

"Okay!" he said, "let's kick some ass!"

The noisy Warthogs flew off after their final simulated strafes, and the helicopters hovered into position to light up the prison from above.

*

Fritz Gargano now had all his men at Bill's and Catherine's, and the cars lined up at the ready. The Caterpillar was working out well. Five men were scanning ahead of it with their detectors, and others were prodding the ground as deep as they could with long steel rods. But so far, they were getting nowhere. It had been two and a half hours already.

"There's nothing here, Boss," reluctantly concluded Carmine.

Luckily for his lieutenant, Fritz had already come to the same conclusion. Short of destroying the house and its outbuildings, which made little sense because they had obviously been in place for decades longer than Lenny had been there, they thought they had covered almost every inch of ground around.

He was desperate. He wanted one last try. He told Carmine and Gin Bottle to round up the men and robot and head back home ahead of him. He would stay just a few more minutes with two detectors to check under the garage.

As one man pulled back the wire netting and crawled under the garage with a detector, Fritz watched the others return to their cars. One of them had served time with him in upstate New York. He considered him the meanest of the lot, even meaner than Carmine. But those times had been long ago. His old cellmate was hobbling along, stupidly negotiating his way with one foot on the sidewalk and the other the roadway. He felt sorry for him. They had both known better times.

All but one car quietly started up and drove off as Fritz and his two companions carried out their ultimate check. They were halfway through.

They heard boots coming down the road from the center. It was time to go. The man under the garage climbed out and Fritz hurled the detector as deep as he could underneath. They ran to the car and drove off just in time.

They turned onto the main road that headed south. They passed where they had tied up and concealed the sentries. Fritz was heaving a sigh of relief just as they ran straight into a roadblock. It was hopeless. The soldiers were aiming their rifles straight at them.

*

The Caterpillar had stopped, its light switched off, and the shadows had all disappeared. Despite the promise, no police car had turned up. Tom decided it was now safe to go and look. He got dressed and had the reaction of putting on his hard hat without really knowing why. Making sure that Mary Lou and the kids locked the door behind him, with the long flashlight in her hand for protection, he crept towards Bill's and Catherine's in the dark.

There was total quiet. He scanned the ground in front of him and headed towards where he had seen the outline of the Caterpillar. He saw a car drive away.

The Caterpillar was still warm. He turned to investigate the back further when several men in helmets jumped out of the shadows near the road and shouted for him to put his hands in the air. He ran. Suddenly, he fell into a pit that had not been there before.

*

They had searched the entire prison. The only prisoner left was the wood-chipper doctor who had decided not to profit from the breach. The Warden helped release the guards who had been tied up in one cell, and they went around together to assess the damage.

Harry let his colleagues return to the barracks while he headed towards Bill's and Catherine's to see what had happened. Troops were escorting Fritz Gargano and his remaining colleagues up the street. By the time he got to the house, Tom the builder had been hauled out of the hole and arrested. He tried to explain to Harry what had happened, but Borto's Second-in-Command insisted that he remain under arrest until they had sorted it all out.

As the Gargano escort disappeared out of view, Harry stayed to look around with the others. They turned on the Caterpillar searchlight. They saw all the massive holes in the ground and the rods lying nearby.

"Someone has been looking for something," said a lieutenant.

Harry could not believe what he saw. Bill and Catherine would be devastated. And why this? Most of the back yard had been littered with pits that went down at least six feet.

Tom said to everyone that Bill and Catherine were away, and that whoever it had been must have known it.

Harry wondered if they had been looking for bodies. Then he thought of Josh Villeneuve. It had to be his Caterpillar. But where was he?

They ran up the road and knocked on Josh's front door. The lieutenant discovered the back door unlocked, and they switched on the lights and went inside. Two minutes later they found Josh and Emilia pinned to the basement floor with twelve-inch nails through the arms and legs of their clothes.

23

General Borto held a breakfast meeting, and they looped in the Governor. His boss had beside him the heads of the state police and prison service and the State Attorney.

Borto said that he still did not know who they were up against. He described the situation as he understood it. The prison had been emptied of one hundred and three prisoners, with only one remaining who knew nothing, and there was no saying how many of the escapees were still hiding nearby. The National Guard helicopters were still periodically sweeping the town but would soon have to head back to refuel. It would be necessary for his troops to scour every one of the thousands of homes and the land all around, including the large wildlife sanctuary which provided plenty of places to hide.

"What's the bottom line, Eugene?" asked the Governor.

"It could take a week, Sir."

The general spelled out what had yet to be uncovered. Why had the prison been attacked? Was it linked to the street protests? Who were the ringleaders of those protests? Three known and armed criminals had been picked up trying to escape Broadacre but, so far, any connection had not been established.

They talked about the strange digging up of a garden not far from where they were, and the sequestration of the owner of the Caterpillar and his wife. Unknown persons had been obviously looking for something. Could it be buried bodies?

The Governor wondered aloud if the prison break been a diversion. Borto said he needed more time to establish that. What they knew, he said, was that the town had been on the edge of an insurrection that had needed to be quelled right away. The rest could follow.

"We have to lock down Broadacre," boomed the Governor over the speakerphone. "We have to stifle any form of resistance until we have figured it all out."

Borto said his troops should remain dispersed around the town perimeter to make sure no-one entered or left. He said they should cut off all communications to prevent organized opposition.

The Governor agreed. All internet, telephone, postal services had to be taken down, as well as any form of mobility. Any wireless communication other than military should be jammed. All members of the local press should be placed under house arrest under threat of being thrown in jail.

"The whole nine yards, Governor," said Borto. "We should stop all deliveries at the boundary line and bring them in ourselves," he said.

"Yes, General."

"We'll also have to remove potentially dangerous non-essentials like paper and ink."

"Huh?"

That suggestion surprised the Governor. Borto described some of his experiences with insurrections abroad.

"The first thing they'll try is to smuggle out messages and papers," he predicted. "We have to make the town perimeter airtight. We have to do that with people who are beyond any susceptibility to bribery."

Borto then reminded his audience of the protests. More civil unrest could be predicted, and for that his National Guard was best equipped in numbers to deal with it.

He did not mention the horses.

The Governor said Borto should stay in place and carry out all that he had mentioned. The state police commissioner said he would take responsibility for the countryside around, and Borto offered him his helicopters and additional troops that he could call up straight away.

"There's a civilian helicopter around here somewhere, and I'll use that for my needs," he announced.

The police commissioner asked if he needed any other help. Borto said he wanted to keep Harry and the team at the barracks.

Their final agreement was that, for the time to complete the task, Broadacre should remain under martial law and lockdown in order to give Borto the freedom and flexibility to act as he saw fit.

"We can't afford to fall behind the eight ball for one minute, Governor," said Borto. "We need to get this over and done with."

Their groupthink successfully consolidated, they tackled the question of how to present all this to the outside world. The Governor believed the less said the better. For the time being it should all be put down to an unspecified security alert.

"If we give a specific reason for it," he said, "we'll be soon outnumbered by experts."

*

Carmine, Gin Bottle and the surviving crew arrived back on Long Island well after sunrise. As they stepped out of their cars, they looked despondent and exhausted. It had been a tense night for no reward, and to make matters worse they had failed to stop at Macdonald's on the way back.

Carmine ordered the men to take their weapons and head home. He gestured to Gin Bottle to unhook the flying robot and bring the remaining metal detectors inside.

Two hours later, there was still no sign of Fritz. Carmine became seriously worried, but he knew not to call his boss's cellphone.

"Get rid of the detectors, quick!"

Gin Bottle looked concerned.

"Carmine, what about the robot?"

That looked more legit. Carmine decided to hang on to it until Fritz resurfaced.

*

Harry the trooper recognized Winston when he arrived at the barracks with Barbara. He made a negative comment about him just as Barbara was on the way out alone, but she turned around and angrily swore that Winston was far better than he thought.

"He's given himself up, for crying out loud, Harry!"

She soon got home after that. She had Winston's key but there was nothing she could do with it right then. She studied the card from the envelope. It was unmarked except for the anonymous handwriting. If she could get someone to recognize to whom it belonged…

*

The following morning, five military grade metal detectors appeared for sale on the internet. They caught the attention of the FBI, fully up to speed over what had happened at Broadacre, let alone at the National Guard barracks a short drive from the Gargano residence.

The head of New York headquarters called General Borto to make sure that they were onto something useful. He told the general that he would send in an undercover buyer and keep him informed.

24

It had been a week already. Time had flown, and life along with it. Normality had disappeared from Broadacre, and the once cheerful town had become forlorn, even dystopian, way beyond recognition.

The state of emergency and martial law had brought an immediate end to the protests, and the citizens of Broadacre had soon become inured. To all extents and purposes confined to their homes, they were nevertheless taking their occupiers' invidious behavior in their stride.

Any goings on in town had frittered away to a trickle, mostly of patrolling troops on horseback. The men were new to it, and so General Borto organized daily training exercises close to the pond. Junior would watch in envy as the horsemen practiced encircling groups of faux protesters in a pattern that was eerily reminiscent of the geese learning to fly only a few months before.

The pond itself was one of the first casualties of the unwelcome invasion. Noise from hooves on the tarmacadam had scared and scattered its population. Even the nighttime fireflies had fled. During the daytime, traumatized frogs were being trampled on by the hundreds as they escaped. The only two fishermen, a pair of American Indians nobody had seen before, leftovers from the fevered spring, had soon given up. They had been replaced by half a dozen inmates from the old people's home, allowed to watch the equine spectacle from their wheelchairs, aside their saintly nurses.

With so many troops around imposing their controls and curfews, the general ambience was first of wait-and-see. As the people of Broadacre confined themselves to their homes, the only activity that seemed to attract their attention, and provoke the occasional flutter of window blinds, was that of the passing horse patrols, more and more experienced, and flaunting their presence.

Time had receded hundreds of years as civilian cars and wheels of any form remained banned. Apart from the sound of hooves, the clatter of paraphernalia strapped to saddles constituted practically the only sound of the street. Quite by chance, Mary Dunne and Anne Kaplan had gotten what they had wanted.

General Borto had immediately imposed his rule of law. He ordered that anyone who had been in any sort of trouble before his arrival be rounded up and placed in the prison that had been repaired by its latest occupant, poor Tom the builder.

"And the lawyers can stick their habeas corpuses up you know where," Borto had uncouthly declared to a Judge Cipriano rendered timid for the first time in his long career.

To emphasize his point, the General waved in front of the Judge's nose the Governor's outrageous orders. In fact, it was unnecessary. There were no lawyers left in Broadacre. No-one had been allowed in, Mary Lou did not practice, and Elliot's budding career had already been brought to an abrupt end.

After General Borto's Second-in-Command discovered the hoods and cloaks in the basement of the town hall and unearthed the weird truth about the Historical Commission that had kicked off the fiasco in the first place, his commanding officer went ballistic. In a flurry of activity that followed a long session between Harry the trooper, Borto and the Judge, there followed a succession of rapid and mendacious hearings presided by Judge Cipriano and an ad hoc military jury. Tom the builder, Winston, the wood-chipper doctor, together with Fritz Gargano and his two men, found themselves joined in prison by Elliot and Susan for their drug offences, Peter Drake for attempted extortion, Barbara for safety and environmental contraventions, Paul Rodier for leaving his premises without permission from the Fire Chief, and Josh Villeneuve for keeping the Caterpillar in his garden against community rules.

For good measure, the prisoners were joined by Harry's colleague who had cheated on her medical insurance and had just carelessly returned to Broadacre. If nothing else, what little remained of her professional instincts could be exploited to keep an eye on her fellow inmates.

All escaped prisoners who had so far been rounded up were whisked off to prisons elsewhere in order to leave Broadacre menacingly free for locals. The community understood perfectly well what was going on. The citizens of Broadacre avoided pronouncing themselves in public or in private whose side they were on.

As for the onetime protestors still free, Tom's Mary Lou, Emilia Villeneuve and Eli Mendelsohn, together with gardeners Jesus and Maria, who took up residence with Emilia for the duration, all felt they should somehow continue to resist with what little means they had. Jesus was outraged more than any of them. Broadacre had in effect transposed itself to a part of the world he thought he had long escaped.

The only safe way to communicate was by face to face. The Villeneuve home became a daily stopover in order to catch up with events and share news. The small clan was gravely concerned about the declivity their town was being exposed to.

The first significant stirrings, however, came from elsewhere. One morning, Father Arnold turned up at General Borto's headquarters. He announced that after Sunday Mass he had been approached by angry residents complaining about the behavior of the mounted troops. Not only did the cavalry behave roughly, but they also disrespected private property, and no-one had been assigned to clean up the accumulating mess left behind by the horses. It had prevented people from going outside.

Borto wisely didn't mention that Tom the builder, trying to find favor with his jailers, had volunteered his snow thrower in order to disperse the foul odor even more to discourage people going out into the streets. Father Arnold reported that some residents, who needed to visit their relatives in the old people's home, had been beaten back by the smell.

"I don't know what you're feeding your horses, General, but the heat and humidity are making it worse. Much worse."

Borto tactfully listened and said that he would look into it.

"Perhaps we could put down wintergreen oil."

Father Arnold detected insincerity in the general's answer. He realized the smell was intentional and trying to mask it with something else, especially as pungent, would only make things worse.

As soon as the priest had left, Borto called the Governor to suggest that religious gatherings be banned as well, but the Governor was mercifully not available.

Once he was alone with his favored bourbon that evening, General Borto thought about it again. He had always been a devout churchgoer, and this spelled the first sign of serious revolt. He had already made sure that his spies, informers and hidden mics and cameras covered any gatherings in places like the church halls, schools and supermarkets, but in all truth, he had least expected representation from a priest, especially a Catholic one. He was well aware of what Father Arnold was talking about. The excessive patrol activity had been of his own making. He had to kill any gangrene that threatened his authority and, just as important, he also had to keep his men busy. Nothing would be more dangerous than under-occupied occupiers sinking into bad ways, distractions, subgroups and corruption induced by boredom. He knew that times of slack would become his worst enemy.

He had a thought. Perhaps the timely stirrings among the locals would suite his purpose. He decided to challenge his teams more than ever, step measures up a notch. In the morning, he would give his lieutenants task checklists and grill them enough to make sure that none of them got away with or allowed cursory checkoffs. Each street would have to be regularly and frequently scoured, unauthorized assemblies, of course, dispersed, premises searched, people stopped, frisked and questioned, and during all those efforts escaped prisoners continually looked for. But he would stop short of closing the churches after all. Perhaps even the contrary.

He knew he could only press so far. If he encouraged too much of an informant economy among the citizens of Broadacre, history told him that people would invent plots simply to be paid off. Conspiracy theories would abound, *agents provocateurs* would end up reporting on each other, and 'approvers' would even organize crimes in order to report on them to gain reward money.

In the end, he was confronted by the need for a delicate balance that he would have to fine tune every single day. All it would take would be a single sign of weakness, one critical mistake. If he allowed too much freedom, he stood to lose control. Even if he managed to keep the locals under control, outsiders might find ingenious ways of sneaking across his lines and spreading an entire gamut of revolutionary ideas and propaganda. They could capitalize on what had already stirred up trouble. Lies would be spread. People might even be encouraged to suspect that a secret clique had gained control of Broadacre for its own ends. That would spell disaster.

Borto took another swig of bourbon. He had to be constructive, to resurrect some vitality in the community. The people of Broadacre needed to prefer the present to what had gone before, to be encouraged to remain optimistic and no longer have something to hide, discouraged from looking for new challenges that might end up boomeranging back at the overall stability of the community and his authority.

He took yet another swig. He had to provide example. If he ever allowed his own morale and appearance to degrade, the worse others' failings would have to become for him to notice. He had learned that before. It was called Weber's Law.

He remembered once hearing that submariners became cross-eyed after months in a confined space. They could not drive until their eyesight had corrected itself enough to gage longer distances. He had to avoid myopia. One thing he could do would be to allow in selected individuals from outside. It would be gradual. They would be vetted to be sure that they were harmless. Father Arnold would not get what he had argued for, but he and the citizens of Broadacre would find themselves confronted with a torrent of initiatives to keep their minds occupied.

It had been a productive session. Major General Borto fell asleep in his chair.

*

It was mid-morning and sunny outside. Rabbi Siegel zestfully entered General Borto's office. He had the General's new list in his hands, the proposals for compulsory communal activities, the daily exercises on the green, the twice weekly soccer practice for everyone under sixty, and the afternoon reading groups in the library, the daily lectures in the church halls by experts on whales, spiders, horticulture, travel and music.

He found Borto an amiable person and was drawn to some of what he was doing. Borto had regained any confidence he might have lost through his slight hangover from the previous night's excesses.

"They'll comply. There's nothing like the threat of a Dickensian prison to make them comply."

"Let those people out of prison, General. It does us no good to think of our friends locked up so close to us. The place is a horror."

Borto firmly believed that he had set a good example to others who might contemplate wrongdoing or stirring up trouble. Time would work for him, he argued.

The rabbi asked what he meant and Borto grinned.

"Scientists have discovered that a population's IQs increases every year, Rabbi. If I keep them there long enough, they will come to their senses."

"Or gained a high enough IQ to allow their execution," retorted the rabbi, clearly appalled at Borto's frivolity.

"I'm afraid of suicides," he said. "These people are not used to this kind of humiliation. They are good Americans. They're more used to congratulating themselves than being oppressed."

Borto ignored him and turned his back so that the rabbi would take the hint and leave. He looked out of the window with his hands firmly clasped behind his back like another of his heroes. After Seigel didn't budge, he said he was thinking of adding religious attendance to the list of compulsory activities for the residents of Broadacre.

The rabbi pretended to be deeply shocked.

"That's going back over 400 years, General! Father Arnold will tell you that."

Secretly, he thought it was not such a bad idea after all. It might put an end to the general decline he so abhorred.

Borto had already done his thinking for the day. After the rabbi had finally left, he went around to visit the Warden to ask him his opinion on the danger of suicides. The Warden preferred not to commit himself, and instead leave the entire responsibility to Borto and the Judge.

"Listen, Warden," Borto said, "we can't afford any adverse publicity. It will fall on you personally."

Since the Warden was clearly not about to take any initiative, Borto returned to his headquarters and issued an order that, in the event of a prison suicide, the inmate should be discovered with a photograph of a secret amour among his or her belongings. It would at least help to obscure the true reason.

Then there was something else he had just read. He ordered the daily administration of pain killers to all the prisoners, as he had just read that they reduced depression.

*

Harry the trooper went around to Bill's and Catherine's several times to figure out why their garden had been raided. He still did not believe Tom the builder had anything to do with it, and the debriefing of Josh and Emilia Villeneuve had yielded nothing. He had talked about it to General Borto.

"They were there with metal detectors," the general said, "so it wasn't for bodies."

And then he gave him the news from the FBI. Soon they would know more.

*

From her prison cell, Barbara tried to think of a way of finding out more about Winston's intrigue. They were exercising in separated yards and could talk across the wire barrier common to both sides.

"Father Arnold," Winston said when she beckoned him over. "Ask to see Father Arnold."

Back in her cell she called the guard and asked to be allowed to have confession on Saturday.

It was more than a little strange for those who knew her, the priest as much as any, as she had never been to church in her entire life.

*

About fifty people from all parts of town tiptoed their way to the church hall by crossing gardens in the dark. Each time they heard horses they ducked behind hedges or trees.

Father Arnold had taped the hall curtains and removed two hidden microphones, and he now stood by the back door of a blackened hallway to greet them. While others continued to arrive in the distance, the first of them cheerfully gathered in a circle inside the lit-up hall. They compared how they had caught on to the hidden messages the priest had given them during their previous Saturday's confessions, and repeated in a coded manner during his sermon at Mass.

The atmosphere was excited.

Father Arnold studied the assembled congregation. There were many newcomers. People were dressed more extravagantly than before, covered in multi-colored fripperies, a sure sign of insurgence. He wondered why people dressed up when in revolt.

"After all those decades of books and films of spies and revolution," one of them said, talking about their decision to attend the secret meeting, "we still do not know where to turn."

Someone announced that General Borto's Rough Riders had now cruelly taken to patrolling the pond in order to preventing fishing. People were in danger of going hungry.

There was an uproar. Father Arnold quieted them down with a spread of his arms in holy configuration to talk about arrangements. He assured them he had bolted all the doors. If ever they got a surprise visit, he would put out the lights and everyone should wait for instructions for escape.

They discussed how the troops were behaving and the things that were being forced upon them. All communications had been cut, even down to paper supplies. Enough was enough. They had to get back their town, warts and all.

They turned to tactics. They had to scare off the horses or create confusion among the troops or at their headquarters. One hard-liner crassly suggested deploying Barbara's yellow-green smoke that had become public knowledge due to Broadacre's onetime press. Mary Lou reported they had quite a few fireworks leftover and could set them off around town when patrols passed by.

At that point a scraggly figure in the back row stood up. It was Randy the skunk catcher, already become a hero for what he had done to Anne Kaplan. He did not even have to make his suggestion.

Father Arnold thanked them all for coming but insisted that they had yet to find a serious and viable idea. He asked everyone to keep thinking and said they should have another meeting in three days' time.

*

Father Arnold had only one appointment at the prison that morning. Given the crop of new inmates, it was not surprising at this early stage, and he was confident it would soon change.

The guard entered the room with Barbara and removed her restraints before closing the door behind him. Barbara asked if it was safe to talk. After getting over his surprise at seeing her, the priest assured her that a recent high court hearing had reiterated that they could not tape conversations, and even if the martial law allowed such things, they would not have yet had time to install equipment.

"I think we're safe, Barbara."

Her almost innate anti-clericalism meant that she first needed to know how much he could be trusted. Sure, he had lent the church hall for the protest and had been there during the meeting, but whose side was he really on?

They talked about the situation, the abuse by the Historical Commission, the protests, and now the unpardonable actions of the military authority that had been forced upon them. Father Arnold solemnly and cautiously replied that his position was supposed to be to represent his flock, which undoubtedly found itself split between the two sides of the affair. Barbara quizzed him what he felt personally, and the priest let go enough for her to understand that he was firmly for the protestors.

"Had it not been for the roughshod behavior of the Commission, we wouldn't be here."

25

Randy the skunk catcher was stinking of skunk, but this time of the herbaceous kind. It was his only way to mask the omnipresent smell of horseshit in the street. As he staggered along and auto-fumigated the sidewalk next to the redundant newspaper store, the fire-breathing unicorns cantering towards him appeared to whip the rare passersby with their swinging tails.

And he was right in their line.

He needed to escape, perhaps across the road to in front of the prison. As he squelched across, he spotted the row of faces peering at him through the barred widows that had been closed to keep out the smell. He mocked them with a raised finger of defiance. He was free, and he was high.

He turned back. He would brave the approaching unicorns and show them. Opposite, his demonstration had had no effect at all. The expressions on the prisoners' faces remained lifeless. The only thing that moved was the horizontal line of windows, with a gentle ripple.

Another posse of panting unicorns charged right in front of him. They had come from behind, almost causing him to lose balance. The riders were spreading their legs as if on Choppers, and they screamed themselves onwards.

Man, this was fun!

*

Eli Mendelsohn had always been disinclined to walk around town because of all the paving stones, railings and sea of faces that he was always compelled to count. But for once people had become scarce, the stones were more freely negotiated, and he had brought along the dog to calm himself down.

He had been losing weight and was still getting used to his shoes feeling looser on his feet. His sense of disorientation had become accentuated by a new pair of glasses that made him feel taller. At least these small contretemps were distracting him from his usual paranoia.

He spotted Randy ahead and slowed down. He watched him swaying erratically while trying to negotiate the corner in front of the store. And why was he shouting at the prison opposite?

He felt more like a stranger there than ever. He tried in vain to blank his mind. He tried to recall the cognitive behavior sessions that his New York psychoanalyst had put him through. His mind only got more out of control.

The awful smell had to be doing something to his brain. Perhaps that was why Randy was behaving weirdly. Everything and everyone around him looked strange. Besides Randy and the uniformed patrols riding up and down the street, even the few other pedestrians seemed from elsewhere. Broadacre had been invaded by strange outsiders. What was the General up to?

Without mentioning Winston's name, she told him she had uncovered something important that needed to be investigated, something that involved Anne Kaplan and an unknown benefactor who had secretly passed her a large sum of money.

"Father, we need to find out who this secret benefactor is and why the money was handed over."

"What would that change?"

When she said it might prove corruption that had led to their predicament, Father Arnold was eagerly on board. By the time Barbara had said that the money had ended up in Elliot Kaplan's hands for a drug deal, he was begging her to assist.

This was no good. He had to get home.

He recognized the Japanese family who owned the restaurant in the main town. What were they doing there? How had they got through? They were wearing face masks to keep out the smell as they always did back home.

Beyond the Japanese, he spotted the woman with a bucket on her head. Surely a bucket would not keep out the smell. Why had they all been let in to Broadacre?

The place looked different as well, even oppressive. Panels had been erected at hundred-yard intervals across the center of town with a large portrait of their supposed savior superciliously mounted on Bucephalus. They made Eli shiver with paranoia. They reinforced his long-held suspicion that most of his neighbors had at one time or another been spies in their life. This was the new nineteen eighty-four, a decade-and-a-bit later. Now they had blatant dictatorship but, worst of all, he had become condemned to count each of the scary signs as he passed them by.

His dog sniffed every single doorway they passed. Eli became afraid of being noticed, of been singled out, and turned around to head for home. His dog, having already sniffed out the route they were taking, impatiently pulled him along.

He heard a buzzing noise and looked up. The spies were in the sky as well. He spotted the general's commandeered helicopter hovering over the next street for a minute, and then pull away in his direction. It crossed directly overhead and swerved dangerously in order to avoid a flock of geese flying in a much more orderly fashion.

Eli had had enough. Something had to be done about it all, and he would say so at the next meeting.

*

Rabbi Siegel returned inside for a breath of fresh air. He thought that perhaps it was all a big mistake. He had lost his hall and therefore the wherewithal to hold his religious education sessions, not to mention the all-important bingo fundraisers. But he was not about to ask any of his Christian colleagues to help him out.

He heard horses outside once again. Each time he looked out there was hardly anybody on foot. The effect of the twice-daily demonstrations of power by the general on Bucephalus had already worn off and drew nobody. The helicopter too had become a footnote.

He saw that General Borto's attempts to revive the town spirit were dismally failing. No-one wanted to be one of his guinea pigs for social resuscitation, or puppets for his ideas, and the attendance at each of his other events had plummeted from their initial mediocre levels. This general only knew how to corral his own underlings and had misread the spirit of defiance and enterprise of the people of Broadacre. Something had to be done to put things right.

*

Mary Lou arrived on foot to buy provisions. She resented the stink like everyone else, but she resented even more the lack of attention she had usually enjoyed when times had been normal. Her only hope had become that Tom was desirously watching her wiggles from one of the windows opposite. She missed his attention more than anything.

She bumped into Emilia Villeneuve, with Jesus and Maria the gardeners. Emilia asked her if she felt bereaved. She heaved a telling sigh, and they all separated in their lugubrious states.

*

Anne Kaplan stayed at home as much as possible. Although she was not put off by the smell of horses, even as bad as this, she had no reason to go into the center of Broadacre. Rosa went on foot for her instead. The eternally proud Anne was also suffering the humiliation of having her son and daughter-in-law imprisoned in the middle of town. It made it impossible to contemplate running into anyone she knew out in the uncontrollable open.

She remained positive, however, about what was happening to the town. She believed that good would come, and this she shared with Mary Dunne in their occasional guarded séances that lasted hours, and during which both spoke at the same time.

She had, however, twice called on her son Elliot since his incarceration, but only recently. She told him that the twins were fine with Rosa. Susan seemed to hold out as well as expected. General Borto, Anne reassured him, couldn't go on forever, and eventually lawyers would be allowed back in.

Elliot apologized to his mother for letting her down. Anne did not want to hear it. In her world one had to uphold one's own actions, however despicable. She felt her son was belittling himself.

"Don't you dare say any of that in front of the judge!"

Anne had had one recent conversation with Rabbi Siegel. He had sounded as disillusioned as her son. She realized Mary had become the only person in her world who seemed to stand ground.

How mediocre other people were.

*

BAD DAYS IN BROADACRE

Tom the builder woke up forgetting for an instant where he was. The prison coffee had oddly sent him into a deep sleep, and his arm muscles felt strangely tense or relaxed, he did not know which. Perhaps it was not the coffee either. It could have been his energetic plastering of the canteen the Warden had put him on the day before.

He sat up and looked outside and saw both Randy and Eli Mendelsohn make their separate ways, and the helicopter above them make its escape. He thought back to the days when Broadacre had been free. He thought about Mary Lou and prayed that she could visit him again that afternoon with the kids.

The patrols were intensifying. He and the others had been counting them and making bets which Barbara nearly always won since Eli Mendelsohn, who mastered such predictions, was not among them. The authorities had to fear something. He only hoped that his friends were right.

He leaned over to see if Josh Villeneuve was awake on the lower bunk. His feet dangling over the end of the bed, he was reading Tom's bible, but he was still only at Genesis. Tom needed it back before long. It was the best thing he had to see himself through.

Exercise time was coming up in five minutes, and he climbed down to slip into his cordless trainers. The guards would let everyone out at once, so he could converse with Barbara through the fence that separated them.

"Is it time already?" Josh asked, his eyes bypassing the tops of his glasses.

There was the familiar noise outside, and a guard unlocked the door. They filed into the small yard. Barbara was leaning against the wall on the other side, uncharacteristically peering blankly ahead of her as if life had ended. She was sharing a cell with Harry's colleague, who never went into the yard, and about whom she was naturally suspicious. Barbara had lost anyone to talk to, the Warden was not asking for any painting work yet, and she did not have any writing materials with her, but at least she had gained the upper hand on the bets and looked forward to all the money she would recoup once they were all out.

They collected at the fence. Barbara finally unstuck herself from her position against the wall.

Fritz Gargano wondered how long it would be before his daughter found out, and what she would do. She knew New York lawyers who were also admitted to the local bar, he told everyone, and they would have an easy time proving that the authorities had no proof whatsoever against him. After all, how could three guys have done all that destruction? But the others were already fed up with his complaining. The day before he had been bitching about the prison food, and before that the treatment by the guards. It had never stopped.

Paul Rodier and Peter Drake came out and joined them. The guards did not attempt to intervene or break up the gathering. This was much freer than outside. From the far wall, Winston walked over, leaving the wood-chipper doctor on his own.

Fritz asked Paul how much he charged for dental treatment in the prison infirmary that had been specially prepared for him. He winced when Paul gave his rates. He turned to Winston.

"How did you escape, Winston?"

He was teasing. Winston knew what they all felt about his volunteering to return. But it had kept him in Broadacre. Only Barbara continued to support him. However, by now every one of them had their minds focused on the outside without realizing quite how depressed it had become.

Josh Villeneuve made the proposition he had been thinking of for several days but keeping to himself.

"We have a unique situation. General Borto has closed off Broadacre and taken away its life. We are isolated from all his oppression, and yet we are right in the middle of the town we love."

Fritz Gargano cleared this throat and said he had no allegiance whatsoever towards Broadacre. No-one paid attention. For once in his life, he felt he had lost control over those around him. Even during his many previous incarcerations, he had kept the upper hand over his fellow inmates. For self-reassurance, he felt for the shiv secreted behind his pants pocket so that a guard would mistake it for lining.

"What is this f***ing place?" he muttered.

Josh Villeneuve went back to what he had been saying.

"We'll put on a show," he announced. "I can get a piano brought over, I know the Warden would accept it, and we'll make everyone outside think we're having a whale of a time. Hey Barbara, can you write something for us?"

Fritz Gargano rolled his eyes. These were the people Lenny the Limp had to put up with all those years. Perhaps he had deserved to keep the gold after all.

He spotted a golf ball lying next to the perimeter fence and pointed upward.

"F***ing seagulls!"

But no-one was listening.

He called in at Mary Lou's. She opened the door and asked if he had any news of Tom's case.

"I'm working on it," he said.

He showed her the card, and she reacted. Father Arnold knew he had struck gold. If only he could get it out of her.

"Why are you asking, Father?"

"To help your husband. But I cannot say any more right now."

She continued to hesitate.

"Does he have to know?"

Then she said to herself that the man in front of her could be trusted. He was her father confessor after all, and he already had plenty on her.

"Just a minute, Father."

She rapidly left the room and Father Arnold heard her scampering upstairs. She seemed as fit as ever. A few minutes later she returned, her composure regained as soon as she had quit the final stair. She was holding a bundle of envelopes wrapped in a pink ribbon. She undid the ribbon and opened the first envelope to pull out the letter inside. She placed it down on the table next to the card. The handwriting was identical.

"Father, you promise...."

"Yes, of course, Mary Lou. Who is it?"

She was blushing.

"The First Selectman."

*

A patrol of twelve riders was heading from the crossroads down South Street. It was about their usual time, and at first it looked routine. Quite by chance, several people happened to be standing on the grass verges along the route, braving the smell while soaking up the sun. The riders split into two groups and aimed for the curb on each side. As they approached the impromptu spectators, they swung their batons and cudgels.

As soon as she heard the commotion, Emilia Villeneuve ran out of her front door to see for herself. There had never been any incidents quite like this before, and she was shocked by the patrol's provocative behavior.

She looked in both directions but saw nothing else happening. She heard the faint sound of singing coming from the prison that was being masked by what was happening out on the road. She felt safe behind her white fence that would act as a palisade against the horses. She was belatedly hit by the revolting smell of the manure that had accumulated by the roadside. She put her hand to her face and turned to go back inside.

Just as she was making one last glance up the street, she spotted a young man throw something onto the roadway. She heard the telltale sounds of ball bearings.

People shouted as if they had been waiting for it. One horse lost its grip and threw its rider. Everyone cheered as his frenetic colleagues rode over and surrounded the horse. Two of the riders rapidly dismounted to come to the rider's aid, but he just lay there.

They dispersed the onlookers even more aggressively than before. Two people got clubbed. Others were rushing in from side streets. The growing crowd retaliated, and two more riders were brought to the ground.

Someone shouted that more troops were on the way. They all looked up the road. Fifty yards away, two patrols were galloping in their direction. The sight of them was awe-inspiring, and they would look for revenge.

The crowd dispersed in every direction possible. By the time Emilia had locked her front door, at least twenty protestors had jumped her fence and invaded her front garden and were running past the side of her house.

Once the troops had regrouped, no-one was left. Through her window, Emilia watched the last of the fallen riders helped back onto his horse and his two colleagues hauled off in Humvees that had just pulled up. After a while, several of the troops returned on foot to gather up the ball bearings.

When they informed General Borto about the incident he flew into a rage. He lost his usual self-control, felt nauseated, and openly doubted everything he had been doing so far. He excoriated the citizens of Broadacre like never.

While his Second-in-Command urged him to take a step back to reflect, his famous resistance to 'will-fatigue' continued to falter. It was rare. He ordered a tripling the horse patrols and a rounding up of twenty suspects to be imprisoned straight away. To frighten Broadacre even more, he ordered that Judge Cipriano be seen to head for the prison with a black cloth over his head, the machine gun practice intensified, and the lights in the whole town to be flickered for two full hours after dusk.

This was total war, and his rage did not stop there. He called for Bucephalus to be saddled earlier than usual and had his Second-in-Command muster fifty riders.

They cantered around town making as much noise as possible and causing any daring stragglers to run for cover. By the tenth time they were riding down South Street, one of the remaining ball bearings had found its way back into a slight dip in the road. It was too late to be spotted. Bucephalus came to a rapid halt and Borto lost his grip and went shooting over his horse's head.

He thought of his retirement. How would it be? Despite his long career of action, he had never fished. Soon he would have more than enough time to do so. He craved to use one of those fluorescent fishing rods.

He looked over to the horizon and thought he spotted funnel clouds coming in from the west. He did not think they would call him in this time.

As he rose in the air and pulled away, he decided to hand over to his Second-in-Command and spend his last days in Broadacre training with Junior at the pond.

27

Epilog

Channel Thirteen drew the limousine up to the curb and jumped out to open up for Catherine. She gave a brief but telling glance to her husband who never did. Bill guiltily surged ahead with the keys, and within a minute the front door was opened to reveal a familiar musty smell.

They had not been there for eight weeks. Outside, the summer growth and the sun had tired the leaves on the bushes and trees all around, and the grass, although well cut, had also lost much of its color and lushness. The vegetation in front looked in order, albeit a little overgrown.

Catherine overtook Bill inside to open all the windows protected with their wooden-frame mosquito nets. As Bill emptied the mailbox in the front, Daniel checked out the back yard. Channel Thirteen ferried in the suitcases and took his leave after discreetly dropping his invoice on the hall table.

Daniel crossed the lawn to see if the neighbors' kids were using their pool. Bill and Catherine meanwhile hauled the suitcases into their bedroom in order to be over and done with the unpacking, occasionally contentedly peering outside into the garden. They felt glad to be back.

Two hours later, Bill and Catherine went outside to hunt down Daniel. Catherine wailed as she gazed at her congested back yard.

"We've been invaded by triffids!"

Here, it had indeed become a jungle.

The windmill was turning smoothly behind their neighbors' house. Harry the trooper was there, happily mowing the lawn in front, and they spotted Tom at the back watching a flock of murmuring starlings high in the sky beyond.

"DotTom!" said Catherine.

Bill reacted.

"For Christ's sake don't ask him about religion, computers, or his investments. Take it easy, darling."

Saying hi to Harry, they walked toward the back to greet Tom. Bill asked him how things had been. Tom reached out his hand.

"Just great, folks!"

Not for the first time Catherine mumbled something to the effect that Americans would say that even in the middle of a hurricane.

She walked up and gave Tom a generous hug all the same. She then returned without Bill to take a walk around her own garden. She glanced at the tomato plants she had planted. Her well-trained and suspicious eye told her they had only recently been watered, and massively at that, so she would talk to Jesus and Maria about it.

Tom gave his latest news to Bill. He had purchased a new printer and wanted to show it off because it was the start of a modern Gutenberg revolution. He was making such heavy weather of it that Bill wondered if Tom would give himself to printing Father Arnold's boss's bulls at the same time.

Tom completed his monologue. He announced that there was to be a new Japanese sushi restaurant in town, but without the noises Bill had talked about. Barbara had purchased a secondhand Bronco that Bill might recognize, and an ex-inmate from the prison called Winston had taken over the bookshop.

"What happened to the First Selectman?" asked Bill.

Tom did not know. Anne Kaplan's son and daughter-in-law had also mysteriously disappeared.

Bill was still coming to terms with how fast things changed when Harry joined them and helped himself to a beer from a cooler on the ground. He reported that, so far, they had had an excellent summer, with parking fines at record levels.

Tom remembered something.

"Oh, and good news. We're back to the old Historical Commission boundary."

Bill asked how on earth that had happened.

"It's complicated."

Daniel reappeared, they rounded up Catherine, and all three returned to the house for supper. Bill called Sam Rosenbaum a short while later. He received the usual welcome.

"A bit of a drama while you were away, Bill. That guy Gargano got arrested."

Sam said it had been for some misdemeanor up north, but he had not been following the story, and he was still trying to get the flying robot back from him. Bill asked what all that meant for the production and Sam confirmed that shooting was still going to start in a week's time.

Neither of them would ever imagine in their wildest dreams that Fritz Gargano was in Broadacre Prison.

*

The restored peace in Broadacre soon brought Rabbi Siegel and Father Arnold back together again. Over the restored phone line, the rabbi had mawkishly showered his colleague with paeans for what he had done.

"Shalom. I think we should meet."

The priest said that their first encounter should take place on the neutral territory of the boardwalk in the wildlife sanctuary in order to get a bit of fresh air at the same time.

"We need to forget this malaise that hit our community," offered the rabbi as they walked side by side along the creaking slats that only just stood above the water. "A re-joining of the forces of morality."

"The *crise de foi* that descended among us," said Father Arnold, remembering what Bill and Catherine had talked about.

"Exactly, Father."

They held their private truth commission as they toured the lake beyond. They talked about each of the personalities who had played a role in what had happened.

"I won't hold Jesus against you," Siegel said, "despite what he and the others did. I always suspected there was something suspect about the schmuck."

Father Arnold didn't deign to respond. In everyone's attempt to downplay and hide everything that had happened, Jesus's contribution to the troubles had become exaggerated since he and Maria had momentarily been the only foreigners around. Siegel never missed an opportunity to 'Villafy' him, as he wittingly called it, and he was at it again.

They strolled along saying nothing more. In his mind, Father Arnold ran through all that had happened. There were still differences. Elliot Kaplan and his family, as well as the First Selectman, may have gone, the Historical Commission may have been returned to its origins, but it could all so easily start again. Leopards did not change. Blaming Jesus made it even more likely.

But part of avoiding that was up to him. Now he had to keep close to his associate to discourage any more polarization of their community. They had to exploit their common ground.

"At least we agree on the Ten Commandments, Rabbi."

"More or less," came the guarded reply.

*

One of the dozens of letters that had been waiting for Bill and Catherine was a missive from a very contrite Peter Drake. In it he announced the reduction of the price of his slither of land to something uncontroversial. Catherine showed her relief. Bill suspected Drake might be up to something wily and went around to consult Tom.

Mary Lou had turned to putting her energies into returning to practice and taking over Hughes' customers to fill the void, as well as duties for the community. She offered to oversee the signing of the new contract and modification of the survey.

26

Father Arnold found the key and the note where Barbara had said. He thought long and hard about how he could discover more. He remembered what a wise parishioner had once taught him. It went in the sense that when confronted by an unsolvable problem, find another one and use it to work on the first.

He had his two problems. Broadacre needed to be ridded of the ridiculous martial law provoked by the actions of the Historical Commission. Its most prominent member, Anne Kaplan, was suspected of being involved in corruption. If he could find a way of exposing Anne, the martial law might somehow go away.

He had another idea, as if good ones always came in pairs. It would call for a bit of brinkmanship, but it was worth the risk. The envelope had on it the numbers of the hundred-dollar bills. If he read them out to Harry, he could test his reaction.

He picked up the telephone. Harry's was one of the few numbers still operating.

"I have some information that might relate to the Elliot Kaplan affair," Father Arnold said.

He read out the numbers of the first and last notes that Winston had recorded. Harry thanked him.

"I'll call you back in ten, Father."

It seemed the longest ten minutes that Father Arnold ever had to wait, but the return call came.

"Father, where did you get those numbers from?"

Harry did not need to say any more. Father Arnold knew the cat was in the bag, and he had to move really quick.

*

The secret meetings, that had now become more frequent, had been the inexorable harbinger of a revolt against the martial law. There were increasing stirrings going on all around Broadacre, with the notable exception of the prison from where everybody only heard singing.

Seeing his hegemony threatened, General Borto convened a crisis meeting over a special telephone line to the Governor. At his side was his Second-in-Command, along with Harry the trooper and the First Selectman.

He announced they were certain that serious trouble was about to break out again in Broadacre. Everyone had stopped being intimidated by the horse patrols and all the other measures of repression he was taking. In the prison, they even appeared to be enjoying themselves. He had employed every psychological method he could think of. The machine gun practice in the wildlife sanctuary was getting more attention from the woodpeckers than the residents. Even the effect of the daily flickering of the lights had long worn off.

"Won't that burn out all the computers?" asked the Governor, distracted by the flickering lights.

Borto said that the internet links had been cut from the beginning, so it didn't matter. The Governor grunted. Borto sensed his boss was losing his resolve and was about to shift position.

"If I may say so, General, I think you may be setting yourself up for trouble with all this. You may find yourself marching backward into a deleterious future."

But Borto demurred. He was convinced that he had to show force. The Governor showed his concern.

"And what about the prisoners, General? Could they go on hunger strike? What if any of them dies or commits suicide?"

Borto confidently said he had that covered.

*

Father Arnold gradually got there. The hundred-dollar bills had been secretly destined for Anne Kaplan, but had somehow ended up in her son's hands, without her knowing. They had become linked his involvement with drugs, but Anne would have known none of that either. It did not matter. The link still had the potential to cause a scandal if it became known. But the bottom line was that he needed to find out where the money had come from in the first place.

There was no-one inside his church. He made his way to the second pew on the left, his favorite place for reflection, and kneeled on a time-worn hassock to pray and meditate. Before long, his conscience ended up telling him that, just as long as it benefitted the community, he could pursue and exploit whatever he might find out. At last, his priesthood would serve the cause of justice instead of just talking about it.

He had several leads. There had to be ways of finding out who had withdrawn the brand-new notes from the bank and rented the post box. But finding out either would require official authorization, and that was a problem in the present environment.

He had a simpler idea. He would try to find someone who would recognize the handwriting on the card. It would give him an excuse to do the rounds of his parishioners.

He started with Eli Mendelsohn and Emilia Villeneuve. Gardeners Jesus and Maria were at Emilia's, so for good measure he asked them too. But the more he pursued his quest, and nobody seemed to know, the more he wondered whether the culprit had been an outsider.

They carried the half-conscious general back to headquarters, a hundred and fifty yards away. His face was bleeding profusely, and his nose had been seriously smashed.

Borto's assistant Beth came running into the church, throwing the doors open and inadvertently letting in the stink.

"We need you urgently, Father!" she said. "The General is dying."

Father Arnold rushed to his sacristy to fetch his gear and followed her out as she said what had happened. They ran over to the synagogue hall. He saw the mess the general was in and prepared for last rites.

One of the general's medics was standing over his commander when the Warden ran in with two of his guards handcuffed to the wood-chipper doctor.

As they all looked on in deathly quiet, except for Beth's gentle sobbing in the arms of her husband, the doctor carried out a series of checks on the general. Junior rushed in and stood by them, his face whitened, his eyes reddened. The doctor checked the general's eyes. Outside, the commandeered helicopter was landing at the crossroads for an emergency evacuation.

The doctor looked over at the Warden.

"Get Josh Villeneuve over here."

Junior had helped calm Beth and had remained exceptionally brave. The only sound from the group assembled around the general was that of Father Arnold idly fumbling his beads.

The doors opened, and a guard arrived handcuffed to Josh Villeneuve. Once freed, Josh walked up to the general, felt around his nose and asked to see what instruments were in the medic's bag.

"OK, everyone out of here!" brusquely ordered the Second-in-Command, leaving the wood-chipper doctor and Josh alone with the patient.

As he helped himself to a pair of grips, Josh could not resist a smirk. The careful attention he now gave to the general made him recall his countless performances in *Androcles and the Lion*.

*

Father Arnold sneaked away. He followed the First Selectman to the town hall nearby. As he slipped the rosary back into his pocket, and negotiated the steps, his heart was beating. This would be it.

He tried to anticipate the First Selectman's reaction when he showed him the card. As he climbed the wooden stairs inside, he became convinced that his prey would lie himself out of the whole affair.

The First Selectman had just sat down

"Come in, Father. How can I help?"

Father Arnold said he had an extremely delicate matter to discuss. He reached for his pocket and pulled out the small card.

The First Selectman's face told it all. He stuttered.

"What is this, Father?"

"You tell me. It's your handwriting, isn't it?"

The First Selectman prevaricated as best he could. He asked where Father Arnold had gotten the card. The priest responded with the sort of white lie for which his earlier session in the pew had given him permission.

"It came with a key and a lot of money destined for Mrs. Kaplan."

The First Selectman was about to ask the priest what he had done with the money, but wisely held back. He said that the handwriting had been forged and warned the priest against going further with the affair.

As he left the building, Father Arnold was deep in thought. He had hardly extracted an admission from the First Selectman, but the man's reaction had made matters clear. Sure enough, he had met with pure obfuscation, but what had he expected?

He now had no shred of doubt that the First Selectman was up to his neck in something louche and would cover his tracks.

*

Anne Kaplan was far from being too old to saddle up and ride over to Mary Dunne's. She intended to copy General Borto's tactics in order to intimidate her friend. She trotted past one of Borto's patrols on the way as they eyed her with bemusement. She passed the cemetery, and for an instant wondered how soon her own time would be up with all the trouble that was going on. It was all becoming too much. It never used to be like this, and it was all Mary's fault.

Mary's gates were closed. Anne edged up to the intercom and pressed it with the tip of her riding stick after missing it several times. The gates opened, but Mary did not appear at the door.

She tied the horse to a faucet next to one of the Doric columns that sided the front entrance and walked straight in. Mary appeared from her living room and pretended to be surprised by her friend's appearance in breeches and riding coat, even though it had only been days.

Anne menacingly stood there with her riding hat under one arm and the stick in the other.

"Anne!"

"Mary, we must have words!"

The mynah made a squawk from its refuge in the conservatory. Mary chose for them to go outside to the back without offering her friend anything to drink.

"You sent me money. You sent me a bribe over the Commission business."

"I didn't! What gave you that idea?"

"You sent everyone money."

Mary concluded that the First Selectman must have talked.

"Who told you this?"

Anne told her she had just learned that the secret bribe had been discovered. Mary sank into her seat and invited Anne to do the same. She was obviously shaken but trying not to show it.

"You have ways of getting things done, Mary," Anne pleaded. "I want you to get the troops in Broadacre recalled and the martial law abolished right away."

Mary wanted to protest. She had thought they were both on the same page.

"Don't argue with me Mary. I have my reasons."

*

It was early morning. General Borto's head was heavily bandaged, almost making him unrecognizable, and he was still suffering from whiplash and concussion. But a week in bed had almost brought him back to normal.

As his commandeered helicopter approached the Governor's home, he swore he spotted Marine One flying away in the distance. That was very unusual. Perhaps he was not so well after all.

He touched down on the pad in the center of the lawn and was met by one of the Governor's older aides with his hand over his obvious toupee. It was strange that he had been already standing there and looking so smart.

The aide read the general's name from his badge and silently escorted him into the mansion and up to the second-floor office. Borto detested the cohort of acolytes and lictors that made up his boss's entourage. They were politicians, every one of them. He saw them as feral.

The Governor was standing there also looking very smart but strangely ruffled at the same time. He led him over to a small table. As coffee was served by the aide, he asked Borto how things were going and how he had received his injuries.

"As well as expected, Governor."

He avoided talking about his accident.

"Eugene, I'm getting reports that resistance in Broadacre is getting worse."

The Governor had adopted an I-told-you-so look.

The very word gave Borto the frissons. *Resistance, Resistants*, not only gave a legitimacy to people who did not even deserve to have their own label, but also brought back bad memories. They included the one where he had lost the very finger that should have supported his wedding ring. He would not allow Broadacre to figure among them. This was no foreign land, it was America itself, even if not exactly its heartland.

"I would not deign to use such a word, Governor!"

But the Governor insisted facts were facts, and that Borto was not getting on top of the situation. He was even believing that sending him in the first place had been a mistake.

"My mistake, Eugene. I think you should pull out right away."

Borto told him it would be a grave error. The Governor said he had already decided. It was now just a question about how the changeover could take place.

Borto took it to be a personal attack. No-one, he said, could do a better job than he.

"*No-one* is the operative phrase, General. We'll let Broadacre get back to normal on its own."

"But there will be chaos. We have just arrested the only civilian who had been voted for."

"What!"

The Governor got to his feet. He looked as though he was about to go off the wall again.

"We arrested the First Selectman last night. For drugs and corruption."

"This is not one of your schemes?"

"No, Governor. He had provided the money for the purchase of influence and cannabis. He had bought the Broadacre Historical Commission."

The Governor sat down again. He had not expected this last-minute surprise. The local population would never believe it. They would see the arrest as a machination in order to reinforce martial law.

"Get him released, General!. Smother the affair. Do whatever is needed to make it go away."

Borto did not resist. This was an order.

"Get out of there! You have a week to get Broadacre back to where it was before this mess started."

Borto did not know how to react. Going backward had never been part of his abilities. The Governor resumed.

"And that business of the Historical Commission, the digging up of the garden belonging to the English family, the arrests, everything. It must never have happened."

Eugene Borto walked out to the helicopter knowing his time was up. He was stooping, although it had not yet started up. His mind started wandering, perhaps because of the concussion, perhaps because of his impending evanescence.

It was all done within a fortnight. Bill and Catherine took a little more land than planned in order to allow the planting of a row of shrubs on the far side of the shed.

It was while they were all in the garden, watching the surveyor at work, that Daniel, bored, sat on the ground and peered under the garage. Perhaps the skunks had sneaked their way back, he was thinking. Then he saw that deep inside there was something metallic under there, as big as he was.

*

Josh Villeneuve held a welcoming party for Bill and Catherine. It was warm enough to stay outside and, after the usual piano session, he had put on a Boston PBS jazz program. Bill's quip that the station's initials stood for Grievous Bodily Harm went nowhere.

Bill spotted the Caterpillar at the back and Josh noticed.

"You heard about the Historical Commission?"

Bill confirmed Tom had already mentioned it. Josh announced that for some unknown reason the Equus restaurant in town had changed its name. Eli Mendelsohn thanked Bill when he handed him back his book on Massachusetts and said he would shortly start soccer practice again. He asked if Bill would be interested in helping.

Barbara extolled her enjoyment of the Bronco, despite the Bowie tape, and she and Paul Rodier discussed the possibility of an outing to Arcadia to ogle at the busty mountains.

"Use the sea temperature to cool off afterwards," advised Mary Lou laughing.

For fun, Catherine had brought along everyone's portraits she had completed so far. Josh said he would speak to the librarian to see if she would be prepared to put on an exhibition. Paul Rodier intently asked Bill and Catherine how they found Broadacre after their vacation.

"We're so happy to be back," said Catherine.

Bill said Broadacre had not really changed except for the vegetation and, oddly, a metal detector that Daniel had pulled out from under the garage.

Neither Catherine nor Bill, nor Daniel, picked up on the telling glances that the others were making to each other.

Barbara was feeling philosophical. In a repeat of that very first party at Tom's, she and Bill ended up sitting together at the bottom of the garden.

"It's all about goals, Bill," she said after mentioning that she had started a new self-help book. "Everyone needs goals."

She thoughtfully looked over to Father Arnold who was locked in conversation with Winston and Eli.

"Your goal can be to help others and get closer to God," she went on, "or it can be to make money by any way possible or become an expert that everyone looks to."

"You mean those three over there?" asked Bill.

"Exactly. Someone like Josh juggles his different goals for breakfast. Others like Anne Kaplan become fixated on their own power and wealth and create havoc for the lives of others. You, Bill, want your Golden Globe. Tom wants to make electricity out of his windmill and millions out of his investing. But if you add up the different goals we each have, most of them are innocuous and somehow contribute to the common good. It's only the few like Anne Kaplan that damage it."

Bill was not so sure. Goals meant targets when groups of people were involved, and individuals often found ways of cheating on targets and cheating on others to get there.

"So how do we channel everyone in the right way?"

"I don't know, Bill. But when you see it like that it becomes easier to imagine solutions."

The front doorbell rang from inside, but all the guests were already accounted for. Eli was closest and Josh asked him to open up.

It was Tanya Gargano.

"Eli!"

"Tanya!"

She looked ravishing. Eli led her over to Josh who was talking to Bill and Catherine and introduced her. Bill asked what brought her to Broadacre.

"I know what happened," she said. "The FBI came to the…"

Eli and Josh each took an arm and led her away as she struggled, leaving Bill and Catherine bemused.

"Well," said Bill, "let's enjoy the party instead."

*

Jesus and Maria were as busy as ever. They had worked harder than anyone to restore the streets of Broadacre to their pre-equine cleanliness and to help Tom and Josh fill in the pits and seamlessly level the ground and replace the grass at the back of Bill's and Catherine's in time. Everyone in town had said that they had achieved little short of a miracle that would be strictly kept to themselves.

The Town Clerk had taken over the First Selectman's responsibilities until new elections could be organized. One of the surrogate's first decisions was to ask Jesus and Maria to help with areas belonging to the community. It explained why they hadn't had the time to pay attention to Catherine's overgrown plants.

"We want to make our wonderful Broadacre attractive to tourists," he announced to the first of the new-style-old-style Historical Commission meetings.

To support everyone's wish to move on, and forget what had happened, Elliot Kaplan's and Fritz Gargano's trials were slated to be held far away in the state capital, although they were both being held in Broadacre Prison in the meantime. After a broken Judge Cipriano had announced his retirement, the decision was made by the local cable company to stop broadcasting proceedings from the courthouse and replace them with a children's program instead. Broadacre would finally be spared its gore.

*

Mary Dunne had missed her friend Anne Kaplan after only one week of separation. She had been number five on her speed dial which was at last working again. She had no-one else to complain to, or about. She decided she had no choice but to make peace and forget the ephemera that had provoked their breach. But for the present the only route was through seconds.

She called Father Arnold. He called Rabbi Siegel, and the next day she spotted Anne's limousine idling in front of the gates. In a rare but hidden display of lack of equanimity, she rushed to press the button, although without been seen.

As Anne gracefully parked her car, Mary remembered that she was about to be exposed to torrents of deleterious tears over what had happened to Anne's son. Her thoughts metamorphosed into a warm feeling. Anne had lost those who had been keeping her company at home, and so she would look to compensate for it with her friend.

"Have we lost everything?"

Mary gave no consideration for Anne's dramatically changed situation, her son, his wife and their boys, the historical village project and the sale of her land.

"I will soon own the Town Clerk," she said instead.

*

The TV pilot triumphed three months later, and the green light was given to continue filming, so Sam Rosenbaum kept Bill on for another season. With the absence of Fritz Gargano, Bill's meetings in New York amid all the glory had become more enjoyable than ever. At home, he and Catherine discussed improvements to the house with Tom the builder and Barbara the painter, and Catherine sketched what they had said they wanted.

It was now late fall again. Bill was at the computer working on his script. Catherine had just returned from her calisthenics class and had once again slammed all the doors, oblivious of her latest self-induced problem.

Catherine went outside with Daniel to work under the watchful eye of Oswald the cat. She was in her gum boots preparing to plant the row of shrubs that would front the revised borderline of their property. Daniel, with outsized headphones that constantly slipped off his head, was experimenting with his new toy.

The ground was soft and soggy because of that morning's rain. It had become warm. Oswald had left to drink from Mary Lou's fishpond, not so much for thirst, but because he had figured out that if he drank fast enough the unconsumed fish-food, still lying on the surface, would float towards him.

Catherine, now expecting a sister for Daniel, forced her entire weight on the spade and at first it slid in easily. Then she encountered an obstacle. Daniel came over with the detector which emitted a loud squeal into his headphones that even she could hear.

She had encountered something hard…

Printed in Great Britain
by Amazon

71703597R00119